# NO MISTAKE

The door closed behind them. Her head on Charles's shoulder, her eyes closed, Georgiana gave herself up to her emotions. Her heart was pounding so fast she could hardly breathe. Charles smiled at her and lowered her to the floor, letting her body slide down his. Even through her dress and petticoat she could feel him. Her eyes opened wide. Her hand closed over his shoulder. As soon as her feet touched the floor, he tilted her head up and kissed her, scorching her with his heat.

Georgiana knew that Charles was making a terrible mistake, thinking that she was a married woman eager for a dalliance. And she knew that she would be perpetuating a grave error if she allowed him to persist in this folly.

But even if Georgiana could stop Charles from making so foolish a mistake . . . what could she do about her own foolish heart . . . ?

# A Moment of Madness

by

## Barbara Allister

A SIGNET BOOK

SIGNET
Published by the Penguin Group
Penguin Books USA Inc., 375 Hudson Street,
New York, New York 10014, U.S.A.
Penguin Books Ltd, 27 Wrights Lane,
London W8 5TZ, England
Penguin Books Australia Ltd, Ringwood,
Victoria, Australia
Penguin Books Canada Ltd, 10 Alcorn Avenue,
Toronto, Ontario, Canada M4V 3B2
Penguin Books (N.Z.) Ltd, 182–190 Wairau Road,
Auckland 10, New Zealand

Penguin Books Ltd, Registered Offices:
Harmondsworth, Middlesex, England

First published by Signet,
an imprint of New American Library,
a division of Penguin Books USA Inc.

First Printing, August, 1993
10  9  8  7  6  5  4  3  2  1

# 1

GEORGIANA Carrington sat up in bed, her heart pounding, hoping that she had just been dreaming. Then she heard it again. "Fire!"

Trained by weeks of helping her sister care for sick children, Georgiana moved quickly. Almost as soon as her feet had touched the floor, she put on her slippers and slipped into her blue dressing gown. Stumbling over the small case holding her jewels and money, she picked it up and grabbed her traveling cloak.

Opening the door to the hallway, she threw her cloak over her shoulders and inspected the corridor. Someone was still shouting a warning about fire, but although the sound of his voice was clear and seemed close at hand, no one was in sight. A thick, heavy, foul-smelling smoke crept down the passage, but Georgiana could see no fire. Her heart racing, she noticed that the other three doors that opened on the hall were still firmly closed. She started forward and then froze. Someone was running down the stairs from the story above at the end of the corridor only a few feet from her. "Is everyone safe?" she called. The innkeeper did not even look at her but hurried on down the corridor and down the stairs to the ground floor.

Holding part of her traveling cloak over her mouth as a protection against the smoke that choked her, Georgiana ran back down the hallway to the bedchamber her aunt and their maid had been assigned. "Aunt Flora!" she called as she pounded on the door. It flew open.

"Miss Georgiana, come quickly," the maid said frantically. "I cannot wake her up." Georgiana crossed the room to stand beside the bed where Agnes, an older woman, was shaking her aunt. "She took one of her potions before she went to bed," the maid explained. "We are all going to die!"

"Nonsense!" Georgiana said firmly, hiding her own fears, and trying to convince herself as well as the maid. "Get her cloak and wrap her well. Together we can get her out," she said in a determined voice, thankful that her aunt was a small woman. If only her own maid had accompanied them. However, when her sister had written begging for Georgiana and Aunt Flora's help, Dora had been left behind because she had never had the measles.

Reminding herself that wishing never accomplished anything, Georgiana leaned over and helped the maid lift the older woman to the edge. They wrapped her in her gray cloak and put her slippers on her feet. "Dampen a towel and put it over her mouth and nose. Then open the door," the younger lady commanded. While the elderly maid followed her orders, Georgiana held her aunt, shaking her firmly. "Aunt Flora, listen to me." The older lady moaned but did not wake up. "You get on the other side of her," Georgiana told the maid when she returned with the dampened cloth. For once glad that her height gave her an advantage, she took a deep breath and tried to put the possibility that the fire had reached the staircase out of her mind. She shivered. Then giving the maid a signal, she put her right arm around her aunt and shifted her jewel case to her left. Half dragging and half carrying the elderly lady, the three of them entered the smoke-filled hallway. For a moment Georgiana was tempted to leave her case, but her practical nature would not let her. If the fire destroyed the inn, they would need more than their cloaks to survive.

As they walked down the corridor trying unsuccessfully to hurry, Georgiana shivered again. The smoke was thicker. One man rushed up behind them. Georgiana turned, hoping to enlist his help. His face set in hard lines, the man growled, "Get out of the way!" Georgiana and Agnes struggled to move faster, but the almost dead weight of the elderly lady held them back. Shoving past them, the man rushed for the stairs. Off balanced, Georgiana tried to steady her aunt and Agnes and to regain her own balance. They were forced to stop for a moment to redistribute the weight of their elderly burden.

"Here. Give her to me," a gentleman who had come up behind them said softly. Thankfully, the women watched the man lift the elderly lady easily. "You two hurry on ahead. We will follow you," he told them in a voice made husky by drink.

Even in the confusion of the moment, Georgiana knew that voice, although she had not heard it for almost ten years. Startled, she tripped, her long legs tangled in the full skirts of her dressing gown, and would have fallen except for the helping arm of her aunt's maid. "Careful," the man following her admonished. "Just a few more steps. We are almost out." Georgiana tried to ignore her pounding heart, to quiet the joy that leaped into existence. She dared not turn around to be sure. She had been confused many times before. Even if it was he, he was married, she reminded herself as she hurried down the corridor. They dashed into the clean air of the moonlit courtyard already filled with milling people, mostly townspeople who had heard the alarm and had come to help. As she stopped to take a deep breath, Georgiana blinked and tried to clear her mind. "He is here," her heart screamed.

"Where's the fire?" one man asked as the four of them hurried by, a bucket in his hand.

"What has happened? Where is the rest of the bucket brigade?" another one of the townspeople asked, his pants pulled on over his nightshirt. "Where is Tindle?" He saw the confused looks on their faces and added, "The innkeeper."

"I saw him a few minutes ago upstairs," Georgiana answered. Safe at last, she yielded to temptation. She glanced back at the gentleman who was carrying her aunt. She blinked, closed her eyes, and then opened them again. It was he. She was not dreaming.

"Upstairs? Not Tindle. He would more likely save himself first," she heard someone mutter, but even the confusion of the moment could not erase her excitement. It was he. She took a deep breath, glancing around the innyard, trying to find some safe place for her aunt. As she looked around, the gentleman carrying her aunt waited beside her patiently. Even in the bustle of the moment, he enjoyed watching the emotions flit across her face, smoke grime failing to hide the ivory creaminess of her skin. She was a fine figure of a woman. He could see that even under the brown cloak that she wore. He smiled ruefully. Most ladies of his acquaintance would have had the vapors at the thought of being seen when they were less than perfectly dressed. All this lady seemed to be worried about was the safety of her aunt. He watched her survey the crowd. Then the tense look on her face disappeared when she saw someone she knew across the courtyard.

"Follow me," she said quietly. Still holding on to her aunt's maid, Georgiana hurried across the yard. Her aunt's rescuer followed.

"Mistress Carrington, are thee all right?" asked a middle-aged man, his face worried. He inspected the little group, noting the tall man who held Georgiana's aunt. "And Mistress Gardiner?"

"We are just fine," Georgiana said soothingly. "What about the groom, the horses, and the coach?"

"Safe. Mayhap thee would like to wait in the carriage," the coachman suggested, pointing to the coach he had pulled to safety outside the courtyard. Their groom stood nearby holding the reins of the matched bays that pulled her brother-in-law's carriage. "Or I could inquire if there are any Friends about. They would take thee in if I asked." Georgiana glanced around the courtyard and smiled at the gentleman holding her aunt. He was only inches away. Their eyes met. She blushed and lowered hers. Now that they were safe, she had time to realize how she was dressed. For years she had dreamed of meeting him again, dressed in a gown that made the most of her figure. Instead, she was covered in soot and covered in folds of fabric. Telling herself that there was nothing that would make her more alluring at that particular moment, she carefully moved closer to his side. He held her aunt in his arms easily but Georgiana was certain he had to be tired.

"Our coach is just across the road, Mr. Harcourt. I think we would all rest better there until this confusion can be eliminated," she suggested.

In the middle of a yawn that he could not cover with his hand because of his burden, Charles Edward Harcourt looked up, startled to hear his name. "You have me at a disadvantage," he said quietly, searching her face and her hands for a clue to her identity. She pretended not to hear him.

"Mistress Carrington, doth thee wish me to pole up the horses and find another inn?" the coachman asked, not realizing that he was interrupting. "That wheel would hold up if we drove slowly."

"Not yet," Georgiana said quietly. Rather than reproving her servant for interfering, she breathed a sigh of relief. "Let us see if we will be able to rescue anything else of ours first." Explanations could wait. The gentleman who still carried her aunt gazed at her with a puzzled frown, running her name through his mind.

Surely he would have remembered such a striking lady if they had been introduced. Even under her nightcap, her long braid was a vivid russet color, and her skin under its trace of grime was a creamy ivory. And even though he could have forgotten her face and her coloring, her height would have made her impossible to forget. Although he was considered a very tall man, her head reached his chin. She was taller than some of his friends. While he stared at her, he tried to remember when they had met.

"This way, Mr. Harcourt," she said quietly.

Realizing that his most immediate need was finding

somewhere to put the still sleeping lady, Harcourt said, "If you will show me the way to your coach, I think your coachman is right: the lady would rest more comfortably there. Then I will search out the innkeeper to see what has happened."

The coachman led the way across the innyard to the large traveling coach. As she followed Charles Edward Harcourt across the yard, Georgiana wished that she were wearing anything but her dressing gown and her oldest traveling cloak. The coachman opened the door to the carriage and then stood back. He returned to his mistress and took the small valise from her. "Take very good care of that," she told him quietly. She turned back around, vividly aware of the tall man nearby. "Here, Mr. Harcourt. If you will lay her on the seat, Agnes will care for her."

Quickly, Charles followed her advice, putting his thin, fragile burden on the seat. Stretching for a moment after putting the lady down, he looked around at the milling group that filled the courtyard. Then he glanced back at the inn. He could see wisps of smoke but no fire. He stretched again, inspecting Georgiana's face closely, trying to remember her. Realizing the futility of trying to remember something in the confusion that surrounded them, he drew a deep breath. "You have me at a disadvantage. I do not remember your name," he said.

"Georgiana Carrington. And my aunt, Flora Gardiner," she said, her eyes fixed on the ground. She glanced up to see if he remembered her. She had never forgotten him. During her disastrous Season, he had been the only brightness in the darkness of unpopularity. Whenever he was present at a ball, she was assured of dancing at least once that evening with someone other than her aunt's old beaux or her mother's friends' sons. Maybe he had only asked her to dance because he had felt sorry for her, but she had not cared. As soon as she saw him walking toward the corner in which she tried to hide, her heart raced. And when he took her hand to lead her to the floor, her heart pounded so hard it was a wonder she danced to the beat. At first he had tried to converse with her, but she stammered so trying to answer him he soon stopped asking her questions. Georgiana had not cared. Being close to him had been enough.

Then one evening he had not appeared. Creeping away from her aunt on a contrived errand, Georgiana had slipped out onto the terrace where she knew a group of young men would congregate to blow a cloud. Keeping hidden in the shadows, she heard one ask, "Where is Harcourt?"

"Heard he's gone to the country to visit the. . . ." The rest of the reply was covered by a cough.

"Another one leg shackled," the first complained. The men moved further into the garden, chatting among themselves.

Georgiana leaned back against the stone of the house. Charles was going to be married, she thought, her hand pressed to her lips as though to hold back the pain that riveted her heart. Blinking back her tears, she slipped back through the doorway and into her seat beside her aunt.

The next day she had begun her campaign to convince her mother it was time to return home. Her aunt, as embarrassed as her niece at the chit's unpopularity, was her unexpected ally. She convinced Georgiana's mother that the girl was too young, that a girl who towered over most men and who had reddish hair and was as thin as a rake needed more time to develop, and, as she explained to a friend later, more than a modest dowry to send her off properly.

Always well-mannered, Charles Harcourt did not let his lack of recognition show. He smiled at her. Then he glanced around the innyard once more, concentrating on the small group of men closest to the inn. "Stay here," he said firmly. "I will find out what is going on and return." She could smell the faint odor of liquor on his breath, but his walk was still steady as he crossed the innyard.

Georgiana hid a smile at his tone of voice. After managing her own household for the last few years, she was more accustomed to giving orders than taking them. At least that was what her brother-in-law said. The thought of what her sister and her husband would say if they could see her at that moment brought a smile to her lips. Her sister claimed Georgiana's life was dull. If she could only see her "little" sister now, Georgiana thought. How she would tease. Her older sister campaigned constantly for Georgiana's reentry into society, but Georgiana had always resisted.

Georgiana looked across the innyard, keeping her eyes on her aunt's rescuer. As it had long ago, the sight of him made her heart pound with excitement. He was still as handsome as he had been then. His golden brown hair seemed darker in the moonlight. He towered over most other men, his brown eyes staring directly into theirs. His shoulders, already broad ten years earlier, seemed wider. In his shirtsleeves, pantaloons, and boots, he was as muscular as he ever had been. Unlike many men of his class, he had not added weight with the years.

Georgiana sighed, wishing she had her sketch pad so that she could capture him on paper. He was more handsome today than he had been as a young man. After almost ten years, she had convinced herself that he had only been a dream, that the feelings she had had for him had disappeared. Now only a few words from him proved her wrong. And as usual he was seeing her at her worst.

After her disastrous Season, her dream had been to see him again, to have him recognize her, think her beautiful, shower attention on her. She glanced at the bedraggled garments she wore. Ineffectually, she brushed at the grime on her clothes and face. Then, realizing her folly, she laughed ruefully to herself, putting her dreams aside and turning to check on her aunt. "Is she all right, Agnes?" she asked, noting that the elderly maid looked more herself.

"Still sleeping, Miss Georgiana," the maid said soothingly. "There is room for you inside the coach, too. You should come in out of the night air."

"I will be fine." She wrapped her cloak about her more carefully and stood looking at the group of men closer to the inn. "Can you see any sign of a fire?" she asked the coachman who stood beside her protectively in spite of the fact that she was a head taller than he was.

"Not a sign, mistress," he said. Something in his voice caused her to look at him again. They exchanged puzzled glances. "There is something peculiar going on here," he said.

"I fear you may be right," she said quietly, her eyes firmly fixed on Charles Harcourt. He had found the innkeeper. Georgiana watched them as they talked. Then she saw the innkeeper hesitantly approach the door of the inn. He stopped. Harcourt said something, but Georgiana was too far away to hear. The innkeeper gave him a resentful glance and scurried through the doorway.

Minutes dragged by. Georgiana stared at the building, inspecting it for fire, her heart thumping loudly. Her coachman muttered under his breath, the words too low for her to hear. The longer the innkeeper was in the building, the more he mumbled and the louder her heart beat. When after a few minutes the innkeeper did not appear, she was horrified to see Charles striding to the door. Then it opened.

"Danger is over," the innkeeper called from the hallway. He hurried toward the group of townspeople and began thanking them. As soon as they began to disperse, Harcourt confronted him. Not willing to be left out, Georgiana hurried to his side despite the coachman's objections.

"You stay with my aunt," she told the older man. "I will return as soon as I know what has happened." He glowered at her but did as she said.

"What has happened?" Georgiana asked as she reached Harcourt's side.

He merely glanced at her, noting once more how tall she was, a decided contrast to the young ladies with whom he was accustomed to dance. "How much damage has been done, Tindle?" he asked the innkeeper, fixing him with his eyes.

"Ah, hmmm, ah."

"Get it out, man!"

The smaller man shifted nervously, his eyes darting from one side to another. He looked anywhere but at the two of them. He mumbled something they could not hear.

"What did you say?" Harcourt asked. His voice was deep, his tone angry. Georgiana moved closer to him. His arm went around her, and she let her head rest against his shoulder. She moistened her lips with the tip of her tongue. Harcourt, glancing at her, tightened his arm around her unconsciously. Her heart raced so that she almost missed the innkeeper's next words.

"Someone must have been trying to scare us. There was no fire. Only smoke," the innkeeper said very quickly, his words tumbling over one another.

"No fire! You mean you had me drag my poor aunt out into the night air when there was no danger?" Georgiana could hardly believe what she had heard. Her normally calm voice rose alarmingly. Her eyes flashed with anger.

Harcourt watched appreciatively as she forgot to hold her cloak together. Her breasts heaved with indignation. When he noticed the innkeeper eyeing the same sight, he pulled her cloak about her tightly. He glared at the smaller man. "No one was hurt," the man declared, trying to soothe them. "Everything will be all right as soon as morning comes."

"If my aunt has suffered any harm because of this, this . . ." Georgiana began.

"You may take her back inside as soon as you wish. The smoke lingers, but it is worse in the hallways than in the rooms," Tindle said. His face was red with repressed emotions.

"I will carry her back inside for you," Harcourt told Georgiana. The innkeeper turned to leave. "When I have done that, I want to talk to you, Tindle." The man nodded and slunk away. "Does your aunt still sleep?" Charles slid his arm around Georgiana as if to shelter her from any more trouble.

The feel of his hand on her waist made her heart race just as it had when he had danced with her so many years before. She longed to lean on him, to let him comfort her further. "I think so," she answered, her words wispy because of her emotions.

Remembering his manners, Harcourt let his arm drop. He glanced at her once more, his interest piqued. Georgiana sighed softly. He looked at her, but her eyes were on the ground. "Send your maid ahead of us to open the windows," he suggested. "With the breeze tonight, the smoke should be gone quickly."

"I still do not understand what happened," she said quietly, her face turned up to his. Her blue eyes were wide, and her lips barely parted. Charles reminded himself that they were in a public place, but she stirred his blood.

"Nor do I. After I talk with Tindle, shall I tell you what I have discovered?" He looked at her, admiring the way she was behaving. Most of the ladies he knew, and he had no doubt that Georgiana was a lady, would have fainted and left him with two ladies to rescue.

Georgiana dropped her eyes before his admiring gaze, willing herself to answer casually. "I would appreciate it," she said quietly as they approached the carriage.

"Doth thee wish me to pole up the horses, mistress?" the coachman asked, his face registering his disapproval at the actions of the evening.

Harcourt noted what the man called her. Some of his excitement disappeared. She was married.

"No. I have been assured that the inn will be safe for us for the rest of the night. We will leave tomorrow as planned. As soon as Mr. Harcourt removes my aunt, you can return the coach and horses to the stable. Agnes, if you will run ahead and open the windows, Mr. Harcourt has offered to carry Aunt Flora back into her room." She smiled at the maid and then up at the tall man at her side.

Despite himself, he smiled back. The maid nodded and hurried off.

Soon the small procession entered the inn. Harcourt let Georgiana lead the way. Under the heavy cloak and dressing gown she wore, the lushness of her figure was a suggestion, and he enjoyed watching her ahead of him, climbing the stairs.

"Her room is the second on the left," Georgiana explained.

"And yours?" Georgiana stopped and turned around. She stared at him in amazement. He hurried on. "So I can tell you what I discover." Of course, if she had a modern marriage, he would not object if she were willing to offer him more tangible thanks, he thought.

"Oh." Georgiana cleared her throat and turned away from him slightly. "My room is the one closest to the stairs," she said quickly before she could change her mind. She glanced up at him under her lashes, afraid of the disapproval she was certain she would see on his face. But his face revealed nothing.

A few minutes later, having supervised her still sleeping aunt's return to her bed, she was in her own room. Throwing open the window, she stood for a moment looking out into the night. Then she looked at the dress hanging on a peg in the room. A traveling gown, it was a golden brown in the latest style. But it lacked the allure that Georgiana wished for. She sighed and reached for it. Beneath it were her stays and petticoat.

Moving toward the door to call Agnes to come help her into her undergarments, she stopped. Quickly, she stripped off her dressing gown and night robe. Wearing a defiant look on her face, she slipped into her zona and petticoat and pulled her dress on before she could change her mind. She pulled the tapes tight under her breasts, noting with satisfaction that without her stays the dress fit more comfortably.

She glanced toward the glass. Horrified, she pulled her nightcap from her head and smoothed her hair. Resisting the temptation to free her hair from its braid, she wound it in a neat coil at the base of her neck. She stepped back to get a better look at herself. She grimaced and picked up a washcloth. Why did he have to be staying here now? All her dreams and plans had disappeared just like the smoke. Her face clean, she began to pace, wishing she had the strength to resist seeing him again. Then she laughed at herself. If it meant seeing him, being with him again, she would walk on coals. She glanced in the mirror once more and bit her lips to give them more color.

Soon she was pacing the floor again, certain that Harcourt had forgotten her. She had just decided that she might as well put her night robe back on and try to sleep when she heard a sound at her door. Retying the ribbons at her neckline, she hurried to the door and opened it. The excitement she felt added roses to her cheeks.

For a moment after she had opened the door, Harcourt stared at her, feeling an attraction that he had ignored until now. The moonlight and light from candles formed a halo behind her, giving her russet hair a glow. He stood there for a moment, saying nothing. Then he smiled. Slowly he took her hand and pulled her toward him until her hands were on his chest. He waited for her to pull away. But she stared at him, mesmerized, her lips slightly parted. He smiled and put his hands on her sides just under her breasts. A shiver of delight ran through her. She smiled shyly. Giving in to an impulse, he bent his head and kissed her softly.

Georgiana, startled by her own emotions, pulled away. She stared at him, her eyes wide. "Are you going to slap my face?" he asked.

"I should," she said quietly, her face flaming as she thought of what she had allowed him to do. She could not tear her eyes from his face, his lips. She sighed. He smiled and pulled her close again, kissing her more deeply this time, letting his hands cup her breasts. She shivered with excitement. Then she pulled back again. "We must not do this," she said, longing to have him overrule her.

"You are right," he agreed, letting her go and stepping back, wishing that she had not pulled away. She licked her lips, tasting on them the liquor he had drunk. He resisted the desire to pull her back into his arms again.

She looked at the floor, trying to regain control over her emotions. "What did you discover?" she finally asked when the silence had grown more than she could bear.

"Someone was playing a practical joke. At least that's what the innkeeper thinks." His voice was carefully controlled and did not reveal his struggle to control his emotions.

"A practical joke? People could have been injured." She looked up at him, her blue eyes wide.

"Yes, but fortunately no one was," he said soothingly. "Someone filled pots with rags and put them in the hallways. After they had burned for a while, the inn filled with smoke. We should be grateful that whoever did it was careful to use materials that would smolder rather than burst into flame."

"Then who warned us of the fire?"

"Probably the same person."

"He must be mad." She stepped back away from the door, her face angry.

He followed her into the room, leaving the door open behind him. "Doubtless it was for a bet."

"A bet! Of course, you men will bet on anything!"

He watched fascinated as her chest heaved with indignation. "I did not say it was a bet. I only said it could have been," he reminded her.

"Whoever did it, no matter what his reason, was wrong," she said angrily. She turned and glared at him, her blue eyes flashing.

"I agree." He walked further into the room, closer to her. Georgiana's eyes widened. She turned and walked toward the window.

When she turned around, she said quietly, "Thank you for all your help this evening." She smiled sweetly. He took another step toward her. She glanced toward the open door, afraid that someone would come by and see him there. "Good night." She held out her hand to him. For a moment he simply stared at her, willing her to change her mind. Then he took her hand. Instead of shaking it as she expected him to do, he turned it over and put a kiss in her palm. Her heart beat so loud she was certain he could hear it.

"Good night." He dropped her hand, turned, and left the room, shutting the door behind him.

As soon as the door had closed, Georgiana began to pace again. "Dolt! Idiot!" she said angrily. "He would have kissed you again, but you were frightened. You had to send him away!" She took a deep breath and remembered his kisses. She shivered deliciously, her lips slightly parted. Once again her tongue touched her lips, hoping for another trace of him. She sank on the edge of the bed, her face dreamy.

Suddenly someone pounded on her door. Startled, Georgiana slid to the floor with a thump, her eyes wide. The pounding came again. "I am coming," she said nervously, wondering what could have happened. She opened the door cautiously. Her eyes widened as she saw Harcourt, his face angry.

"Check your belongings," he ordered. "Is everything here?"

"Why? What has happened?" she asked, her eyes startled. He walked toward her, forcing her backward into the room.

"When we vacated our rooms, someone entered them. Are you missing anything?" he asked, glancing around the room as though he were taking inventory.

Georgiana walked around the room, trying to remember just what she had had with her. "My reticule is missing," she said finally.

"Nothing else?"

"Not that I can tell?"

"Check with your aunt's maid. As soon as you have done so, come downstairs," he said firmly. "I am sending for the magistrate."

"For a reticule?" Georgiana asked, confused.

"For that and for the money that was stolen from me."

"Money? How much?"

"I will explain to you and to the magistrate at the same time. Now check on your aunt. Find out what is missing there." As though it were his room instead of hers, he opened the door and escorted her outside.

"Just a moment. I want to take something with me," she said firmly. She darted back into the room and appeared a few seconds later with her case.

"You had that with you in the innyard earlier. What is in it?" he asked curiously.

"I will explain later," she said loftily, letting him have a taste of what it was like to have someone avoid answering. She walked down the hallway to her aunt's room, her back straight and her head high. He watched for a moment, his lips a thin, white line. Then he hurried down the stairs.

When she entered the common room a short time later, the innkeeper was there, a frightened look on his face. Sprawled in a chair nearby was Harcourt, a glass of brandy in his hand. As soon as they saw her, they stood up. "Well, what did you find?" Harcourt asked as he seated her carefully.

"My aunt's case had been disturbed. Like mine, her reticule is missing as is her needlework," Georgiana said quietly. The innkeeper blanched.

"Her needlework?" Harcourt asked, the confusion on his face echoed in his voice.

"She was making chair covers. She had finished five of them and was working on the sixth. I do not know what she is going to say."

"She still is sleeping?" Harcourt asked in amazement. He poured her a small amount of brandy and gave it to her. She took it absentmindedly, swirling the brown liquid. The scent made her think of his lips. She glanced at him and blushed. He smiled at her, wondering what she would be like as a lover.

"Yes. The potion she took ensures eight hours of

sleep. In a way I am glad she has slept through all of this," she said. Her voice was husky with emotion.

"Why?" he asked, his eyes caressing her. They had both forgotten the presence of the innkeeper, and he was happy that they had done so.

"She would have been so excited that she might have had apoplexy. And the last few weeks have been very tiring for her."

"Only for her?" he asked, hoping that she would continue.

"For all of us. Four children with measles are not the best of patients," she explained. She took a sip of the brandy and then coughed.

"You have four children?" he asked, wondering how she had managed to keep that pristine air of innocence about her.

"Not me." She smiled at him wistfully. If he had only been interested in her ten years ago, they might have had four children by now. And every time she left her nieces and nephews behind she longed for a child of her own. "My sister."

"Oh." He smiled at her, relieved that his original assessment had not been wrong.

"Do you have any children?" she asked, holding her breath and waiting for his answer.

"Me? I am not married," he said with a laugh.

"You are not?" she asked, her blue eyes opening wide. She wished she could have asked what happened to the lady he had been engaged to. Her heart began to pound with excitement. Before he could answer, the door to the inn opened, and a large older gentleman dressed in a greatcoat with many capes entered. He was scowling.

"Who called for me at this time of night? Who are these people?" he demanded, frowning at the innkeeper.

"Not I, sir," the innkeeper mumbled. " 'Twas him." He pointed toward Charles Harcourt, who had risen when the older man entered the room.

"And who might you be?" the magistrate asked angrily. "Could this not have waited until morning."

"I am Charles Edward Harcourt, Mr. . . ." He paused and looked at the innkeeper, who was cowering near the fireplace.

"Squire Lindsey," the innkeeper whispered.

"Squire Lindsey. And this is Mrs. Carrington. This evening we were robbed while we were staying at this inn," Harcourt explained.

"And what do you expect me to do about it?" the squire asked angrily. He had enjoyed a fine port and then retired to bed. When the messenger had awakened him, he was not happy to have his sleep interrupted.

"What you are supposed to do: find the criminal," Harcourt said firmly.

"Are you trying to tell me my job?" Lindsey demanded, his red face becoming even redder.

"Gentlemen," Georgiana said firmly. The two stopped and looked at her. "Perhaps we could tell Squire Lindsey what happened and let him decide what should be done," she suggested calmly.

The two gentlemen looked at each other and nodded. As soon as Squire Lindsey took his seat, Harcourt took his. "Bring me some of that brandy, Tindle," the magistrate said. "Then tell me the details." He looked at the two of them.

Tindle put the glass in front of the older gentleman and began to make excuses. "It was not my fault. Nothing that happened this evening can be blamed on me. I am a helpless bystander. Someone is trying to destroy me; that's what it is."

"Be quiet, Tindle. Now tell me exactly what happened, Mr. . . . ," the squire said firmly.

"Harcourt." He got up and began to pace around the room. "Those of us staying here had retired to our rooms. Then someone started shouting about a fire. When we went into the hallway, it was filled with smoke."

"And had it not been for Mr. Harcourt's help, my elderly aunt might have been injured," Georgiana said quietly, her eyes on the tall man walking around the room.

"And you are?"

"Mrs. Carrington," Harcourt answered for her. "I introduced you earlier." He picked up his brandy and emptied the glass. The innkeeper quickly filled it again. Georgiana smiled at the magistrate but did not correct Harcourt's introduction. She had already decided that the gentlemen would be more comfortable talking to a married lady. She knew that she should have explained and awakened Agnes to be her chaperon but did not have the heart to disturb the older woman's sleep once again. And she was not about to stay upstairs and wonder what was happening.

"You said something about a theft. Mrs. Carrington, what was stolen from you?" Once again Georgiana explained. The squire laughed when he heard that her aunt's needlework had been stolen; she bit the inside of her lip and kept silent. "Needlework." The magistrate looked at the other two men and shook his head. "Imagine the thief will be surprised when he discovers what he has taken," the squire said with a chuckle. "What about you, Harcourt?"

"A case containing one thousand pounds," the man said grimly.

"A thousand pounds?" Georgiana was horrified.

"How come you was carrying such a large sum, Harcourt?" the magistrate asked, his face both curious and disturbed.

"I won it yesterday," Harcourt explained. "At a mill."

"Sizeable amount for this part of the country," the squire said disapprovingly.

"A bet!" Georgiana said angrily.

"Now, Mrs. Carrington, do not be so hard on him. He won," the squire said soothingly, wondering at the presence of the attractive lady and the gentleman at an inn that rarely catered to gentlefolk. He glanced from one to the other, knowingly. His speculations, however, did not show on his face or in his manners. "Tell me more about where you had the money stored."

"In a case with my shirts and small clothes. When I

decided to go to the mill, I sent my valet to my home ahead of me."

"Did he know how much money you had won?" the magistrate asked, delighted to have found a suspect who was not a local.

"No. He left before I won it." Squire Lindsey frowned. "Besides the man has been with me since I made my first appearance in the *ton*. He has never stolen from me before. Why should he start now?" Harcourt looked at the squire. His belief in the innocence of his valet was clear in his eyes and voice.

Georgiana listened to him, enjoying the shared moments together even at the cost of her possessions, knowing that these few moments soon would be over. "Maybe Mr. Tindle remembers someone else who could have done it, a stranger perhaps," she suggested.

All three of them looked at the innkeeper. His face flushed and then blanched white. His hands began to shake. "I do not know what you are talking about," he said nervously. He picked up the brandy and poured more into the men's glasses, his hands shaking so much that the brandy splashed onto the table.

"Nonsense, man. You must know who is staying with you this night," the squire said firmly.

"What about the man who pushed by us. He must have been staying on the floor above," Georgiana said helpfully.

"Only one chamber on the floor above, and he has it," the innkeeper said nervously, pointing to Harcourt.

"Well, it could not have been he," Georgiana said firmly. "He was still behind us when the other man shoved us aside. Who else was staying on my floor?"

"Just you, your aunt, and her maid," Tindle said hastily.

"You told me all the other rooms were let, you scoundrel," Harcourt said angrily. He got up from his chair and crossed to the innkeeper, who backed away from him. "What is going on?"

"Nothing! Nothing! I promise you." The innkeeper moved to stand behind the magistrate's chair.

"Very peculiar," Squire Lindsey said. "You get out in front of me, Tindle, so I can see you." Reluctantly, the man obeyed. "Now no more lies. I want the truth. Do you understand?" The innkeeper nodded his head, glancing warily from side to side. "Well, who was staying here tonight? Besides these people?"

Tindle mumbled something, his mouth close to the magistrate's ear. Then he stepped back. He was wringing his hands nervously.

"What did he say?" Harcourt demanded. Georgiana leaned forward in her chair.

"Hmmm." The squire tapped his fingers together, his face twisted in thought. "Rather awkward, I will admit."

"Stop talking in puzzles," Harcourt said angrily. "If he has any information that will help us get our possessions back, he should be forced to speak up." He glared at the innkeeper and at the magistrate.

"Suppose you are right," the older man said. "Still might be dangerous if anyone found out Tindle had talked." He glanced at Georgiana and then at Harcourt. "I trust you can hold your tongues?" They nodded. "There has been a highwayman stopping coaches around here. Tindle agreed to help spring a trap for him. But something went wrong. Maybe he saw all of you and decided to go elsewhere."

"Or maybe he was warned off," Harcourt said, looking at the innkeeper, his eyes angry.

"Not me. I would not do something like that," the man said stuttering.

"That still does not explain what happened," Harcourt reminded them.

"Or who set that elaborate pretense of a fire," Georgiana added.

For the next few minutes the four of them discussed the events of the evening without coming to any conclusion. While Georgiana drank only one small glass of brandy, the men consumed considerably more. Finally, the magistrate heaved himself from his chair. "Nothing more to do tonight. See you in the morning, Harcourt, Mrs. Carrington," he said. "Do not hold any hope of recovery, though. Too many questions we cannot answer. I will be keeping my eye on you, Tindle," he said gruffly.

"Me? I had nothing to do with this. Nothing!" the innkeeper sputtered.

"You are hiding something, and we shall discover what it is," Harcourt said firmly. He stood up and towered over the smaller man, who seemed to shrink before him. Harcourt turned to Georgiana, who had sat through all the questions, and helped her up. Squire Lindsey's mouth dropped open when he had to look up to her. Fortunately, given Harcourt's temper, he kept his comments to himself. Quickly, the squire made his farewells and vanished into the darkness.

# 2

HARCOURT offered Georgiana his arm. She took it and allowed him to lead her toward the staircase. "The squire is probably right," he told her as they walked up the stairs together.

"I lost nothing that cannot be replaced besides the chair covers," she assured him. "But a thousand pounds? How will you manage?"

"As I managed yesterday before I won it."

"But it is such a large sum." She gazed up at him, a worried look on her face.

They had reached her door. He released her arm. She turned back to face him, her eyes on his. "You are not to worry about me," he told her, reluctant to let her leave his side.

"But what if Tindle insists that you pay the bill?" she asked, still concerned.

"The thief did not take all that I have," he told her. She blushed and hung her head. "But what about you? I would be happy to lend you some money. Do you have enough to settle your bill?"

She looked up at him and smiled. She longed to touch him, to smooth the lines from his forehead. Already unsteady from the brandy he had been drinking, Charles rocked back on his heels, consumed by desire that he had tried to ignore. "Yes," she whispered. Her eyes made promises she did not really understand.

Looking at her, he forgot the question he had asked. He leaned forward and kissed her, pushing her back against the door. Instead of pushing him away as her practical mind told her to do, she yielded to her desire. Georgiana returned the kiss, wrapping her arms around his neck. He kissed her more deeply, caressing her lips with his tongue until they parted. She sighed as his tongue caressed her mouth. His hands encircled her waist and then one crept up to caress a breast. She stiffened for a moment, reminding herself that what she was doing was not proper. Then she reached up to draw him closer, her hands clutching his shoulders, her heart pounding in her ears.

Charles drew back for a moment. He looked at her again, smiling at her parted lips, her heaving breast. He reached behind her for the latch. "May I?" he asked, his lips so close to her ear that she could feel his breath against her ear.

Georgiana hesitated for a moment. Then she nodded, burying her face in his chest, conscious that she was breaking every taboo she had ever been taught. But all the hunger she had been repressing for years had broken free this evening. No matter what she had to pay for this moment of madness she was certain it would be worth it.

Unconcerned about the moral struggle she was facing and determined to plunder the richness he had been drawn to all evening, Harcourt smiled, opened the door, swept her up into his arms, and carried her into the room.

The door closed behind them. Her head on his shoulder, her eyes closed, she gave herself up to her emotions. Georgiana's heart was pounding so fast she could hardly breathe. Harcourt smiled at her and lowered her to the floor, letting her body slide down his. Even through her dress and petticoat, she could feel him. Her eyes opened wide. Her hand closed over his shoulder. As soon as her feet touched the floor, he tilted her head up and kissed her again, scorching her with his heat.

While her training told her she should end this when she still could, her body urged her on. She had never felt like this before, her blood singing in her veins. She opened her lips to him and ran her fingers through his hair. She pressed herself closer to him. When his hand found the tape that held her bodice in place, she did not try to stop him. He released the bow and opened the zona beneath it. Watching her carefully to see if she would object, he pushed her dress from her shoulders and undid the ties on her zona, freeing her breasts. Her eyes widened, but she did not pull away. He bent and kissed the upper slopes of her breasts, smiling when Georgiana shuddered.

He stood back and pushed the dress to the floor. Georgiana stood before him, her breasts bare and heaving and her cheeks scarlet. He smiled and ran one finger over her creamy white breast, circling her nipple. Georgiana gasped. "Do you want me to stop?" he asked. She shook her head violently, praying that he would continue. His face serious, he lifted her free of her dress and carried her toward the bed.

Once more her conscience reminded her that what she was doing would ruin her forever. But after waiting for twenty-eight years, Georgiana refused to listen. She held on to him tightly, afraid that it was only a dream.

Carefully, he put her on the bed and, after yanking his boots off, joined her, pulling down the sheet that she had draped around her. Delighted by the shyness that was not common among the married women of his acquaintance, he kissed her again and let his fingers toy with her breasts. His tongue played with hers as he stroked her. Feeling her relax once again, he transferred his kisses to her breast. She stiffened for a moment and then sighed.

"Like that, do you?" he asked, his face so close to her that she could feel his breath on her breast. She nodded, too caught up in her emotions to speak. He lowered his head again, letting his tongue circle her nipple. She moaned and pulled him closer. Lost in sensations that were new to her, Georgiana was not aware when one of his hands moved beneath her petticoat. But as soon as he touched the inside of her thigh, she gasped, resisting the impulse to pull away. Every time he touched her, it felt as though she were on fire, not just where he touched but deep inside.

She shifted restlessly, but his hands and mouth had her in thrall. "Please, please," she begged, unsure of just what she was asking for.

Then he shifted so that instead of lying side by side, she was on top of him. Her eyes widened nervously as she felt him hard beneath her. "It is your turn, now," he said, looking up at her with a grin. He pulled her down closer to him so that he could kiss her breasts and torment them with his tongue.

"My turn?" she asked, not at all certain that she liked this new position.

"To learn what I like," he explained. She blushed and looked away. She was so still that he shifted nervously, sending shivers through her. "Has no one taught you how to please a man?" he asked curiously, wondering what her husband was like. If he had a wife who responded as she did, he would have taught her carefully. She shook her head, blushing again. Cursing softly but still pleased that in this way at least he would be the first, he pulled her close and kissed her, letting her hide her face on his chest. He could feel her trembling. He put his arms tightly around her. "Then I will teach you," he promised, his voice just a whisper in her ear, his blood pounding in his veins.

Slowly, so slowly that he had to pull away from her occasionally to regain his control, he taught her to touch him, stroke him, letting her set the pace. Enthusiastically, she practiced the moves he taught her, delighting in his reactions. Soon those caresses were not enough. Sliding from her grasp, he sat up and stripped his clothing from him. Her eyes widened as he disrobed, but she did not turn away. Her hands followed the arrow of hair from his chest to the thicket of hair that surrounded his manhood. Resisting the impulse to throw her beneath him and take her roughly, he reluctantly pulled her hands away, took her zona completely off and then removed the petticoat that was bunched around her waist, throwing them both to the floor where her dress already lay.

The flickering candle could not hide the blush in Georgiana's cheeks as she lay bare under his eyes. But as she watched him look at her with burning eyes and touch her delicately, she no longer tried to hide her nudity, instead rejoicing in the pleasure that her body gave him. After taking a moment to look at her, marveling at the creamy white skin and russet curls, he laid her on the bed, bent over her, and kissed her once again. His hand found the nest of russet curls that hid her womanhood. He stroked her gently. As the kiss deepened and he felt her ready for him, he shifted, rising above her. Then he entered her swiftly. Georgiana could not help the small gasp of pain as he pushed his way into her. She bit her lip to keep from crying out.

"So tight and warm," he whispered, kissing her once again. His tongue mimicked his body's actions.

After that first brief pain, Georgiana felt something else. She instinctively met his thrusts, trying for something she had not even known existed a few hours earlier. When he shuddered and collapsed against her, she held him tight. As his breathing slowed, his arms tightened around her. After some time had passed, he began to kiss her softly at first and then more urgently. Her eyes widened as he began the dance of love once more. "Again?" she asked, her eyes wide.

"As often as we want," he said drawing her close. The fire that had not been quenched flamed between them again very quickly. More in control this time, Harcourt drew out their pleasure until Georgiana gasped and collapsed in his arms. As soon as she recovered, he began again. Although he drifted off into sleep between their bouts of lovemaking, Georgiana did not sleep but watched him, storing memories that she knew would have to last her a lifetime.

When the sky outside began to show the first hint of light, she touched him. His eyes flew open, and he pulled her down to him, giving her a warm kiss. Pushing her fears of discovery aside, she surrendered to him once more. Before he drifted back off to sleep, she said quietly, "You must go."

"Why?" he mumbled and put his head on her breast. She ran her fingers through his hair lovingly.

"Someone will see you," she whispered. "Consider my reputation." He kissed her again and reluctantly slid from the bed. He gathered up his clothes and pulled his shirt over his head. He bent to kiss her again. Then he slipped into his trousers and was gone.

Lying there, staring at the door through which he had gone, Georgiana wanted nothing more than to drift into sleep, a sleep she was sure would be filled with dreams of him. But she knew she could not. Sliding from the bed, she picked up her clothing where he had thrown it, moaning slightly. However, even the aches she felt could not quench the glow inside her. For a moment, the memory of the night just past brought a smile to her lips and then tears to her eyes as she realized what she would be missing. Quickly, she took herself in hand, reminding herself that she could not allow her despair to stop her. Nothing would ruin her memories more than having to face Charles Harcourt this morning. Just knowing that he thought her an erring wife made her feel guilty. And if he knew the truth? She shuddered. Throwing her clothes about her and covering everything with her cloak, she picked up her valise and tiptoed to the door. Seeing no one about, she hurried to her aunt's bedchamber to have Agnes finish lacing her up.

By the time Charles Harcourt awakened much later that morning, Georgiana and her aunt were well on their way home.

The morning was already late when he descended. He walked into the common room and looked for the innkeeper. "Some ale," he demanded. "And something to break my fast." He looked around, noting the common workers who sat at the tables around him with their tankards. As soon as the innkeeper set his meal in front of him, he asked, "Have the ladies broken their fast?"

"Miss Carrington and her aunt left as soon as the wheelwright finished repairing their coach," Tindle said and stood back, waiting for his customer's reaction. In the end, Harcourt disappointed him. His mind was occupied with the word "miss." After a few minutes, he relaxed. The lady who had nestled in his arms last evening was no spinster. Tindle probably had misunderstood. Picking up his tankard of ale, he sat back with a smile as he remembered the eagerness with which she had responded to him. Thinking of how quickly she had learned, he wondered cynically what her husband would say when he next made love to her. He hoped she was smart enough to hide her knowledge. To his surprise, the idea of Georgiana in the arms of anyone else made him uncomfortable, a feeling that was usually foreign to him. He had dallied with married women before; in fact, they were his preferred choice for a mistress. However, he had never worried about the lady's returning to her husband's bed. No longer as relaxed as he had been, he finished his breakfast quickly. "Tindle, where can I find Squire Lindsey?" he called.

During his interview with the magistrate, Harcourt had to work to keep his mind on his loss. The thought of the lady's creamy white skin and russet curls kept getting in the way. Finally, agreeing with the squire that they had done all that was possible, Harcourt took his leave.

"I will keep an eye on that innkeeper, sir. And if we do find the thief, I will expect you to return for the trial," the squire said firmly. He held the card that his guest had given him. "A letter to this address will reach you at any time?"

"They will send it on to me if I am not there," Harcourt assured him. "Is there anything further that you need from me?"

"No. I trust you will have a safe journey," the squire

said politely, not at all sad to see the back of this demanding gentleman.

While Harcourt was dealing with the squire, Georgiana was driving over country roads toward her home. Her aunt, revived by a good night's sleep, pelted her with questions. "Why did you let me sleep?" she asked repeatedly.

"We tried to wake you up," her niece explained patiently. "But you would not rouse."

"No one saw me in my night things, did they?" the older lady asked, horrified. She patted the fringe of white curls around her face.

"Agnes wrapped you in your cloak. I am certain no one saw anything improper."

"No one recognized me, did they?" Flora Gardiner twisted her hands nervously. "Oh, I would never be able to hold my head up in public if anyone had seen me."

"You were completely covered," her niece and her maid assured her, almost in the same breath.

"My mouth was not open, was it? I did not snore?" the older lady asked, still worried.

"You were the perfect lady, Aunt Flora," Georgiana said with a smile. "Mr. Harcourt carried you from the inn and put you in our carriage, which the coachman and groom had pulled to safety. No one had a chance to observe you."

"Just Mr. Harcourt. I hope he was a gentleman." A new worry caught her imagination. "You did not speak to a gentleman to whom you had not been introduced?" she asked in horror.

Georgiana thought of how her aunt would react if she had known how her niece had spent the night and blushed. "I had been introduced to him, Aunt Flora," she said in a voice that was slightly husky. "I met him during my Season." She kept her eyes firmly on the floor in front of her, wishing she were anywhere but this coach so that she could revel in her memories. She pressed her hand to her breast, remembering the touch of his lips there. Her lips parted, and her eyes were half closed.

"Well, at least something good came out of your time in London. I hope we never stop at that inn again. As soon as I saw it, I knew it was no place for ladies. And I was right. If only our wheel had not broken." She wrung her hands again. "If only I had my needlework," she sighed, big tears welling up in her eyes. "Why would anyone want that?"

"I am sure I do not know, my dear. Perhaps they thought that was where you carried your ready money," her niece explained once more, not willing to condemn the inn as worthless.

"You were very wise to take our jewels and money with you. I would never have had the foresight to do so. Do you not agree with me, Agnes?"

The maid nodded her head as she had been doing since they left the inn that morning. She smothered a yawn, wishing that her mistress's niece had not awakened quite so early that morning. The sun was hardly up before she was stirring. She yawned again, this time not able to hold it back. Georgiana smiled at her, but her mistress scolded. "I do not understand why the two of you are yawning. You went to bed when I did last night."

"Our rest was disturbed, Aunt Flora," her niece reminded her gently. "The fire."

"I am certain that had you awakened me"—she paused and glared at both women who shared the coach with her—"I would have realized that it was a hoax immediately. And I would still have my chair covers." Her chin wobbled slightly.

Georgiana took a deep breath and continued to smile at her aunt. The years they had lived together had helped her recognize that the constant complaining the lady did was her way of dealing with the insecurity she felt. It could not have been easy for her to be forced to leave her home and live upon the charity of relatives when her husband died. Although Flora's jointure was still secure, it did not provide her enough income to live on her own.

Georgiana had always been grateful that her aunt had been living with them when her parents died. Instead of being forced to live with her sister and brother-in-law when her cousin had moved into the family home, Georgiana and her aunt had retired to a small estate her mother had left her. Of course, her cousin would have permitted them to stay, but neither of them would have felt comfortable doing so.

That afternoon when they pulled up in front of the neat house that had been home for almost eight years, Georgiana gave a sigh of relief. Letting the groom hand her from the coach, she looked around, noting the flowers just beginning to bloom. Her front door opened, and her housekeeper appeared. "Welcome home, Miss Carrington, Mrs. Gardiner," Mrs. Johnson said, smoothing the apron she wore. Georgiana had brought her with her when she had moved into the establishment; therefore, she was not surprised when, with the familiarity of a servant long acquainted with the family, the housekeeper asked, "How are the children?"

"Recovering, Mrs. Johnson. My sister sends you her thanks for the recipe for restorative jelly which you sent with me. We found it especially helpful with the youngest." The woman positively beamed with pride. She stepped back to let her mistress enter. Waving her aunt on ahead, Georgiana turned back to the coachman and groom. Handing them some coins, she told them, "Although our stable is rather small, I am certain my groom can provide for you. Rest the horses before you return home. Ask Benson for whatever you need." They nodded.

Georgiana walked into her own home. She took a deep breath and smiled. Home, she thought. She yawned. Her sleepless night and the journey that day had added to the exhaustion she had felt after looking after four sick children. She yawned again.

Her housekeeper looked at her, noting the circles

under her eyes. "Shall I send a tray up to your room, Miss Georgiana?" she suggested, unaccustomed to seeing her mistress so tired.

"That sounds delightful, Mrs. Johnson. And ask my aunt if she would like the same." She turned to walk up the stairs and then paused. "Send word to Lucy that I will need her tomorrow. My clothes are in disarray." When she had left to help care for her sister's children, she had left her maid behind.

"She was here only today asking when you would return," her housekeeper assured her. "Shall I send for her now?"

"No. Agnes can do for me this evening. All I want is a cup of tea and a good night's sleep." She walked up the stairs, yawning once more.

Before long she was in her own bed. During her absence, Mrs. Johnson had taken all her curtains and bed hangings down and freshened them. The white fabric embroidered with green and gold was sweet-smelling. Georgiana glanced around her room, enjoying the cool greens and golds she had chosen for the walls and decorations. She shifted position as she thought of where she had been the previous evening and what she had been doing. Her bed which only moments before had been so comfortable now felt lonely. She wondered where her lover was that evening and wished that he were with her. That was her only regret, she told herself firmly.

# 3

TWO months later Georgiana was forced to admit that unless something happened quickly, she would have much to regret. Never regular, she had not paid any attention to her irregular spotting, but her maid had. "You must send for the doctor," Lucy insisted. "This is not natural." She was certain her mistress had something seriously wrong with her.

"Nonsense. I would die of embarrassment," Georgiana said. "I am certain it is just the strain of helping care for the children." And perhaps the shock to her system from her evening with Charles. Her eyes widened as she suddenly remembered a possible consequence of that night.

"Better embarrassed than dead," her maid replied. Having served her mistress since before Georgiana's Season, she felt free to express her opinion. And certain of the lady's virtue, Lucy knew that she must be seriously ill. However, Georgiana refused to listen. "I am not ill," she said reassuringly and gave her a tight smile.

After she had dismissed the maid, Georgiana lay down on her bed. She was shaking all over. There was no way to convince herself that she was merely late. A few days either way but never as long as this. How could she have missed something so simple? Having lived close to Lynette during her first pregnancy, Georgiana knew the symptoms. How happy her sister had been when she had missed her first monthly. Her cheeks pink, she had dashed into her mother's morning room one bright morning, not even caring that her younger sister was present. "Mama, I missed this month," she said happily. Their mother had hugged her.

"Have you told Henry yet?" her mother had asked.

"Not yet. I want to be absolutely certain."

"Wait another month," her mother suggested. She drew her daughter to the settee beside her. "Have you been experiencing any sickness?"

"Only first thing in the morning, Mama. And I want to sleep more," Lynette explained with a blush. "Oh, Mama, I am so happy."

Remembering that occasion, Georgiana, overcome by loneliness and fear, began to cry, longing for her mother's comforting arms. Then she thought about trying to explain what she had done to her mother and cried harder. When she had welcomed Harcourt's advances that evening, she had known that what she was doing was not right, that society would condemn her for what she had done if they found out. But she never expected anyone to find out. Now everyone would know. As she thought of what her aunt would say, she began to sob. Finally, worn completely out, her tears at an end, she dried her eyes on her sheet. What could she do, she wondered as she drifted off into sleep.

When she awakened several hours later, the problem was still there. Taking a deep breath, she got up and began walking about the room. She glanced in the mirror and then turned sideways trying to see if the baby had already changed her shape. Although she could not tell any difference yet, she knew that would not be true for long. Her face blanched. What was she going to do?

The question haunted her during the next few days. Each time she washed she stood before the mirror, trying to see the changes that would reveal her indiscretion to the world. Certain everyone could read her guilt on her face, she isolated herself in her room, refusing to come out for any reason. Her maid Lucy, already worried about her mistress, took the problem to the housekeeper.

"What can we do, Mrs. Johnson?" the maid asked after she had explained the problem. She kept her hands clasped so tightly that the housekeeper could see her knuckles turning white. "She will not listen to me."

"No hope of her listening to Mrs. Gardiner either even if I were willing to explain to the old lady. She would go into a decline. Be sicker than Miss Carrington," the housekeeper said thoughtfully. "Are you certain this is as serious as you think?"

"Maybe more."

"Then there is nothing more for it. I will write Mrs. Henry. Maybe she will have more effect on Miss Georgiana." The maid sighed, relieved to have someone else to share her worries.

Less than a fortnight later, a traveling coach pulled up outside the door. Georgiana was walking down the stairs when her sister dashed in. "I came as soon as I heard. Georgiana, you must tell me what is wrong!" she said, hurrying toward her sister. Georgiana put her hand to her throat, lost all her color, and slumped to the floor. For a moment, Lynette and Mrs. Johnson simply stared at her. Then Lynette sprang into action. "Get my groom. We must get her to her chambers as soon as possible."

When Georgiana came around, she coughed at the smell of burning feathers. Then she tried to sit up. Her sister pushed her back. "Lynette, what are you doing here?" she asked. Her voice was so weak it surprised even herself.

"More's to the point; what is going on with you?" her sister asked sternly, a worried look on her face. To both of their surprise, Georgiana, who had never been given to public displays of emotion, burst into tears and buried her face in her sister's bosom.

When the outburst was over and the tears dried, Lynette straightened her rose-colored traveling gown. Giving Georgiana a few more minutes to gain control, she removed her hat and pushed a pin back into her curls. As soon as she had passed her own inspection, she turned back to her sister. Georgiana was pale, her eyes had black circles under them, and she was dressed in one of her oldest gowns, an unbecoming gray. "My dear, you must tell me what is going on. You look positively haggard," Lynette said as calmly as she could. Unlike many other sisters of their acquaintance, she and Georgiana had always been close. The thought of something seriously wrong with her little sister was more than Lynette could bear.

"How did you get here?" Georgiana asked, taking a gulp of air and hoping the excitement would not overset her weak stomach.

"In my coach."

"That is not what I mean and you know it," her sister said, laughing a little. Her laughter had an edge that Lynette did not like.

"Mrs. Johnson and your maid were worried about you. They thought I should know," she explained, inspecting her sister carefully. She did not like what she saw. "Lucy says you will not allow her to send for the doctor."

"Why should I?" Georgiana asked bitterly. "So he can tell everyone?"

"My dear, if you are ill, your friends will want to know," Lynette said soothingly. She knew that from the time she was a small child, Georgiana had never liked having anyone fuss over her when she was sick.

"Oh, they will all know before long, and then I will know who my true friends are."

"Stop speaking in riddles, Georgiana Carrington. I demand that you tell me what is wrong. And do not try to convince me that everything is fine. I will not believe it."

Georgiana took a deep breath and slid from the bed. Her sister could see her consciously straighten her shoulders. "If I had only looked like you," she murmured. She looked in the glass at her rumpled hair and pasty white face. Then she looked back at her sister. The contrast between them was stark. Georgiana was very tall; her hair more red than brown; a feminine version of their father. Lynette, more average in height, had her mother's vivid blue eyes, curving figure, and soft brown hair.

"You have developed quite nicely yourself," Lynette reminded her.

"If only I had developed before my Season," Georgiana whispered. "If only it had not been such a disaster."

"Why are you worrying about your Season now, Georgiana? I have tried to get you to return to London with me every year I have gone. And you have always refused."

"Do you have any idea what it was like to be stared at?" Georgiana asked quietly. "To be called a great Maypole? One of my friends told me her brother had seen my name in the betting book at White's. They were betting on how much dowry Papa would have to provide to find me a husband."

"That was ten years ago. Why are we talking about it now?" her sister asked impatiently.

The door to the hallway opened, and both Georgiana's maid and the housekeeper walked in. "I thought you might like some tea, Mrs. Henry," Mrs. Johnson said quietly. Georgiana turned her back to them and walked to the window. Telling them to put the tray on the table, Lynette motioned them to leave.

Pouring two cups and adding the sugar and milk she knew her sister liked, Lynette walked across the room and gave her sister a cup. Georgiana took a sip and started to take another. Putting the cup down hastily, she ran to the dressing room. Her sister followed to find her bent over a washbowl. Waiting until the heaves stopped, she dampened a cloth and gave it to Georgiana, a frown creasing her brow.

She said nothing until they were back in Georgiana's bedroom. She poured out the first cup of tea she had prepared and poured another but did not put anything in it. "Drink this," she said sternly.

Georgiana sank into a chair and took the tea, her face pale but calm. "I do not know how to begin," she said quietly, dreading her sister's reaction but needing to share her problem with someone.

Lynette picked up her own cup and drank deeply. "Just tell me what happened," she said, bracing herself for the worst. Georgiana plunged into her story. By the time she finished, Lynette had gone from red to white. When her sister's story came to a close, she asked, "Oh, Georgiana, are you sure?" Her sister nodded. "How could you?" Her voice was shaking.

Too afraid that her sister would wash her hands of her, Georgiana said nothing. The silence grew. Lynette clasped her hands in front of her and took a deep breath. Her sister trembled. "We must decide what to do," Lynette said thoughtfully, as though Georgiana had not rocked her world.

"You are not going to cast me out?" Georgiana asked, her eyes filling with tears once again.

"If you do not stop being a watering pot, I may," her sister threatened. "Of course, I do not suppose you have a choice. Whenever I am expecting an interesting event, I weep constantly. Here, wipe your eyes." Handing her sister a handkerchief, Lynette got up and began to walk around the room, unconsciously rearranging the small china figures that decorated one table and the mantel. "You are not a character in a Gothic novel. Let me think."

"I never planned to disgrace you."

"Naturally I know that. Hmmm. I wish you had chosen someone closer at hand."

"If it had been someone I had to see regularly, I would not have done it," Georgiana said and blushed at her own words.

"Well, your red face will get us nowhere," her sister said crisply. "I must consider this."

"There is nothing that can be done," Georgiana wailed, bursting into tears once again. "You will be ruined, too."

"Hush, you foolish child. No one will be ruined." Georgiana looked up, startled. "You are not the first to face this problem, you know." Lynette crossed to stand in front of her sister. "And crying will not solve any-

thing. Let me think." She gave Georgiana a little shake.
"Now, wash your face. Then call for your maid and
dress for dinner. We will talk later."

Refusing to allow her sister's plight to panic her into a
hasty decision, Lynette thought about the problem for
several days. Soothing the minds of Georgiana's maid
and housekeeper without making them suspicious was
her first goal. She accomplished that fairly easily. Georgiana, assured of her sister's support and help, became
her normal, calm self most of the time. Only when she
was alone did her despair overtake her. When she would
awaken in the dark hours just before dawn, she would lie
in bed, her hand over the place where the baby was
growing, dream of having a child of her own to love, and
then think what society would say.

As she considered her sister's dilemma, Lynette asked
Georgiana very pointed questions. "Do you plan to keep
the child?"

"Yes. What else could I do?"

"My dear, you have led a very sheltered life. You
could do as so many others of our class do: arrange for
someone else to bring up the child. You have enough
money to pay them." Lynette's tone of voice was very
cynical.

"Never. The child is mine." Georgiana's voice was
clear and firm.

"That complicates the solution."

"I will leave this place, sell it. Change my name,"
Georgiana said, her arms wrapped around herself as if to
protect the child growing inside her. "But I am going to
keep the child."

"Hmmm." Lynette turned and walked away, leaving
her sister shaken but determined.

Two days later, Lynette walked into the small office
where Georgiana was figuring her monthly accounts.
Dressed in a lemon muslin round gown, she was the pic-
ture of someone without a care in the world. Georgiana

looked at her and then down at herself. Once again she was dressed in gray. It was the most comfortable dress she had. Nothing seemed to fit anymore, and she could not ask Lucy to alter any of her dresses without her finding out what had happened.

"Did you mean it when you said you would leave here?" her sister asked. Georgiana nodded. Lynette smiled. "Good. Here is what you must do." Quickly, she outlined the plan.

"But what if I meet someone who knows us? And what excuse will I give for moving to Harrogate?" her sister protested. Her hands were clasped tightly together in front of herself on the desk.

"It is unlikely you will see anyone you know there. If anyone asks why you did not come to me, you can tell them your husband did not trust the family and demanded you spend your time of mourning away from us. Besides it is a perfectly logical story. And we do have a distant cousin. At least I think he is still alive. He was older than Papa."

"What if someone should know him? What if he is already married?" Georgiana asked. She wanted to agree but could not. She could see all the faults in the story.

"He probably is or was. Since his home is in Jamaica, I do not believe you will need to worry about meeting his acquaintances," her sister said. Her tone of voice suggested that Georgiana was finding fault when none should be found.

"Jamaica? Then why am I in England?"

"Georgiana, are you being a slowtop deliberately? No, do not cry," Lynette said. She handed her sister a handkerchief. "Even I was not such a watering pot. I suppose your tears will stand you in good stead though."

"I cannot help it," her sister said with a sniff. She sat back in her chair, her blue eyes wide. "What advantage could tears have? I hate crying all the time."

"As a recent widow, especially one with an interesting event to look forward to, your tears can be a screen to hide behind. When someone starts asking questions you do not want to answer, let them flow."

"I cannot cry whenever I want to!"

"Then pretend to cry."

"Lynette!"

"Georgiana! If this is to work, you must be willing to do your part!" Lynette stood up. Her back was as straight as a ramrod, and her face was serious. She put her hands on the table and leaned forward. "Tell me now if you disagree."

Georgiana stared at her sister for a moment, considering the alternatives. Then her eyes dropped. "I agree," she said quietly, wishing her stomach would stop rolling.

Lynette came around the desk and hugged her. "I know this will not be easy, my dear. But it is the only way. I will send the necessary letters. As soon as the replies arrive, we can proceed."

"I hope it is quickly."

"So do I. So do I. The sooner you are known as a widow, the more comfortable you will be. You will see." Leaving her sister to her work, Lynette hurried upstairs to find writing materials.

Fortunately for everyone, both the reply from the agency and the letter from Georgiana's solicitor arrived very speedily. In a household where letters provided much of the excitement, two within the same week was a cause for gossip, especially when the handwriting was strange.

Her face carefully unconcerned, Mrs. Johnson took the first strange letter to her mistress. "I hope it is nothing serious," she said as she handed it to her.

"Thank you, Mrs. Johnson. I know how busy you are. I will not keep you," Georgiana said. She smiled at the woman who maintained her home. The housekeeper, disappointed, left the room.

"You have ruined her entire day, Georgiana," Lynette said with a laugh.

"Better hers than mine." She stared at the letter in her hand as though she could read through the outside sheet.

"Well, open it."

Georgiana tore the seal and opened the letter. "He has already found me a house in Harrogate," she said quietly. "It will be ready by Wednesday next." She looked up at her sister. "Are you certain this will work?"

"As certain as I can be. No one knows us there, and it is as far from here and from our home as you could wish." She sighed. "I do wish that I could come for your confinement though."

"We agreed. It would arouse too many suspicions. Besides I will not be completely alone." Georgiana could tell her sister was worried and tried to reassure her.

"A hired companion is not the same as a sister."

"True. But I am certain you will find me someone pleasant," Georgiana said quietly. She smiled at her sister and wondered how she had ever been afraid of telling her what had happened.

"How was he able to find you a place to live so quickly, Georgiana? I hope you are not going to be exiled to some unfashionable dwelling."

"If it were fashionable, it would not be the right place to go, would it?" Georgiana reminded Lynette. For the first time in weeks, she felt like laughing. Her sister threw a small pillow at her, but she ducked out of the way. "You always had terrible aim," she chided, a smile softening her remark.

"I will throw something harder than a pillow if you do not tell me what he said," her sister said with a frown. "How did he find a house in Harrogate so quickly?"

"Apparently he had been to York recently. While he was conducting his business, his wife went to Harrogate to drink the waters."

"She is not there now, is she? It would ruin everything if there were someone you knew there."

"No. In fact, her stay there was brief. He had to return to London unexpectedly, and his wife did not want to let him travel alone. Fortunately for me, however, because he had been there so recently, he did know the general area of the town in which I would be happy and had the name of an estate agent at hand." Georgiana looked at the letter again. Then she looked at her sister. "At first I did not believe your plan could work. Now I am certain it will not fail."

"Do not be too complacent," her sister said sternly. "We still have to convince Aunt Flora."

That very afternoon they began to concentrate on that problem. When Flora entered the drawing room that afternoon, she found Georgiana trying to soothe Lynette, who was almost in tears. "I am certain that Nurse is just trying to frighten you," she said in a voice carefully lowered as though to keep her aunt from hearing.

"What has that woman done now, Lynette?" her aunt demanded. "After she became hysterical when the children were ill, I told you that you needed to hire someone younger."

"I cannot. She was Henry's nurse and would be hurt if I let her go." Lynette sank to the settee, her face worried. "If only . . ." She sighed deeply, noting with satisfaction the interest on her aunt's face.

Despite the way she tried to hide it, the sisters knew their aunt, childless herself, doted on the children. Flora sat down beside her older niece and took her hand between her own. "Tell us how we can help. What has you in such a state?"

"Nurse writes that Edward is very restless lately. She fears a return of the fever," Lynette said with a sigh. "He is so delicate. Why did I leave him behind?"

The sisters had chosen their tools well. Edward was Flora's favorite even though she would have denied it if anyone had asked. Only five years old, he would sit beside her and ask her questions about what it had been like when she was a child. He would listen to her stories for hours, holding her hand and patting it gently. He had been Flora's special charge during the bout with the measles; she had sat with him hours without complaining.

"Do you want me to return with you?" Georgiana interrupted before Flora could respond.

"But your school friend needs you," Lynette protested.

"What school friend? What are you two talking about, Lynette? You are not making sense," the elderly lady fussed.

"Lynette, if you need me, I can write my friend and tell her that I cannot come," Georgiana said. "She can find someone else to support her during her mourning."

"There is no need, my dear. I am certain that aunt is right. Nurse is just overexcited as usual," her sister said in a voice that quavered artistically.

"We can both return with you until you are satisfied that everything is just as you would like," her aunt stated firmly, patting her hand.

"But Georgiana said you and she would be going to Leeds to stay with a friend of hers during her year of mourning," Lynette said, looking from one to the other in confusion. The sisters had agreed that their aunt should not know Georgiana's ultimate destination.

"Leeds? I have heard nothing of this!" her aunt said angrily.

"Lynette, I told you that I had not had time to discuss this with Aunt Flora," Georgiana said, her voice revealing her impatience.

"When did you plan on telling me that we were removing to the north? As if I would go that far away with Edward's health in question. Besides I do not see that it is your responsibility to share this person's year of seclusion. Let her go to her own family or his!" Had it been polite Flora would have shaken her finger in her youngest niece's face.

"Unfortunately, both sets of parents are dead. And her closest relatives do not want to be burdened with a widow of a dead officer who is expecting an interesting event. I am her last hope."

"You did not tell me she was increasing," Lynette said sharply. "I will not allow you to sacrifice her for Edward."

The thought of what it would be like to be newly widowed, increasing, and alone wrenched the elderly lady's heart. "They cast her out, did they?" she asked.

"I believe both sides decided that it would be best if she left," Georgiana said quietly. Lynette glared at her, trying to keep her from embroidering the story more than she needed to do so.

Flora cleared her throat. "Georgiana, I do not see that there is any need for both of us to go to Edward. You know how restless you make Edward, stirring him up with those games of yours," her aunt said. "You go to your friend, and I will return home with Lynette. I have always had a way with the child." The sisters kept their grave expressions only with difficulty. When Lynette glanced at Georgiana, she could not resist a wink. "We must not delay. But if we plan to be away for some time, we must make plans. Georgiana, when will you leave?"

"Leave with us. I plan to stop in London so that I can consult a doctor I have recently heard about," Lynette suggested. She turned to her aunt. "As competent as our own doctor is, I will be happier with a second opinion about Edward's condition."

The elderly lady nodded and said, "Just what I would have done myself. Perhaps we should also arrange for a supply of lemons while we are there. Edward does so enjoy lemonade." Then finally realizing what her older niece had suggested, she turned to Georgiana. "Surely, however, it would be wiser if you left from here?"

"By meeting my friend in London, we can shorten her journey. And I will need more somber clothing if I am to live in her household," Georgiana said.

"Send a letter to your dressmaker immediately," her aunt suggested. "Tell her to have them ready when you arrive." She took her older niece's hand in hers. "Lynette, we can leave immediately if you wish. Do you think it is wise to wait?" She was so worried that the sisters felt guilty for frightening her as they had done.

"I have written to Nurse. She is to send a groom for me if he does not improve," Lynette said quietly. She patted her aunt's hand, wondering how she would explain the robust good health of her children when they arrived at home. Then she smiled. "I know a gentleman who will be happy to see you again," she said teasingly, remembering a neighbor who had haunted their home during their aunt's last visit. Flora blushed.

Letters sent, engagements canceled, and packing finished, they were on the road very shortly, leaving the estate in the hands of their carefully chosen staff. Georgiana breathed a sigh of relief as she watched her home grow smaller and smaller. That relief disappeared during the journey. By the time they arrived in London, she was exhausted and unsure of herself again. As they drove through the streets, she jumped whenever she heard a loud noise.

"No wonder you had such a miserable Season," her aunt said in disgust, "if the least little noise set you off." Georgiana did not answer her but stared out the window at the hustle and bustle of the city streets. When they pulled up in front of her sister's town house, she breathed a sigh of relief, glad to escape into its sheltering walls.

Fortunately for their plans, a host of letters awaited Lynette. Avidly reading them, she smiled. "He is better," she declared. Both her sister and aunt smiled. "As soon as he found out you were returning with me, Aunt Flora, he began to improve immediately." The elderly lady smiled. More tired than she wanted to admit, she followed the housekeeper up the stairs to her room. As soon as she was gone, Lynette drew her sister into a small morning room. "Henry is full of questions, Georgiana. What am I to say?" Unused to keeping secrets from her husband, who had known her all of her life, she waited in trepidation to see what her sister would suggest.

"Tell him the whole. He will have to know sometime," Georgiana said quietly. The thought of Henry's disapproval and the fact that he had the right to force her sister to give up the connection between them made her stomach knot in fear. But she was not willing to come between husband and wife. "Just wait until you are home, and I am on my way to Harrogate."

"Are you sure?"

"I will not ask you to lie to him," Georgiana said quietly. Her sister sighed in relief. "As soon as you find me a companion and a maid, I will leave and you can return home."

Over the next few days, Georgiana did not leave the house except to visit her dressmaker. When she did venture outside, her eyes shifted from side to side, searching for advance warning of anyone she knew in order to avoid them. Unconsciously, she was also searching for a pair of wide shoulders and golden brown hair that towered over the other men. The town was thin of company with most of the families of the *ton* having already left for country estates or Brighton, and so she was able to come and go unnoticed.

Lynette had found her a companion and a maid very quickly. Her companion was to be the widow of a naval officer, Mrs. Thomas, a plump, pleasant, and middle-aged woman. Her only child, a son, was also in the navy and rarely home. The maid, a dresser with some experience who had come highly recommended, agreed reluctantly to leave London, realizing she would have a difficult time finding a better job at the present.

Having made arrangements for the maid and Mrs. Thomas to meet the carriage at the inn, Lynette watched in satisfaction as it rolled up before her door exactly on schedule. She supervised the loading of her sister's trunk. "Oh, Georgiana, I wish I could go with you," she whispered as she hugged her.

Dressed in black, a color that did little for her, Georgiana returned the hug. Then she kissed her aunt's cheeks and walked out the door. Feeling as though she were leaving her old life behind, she turned and looked back. Her sister smiled bravely and waved. Biting her lip to keep from crying, she hurried down the steps toward the carriage.

Letting the hired groom hand her into the coach, she smiled tremulously at the women inside. "I am Mrs. Carrington," she said.

# 4

THE journey northward was a voyage of discovery for everyone involved. As Georgiana told Lynette much later, throwing three unacquainted women together in one small coach was a recipe for instant hatred or a lasting friendship.

After Georgiana had settled herself in the coach, the other occupants of the post chaise had identified themselves. "Mrs. Carrington, I am Mrs. Thomas," the older lady had said. "And this is Miss Miller."

"Just Miller, if you please," the maid had said primly. Her careful assessment of her new mistress did not please her. Unlike the fashionable lady who had interviewed her, this lady had little town bronze and was too tall ever to be fashionable. She pressed her lips together grimly after her inspection.

Georgiana smiled at them both, hoping that her sister had chosen wisely. "My sister has given me your references and told me what she knows of you, but I hope we will become better acquainted." The chaise hit a bump, and she gulped.

"Shall I tell the driver to slow down, Mrs. Carrington," her companion asked. She recognized the white look on the younger lady's face. "Or perhaps you wish to have him stop?"

"If we were to stop each time I grow queasy, we would never reach Harrogate," Georgiana replied with a weak smile.

"I remember what it is like," Mrs. Thomas said, patting Georgiana's hand. "In just a few months, this will be but a memory. As your child grows, you will wonder that he was ever small enough to be part of you." While Miller sat quietly, her lips carefully pursed together, Mrs. Thomas chattered on. She watched in satisfaction as Georgiana began to relax, the white line around her lips disappearing.

By the time they stopped to change horses and eat something, Georgiana knew that she and Mrs. Thomas would deal nicely together. Chattering or keeping silent, the older lady seemed to know exactly what Georgiana needed. The journey was difficult for Georgiana. Besides the queasiness she felt, she was plagued by a persistent backache and cramps in her legs. Although she tried to hide her deteriorating condition from her companions, it was not long until Mrs. Thomas became increasingly aware that something was wrong.

In York, almost at the end of their journey, she tried to persuade Georgiana to rest for more than one evening. "Give yourself some time away from the journey, Mrs. Carrington," she urged, noting with worry the waxen look to Georgiana's cheeks.

"I will be fine," her mistress assured her, stifling a moan by biting her lips. Not even to herself would she admit how worried she was. "We are so close. I will be fine tomorrow."

Mrs. Thomas pressed her lips together firmly to hold back her disagreement. "Miller, see that Mrs. Carrington goes to bed as soon as she enters her room. I will instruct the innkeeper to send up a light supper."

The maid pinched her lips together angrily. Then she nodded and helped her mistress up the stairs. As soon as Georgiana undressed and crawled into bed, she suggested, "Miller, if you wish, you have my leave to spend some time visiting the sights in York. This is a very old city. I had hoped to visit the York Minster myself. It should be light for hours yet." The maid nodded and hurried from the room, her face still set in disagreeable lines.

Alone, Georgiana let her mask slide. She put her hands over her growing child, and a few tears trickled down her cheeks. Before she could lose herself in despair, her door opened, and Mrs. Thomas bustled in, followed by a red-cheeked maid carrying a tray.

"I could not eat anything, Mrs. Thomas," Georgiana said wearily. Lately, nothing tasted good, and more often than not she lost whatever she ate.

"Just tea and toast now, my dear," her companion coaxed. "You must be parched. And I know you ate nothing at luncheon." Reluctantly, Georgiana allowed herself to be persuaded. Sipping on plain tea and nibbling a crust, she was surprised how much stronger she soon felt.

As she watched the color return to Georgiana's face, Mrs. Thomas smiled in satisfaction. "As soon as you have had some time to rest, the maid—I believe she's the innkeeper's daughter," she added, "will bring you some broth. The cook has quite a reputation for tasty soups, I'm told." She glanced around the room. "Where is Miller?"

"Out viewing the town. You should join her," Georgiana explained, hiding a yawn and wishing she were alone so she could go to sleep.

"Nonsense. I plan to sit here by the window and take advantage of this light to work on my embroidery," she said briskly. Georgiana did not reply, but only closed her eyes and was soon asleep. As soon as she realized Georgiana was asleep, Mrs. Thomas lost the cheerful look she normally wore. The sooner they arrived in Harrogate, the happier she would be. Georgiana needed to see a doctor, and the spa would undoubtedly provide several.

When they arrived at their house in Harrogate the next day, Georgiana admitted to herself that Miller would not suit. Her face pale and drawn from the tiring journey, Georgiana greeted her servants and then listened as her maid ordered the groom and footman about as though she were the mistress of the house. However, she was too tired to do more than call Miller to her side. "Order a tea tray in my room for me," she said quietly.

Her companion, noting her pale face, bustled forward,

her gray skirts rustling. "Mrs. Carrington, you must go upstairs immediately," she insisted. "I will do all that is necessary to get us settled in." The housekeeper, a tall, spare woman, bristled at her words. "Think of the baby," Mrs. Thomas said in a whisper that was overheard by everyone in the entrance hall. Georgiana blushed and nodded. And the moment of tension was gone. Suddenly everyone was solicitous.

"This way, Mrs. Carrington," the housekeeper said, leading her up the stairs. "Cook will have your tray ready in the twinkle of an eye. I prepared the mistress's rooms for you. But if they do not suit, there are four other chambers to chose from." Sympathy poured from her as she escorted her new mistress to her chambers.

"I am certain that it will be splendid, Mrs. Smythe," Georgiana murmured, wanting nothing more than a soft bed on which to place her head, and a cup of plain tea to settle her stomach.

More exhausted than she wanted to admit, Georgiana spent the next several days in bed. Removed from the jostling of the coach, her back lost most of the ache that had held her prisoner during the journey.

When she descended to breakfast several days later, she was feeling more herself. The nausea she had felt during the last few days was almost completely gone. And for the first time in several weeks, she was actually looking forward to a meal. The array on the sideboard caught her immediate attention as she entered the room. Selecting a muffin, she ordered fresh tea from a footman who waited to serve her. "And a slice of ham, too," she said.

When Mrs. Thomas bustled in a few minutes later, she was drinking a cup of tea. Her chaperon inspected her carefully, noting with pleasure the improvement in her looks. "Good morning, Mrs. Carrington. I am pleased to see you looking so refreshed this morning."

"Mrs. Thomas. Thank you for supervising our arrival. I am sorry I was not more helpful." After running her own household for several years, Georgiana was not accustomed to having anyone else take charge for her. If truth were known, she was not at all certain she enjoyed it.

"That is what I am here for," her companion said with a smile. As if reading her employer's mind, she continued, "Though now that you are feeling better, I am sure that I will have little to do." She selected her breakfast and sat down. "The servants seem quite competent and the house pleasant. How did you discover such a place in the middle of the summer?"

"Not I," Georgiana assured her. "My man of affairs. The family who had rented it for the summer had to return home to prepare for a wedding."

"A successful venture for them, I suppose," the older lady said with a smile. "Ah, I remember the excitement of preparing for my own wedding as I am sure you do."

As she had done every time the lady had brought up the subject of husbands and marriage on their journey northward, Georgiana ignored the comment. For a moment the room was silent as her companion drew her own conclusions about the state of her employer's marriage. Then Mrs. Thomas asked, "What do you wish to do today, Mrs. Carrington?"

"I want to inspect the house. Since we will be here until next spring at least, there will be things I wish replaced. But you do not have to wait on me constantly." When her companion tried to protest, Georgiana simply went on. "Perhaps you could inspect the shops to see to which we will give our orders."

Mrs. Thomas, who had resigned herself to another boring day inside, beamed. "I will be happy to do so immediately." She started to get up from the table, leaving her breakfast unfinished.

"There is no hurry. You do not have to rush off just now," Georgiana said with a smile. "Have you written your son to tell him of your new direction?"

"Before I left London. As soon as your sister gave me the location, I wrote him immediately. How soon he will get the letter, I cannot say."

"Does it worry you to have him in the navy and so far away?" Georgiana asked, unsuccessfully hiding her own unhappiness at the separation from her family. Lynette would have returned home by now and told Henry everything. She could only hope that her brother-in-law would at least let Lynette write to tell her sister of his reaction.

"The same as most mothers. At least he is away from most of the fighting," Mrs. Thomas said quietly. "You will discover that most mothers worry no matter how safe their children are. It is the peril of having children," she added. "When my son was a child, I worried constantly. He was always climbing trees or borrowing a punt and going out on the river. That is when I knew that he would follow his father into the navy." Georgiana merely smiled and nodded at appropriate places, only half listening to what the lady was saying. Where once Mrs. Thomas's constant chatter would have disturbed her, now she found it soothing.

By the end of the next week, Georgiana had the reins of the household firmly in her grasp, her new servants pleased to discover that she was both fair and concerned. To their delight, she was engaged in refurbishing the house. Her bedroom, originally decorated in red and black, was being redone in her favorite white, green, and gold. While it was being finished, she was sleeping in a smaller chamber. And she had drawn up plans to refurbish the shabby morning room with new wallcoverings, upholstery, and curtains. The room caught the light most of the day, and Georgiana had selected it as her own sitting room. She had unpacked her sketching materials, but had not had a chance to use them.

The only disruptions in her existence were her worry over her brother-in-law's reaction and the turmoil her maid was causing in the household. Puffed up with her own importance, the woman simply refused to make any effort to get along with any of the other servants. After the third complaint by her housekeeper, Georgiana called her maid in once again.

"Miller, what am I to do with you?" she asked in the gentlest voice she could manage. It was their second interview in less than four days. The woman's attitude was beginning to make Georgiana feel uncomfortable in her own home. Nor was her attitude about the other servants the only problem; Miller was not willing to listen to her mistress's suggestions about her clothing.

"It is not my fault, Mrs. Carrington. Had the others the same high standards which I uphold, there would be no problem at all," the maid said, her nose tilted upward. She remained standing before Georgiana's desk, although her employer had asked her to be seated.

"We all live in the same house, Miller. I do not like this strife." When the maid started to speak, Georgiana held up her hand. "No. I think the time has come to take drastic action." Quickly, she outlined her plan: Miller would return to London to seek a new post. "I will pay your traveling expenses. You are here because I brought you here. I will pay you a quarter's wages and provide a reference."

Although the maid had blanched when she first heard that she was being dismissed, the terms of the arrangement were so generous that she was delighted. With three months' wages in her pocket, she would have time to find a post that suited her better. "I am sorry that you have not found me suitable, Mrs. Carrington," she unbent enough to say. "When do you wish me to leave?"

"I will send the footman to inquire about the next stagecoach to London." She frowned for a moment. "Perhaps it would be best if you left from York. You may begin packing, and I will send you word." Determined to have the woman out of her house as soon as possible, Georgiana rang for her housekeeper.

Georgiana could tell Mrs. Smythe was pleased with her actions, although the woman tried very hard to keep her face from showing her emotions. "I will need another maid, perhaps someone younger. Do you have any suggestions?" Georgiana asked.

"I know just the girl, Mrs. Carrington. She may not

have the town bronze of Miller, but she is willing to work," Mrs. Smythe said. The smile she had been trying to hide burst across her face, changing it completely. "I shall send for her immediately."

"Wait until Miller is gone first," Georgiana said quietly. "Now send the footman to find out about stages to London." Before the day was out, Miller was on her way, and Georgiana had a new maid.

With the more relaxed atmosphere of the house, Georgiana regained her composure. Although she had not been out of the house except to walk in its small back garden, she realized that she could not hide there forever. Completely forgetting that she was supposed to be a recent widow, she made a list of the items she needed and made plans to seek them out.

The long-awaited letter from her sister brought her back to reality. According to Lynette, Henry had been furious, forbidding her to see Georgiana ever again. After reading that line, Georgiana closed her eyes and clasped the letter to her heart. A few tears trickled down her face. Mrs. Thomas, looking up from a letter from one of her friends, asked, "What has disturbed you? Is something wrong?"

Quickly Georgiana regained her control. She dashed away the few remaining teardrops. "Everything will be fine," she said in a dull voice. Never to see her sister again. Tears threatened to flood her face, but she shut her eyes in order to keep them back. Finally, she took a deep, shuddering breath and opened them. Putting the letter on her lap, she carefully smoothed away the wrinkles. Then she began reading again, trying to decipher her sister's words. When she was excited, Lynette had a habit of adding extra flourishes on letters. It was even more difficult to read because she had chosen to cross the lines rather than cost her sister additional money.

Her companion watched her reading the letter and wished that her employer were willing to share her burdens. At times her hidden sadness was more than Mrs.

Thomas could bear. She was just about to ask another question when Georgiana gasped and then smiled broadly.

"As soon as he had time to think this through, Henry relented. You know he can never stay very angry for very long. Undoubtedly you will receive a letter from him telling you how disappointed he is in you, but he finally agreed that you are my only remaining family and should not be completely disowned. As if I would. But I am glad I will not have to go against his wishes," Lynette wrote. The rest of the letter relayed the news of the family. Edward miraculously recovered as soon as he saw Aunt Flora. Georgiana giggled. Their aunt was enjoying country society and even had a beau. Squire Longworth, a gentleman a few years older than their aunt, had been calling at least twice a week. And Aunt Flora had agreed to go driving with him. This time Georgiana could not control her reaction; she laughed loudly. Her companion smiled, relieved of her worry, and returned to her own letter.

At the last line of her sister's letter, Georgiana frowned: "Do not forget that you are a widow, Georgiana." She sighed. How was a widow supposed to act? Her mother had died only days before her father. And when Aunt Flora had joined them, she had already put off black gloves. During the mourning period after their parents' death, she and her sister had received friends and attended dinners and small parties, although they had not accepted any invitations to dances. Did widows have to don more than widow's weeds?

For a day or two, Georgiana pondered the question. Then, already comfortable with Mrs. Thomas, she decided to ask her what would be proper. After breakfast the next morning, she followed Mrs. Thomas into the still dreary morning room. Taking up her sketchbook and pencils, she attempted to draw, but soon gave it up when all she produced were lines.

Gathering her courage, she began. "Mrs. Thomas." The older lady looked up from the small shirt she was embroidering and waited for her to continue. Georgiana put her sketch pad and pencils on the table and clasped her hands tightly. She cleared her throat and began again. "Mrs. Thomas?"

"Yes?"

"How must a widow behave?" Georgiana asked quickly, spilling her words over one another so that they seemed to run together. She held her breath, hoping that her companion would not brush her question lightly aside.

"Just as you have been, Mrs. Carrington," the older lady said pleasantly, delighted that for the first time since they met her mistress had shared more than a commonplace remark with her.

"That is not what I meant. I know how I must dress, that in a little more than two months' time I may wear gray or even white trimming on my dresses. What I need to know is what I may do." She rose, a graceful figure in her black gown, and began to pace about the room.

"What you may do?" Mrs. Thomas asked in a confused voice. "I do not understand."

"My mother died before my father. My aunt had been a widow for several years before she came to live with us," Georgiana explained.

"Surely you knew widows who lived near your home."

"Yes, certainly. But I did not know them well. We did not visit. I did not see them often. Do you understand my problem?" The younger lady paused in her circuit of the room. "I am afraid of giving offense because I do not know how to act."

"Oh. Oh, Mrs. Carrington. Yes, yes, of course." Taking a deep breath, her companion patted the chair near her. "Come, sit by me." When Georgiana was once more seated, she carefully asked, "How long have you been a widow? Your sister said only that your loss was recent."

Doing sums quickly in her head and hoping that she had left room for unforeseen delays, Georgiana said,

"Almost four months." She kept her eyes fixed on her clasped hands rather than on her questioner.

"Not a love match, I would guess," Mrs. Thomas said under her breath, remembering how Georgiana avoided discussing her husband. "So recent," she said aloud. Georgiana looked at her clasped hands and hoped she did not give anything away. "Just what did you want to do?"

"Visit the shops; explore the circulating library, if there is one; take a ride in the country," Georgiana said, her words flying from her.

"Yes." Georgiana stared at the lady who provided her position dignity, willing her to continue. "The ride will certainly be possible," Mrs. Thomas finally said. "I will hire a coach. We can go tomorrow."

"A coach? I want to be outside in the sunshine, not closed up in a coach," Georgiana protested. "I had hoped to ride."

"Once we have arrived at our destination, whatever that may be, we will have a picnic. I am certain Cook will be happy to oblige." Mrs. Thomas smiled at Georgiana as if she were offering her a great prize. "Riding in your condition will be out of the question."

"Are you also saying that I cannot visit a shop or go for a walk down the street?" her mistress demanded. She drew herself up and glared at the other lady as if she and not society were to blame for the restrictions Georgiana now faced.

"Of course not. If you wish to be discussed as a person who has no regard for society, you may do as you please," Mrs. Thomas said. Her voice was cool.

Georgiana wilted immediately. "No. I will follow your advice," she said quietly. She sank in a nearby chair. "How long must I remain in seclusion?"

"Society does not regard this as seclusion. If you had family nearby or close friends, you could visit them or they could visit you. And when you go into half mourning, you may go for a walk or a drive or even visit the shops. However, your interesting condition makes every-thing more awkward."

"Oh." Georgiana sighed. If her companion knew the whole, then she would understand what awkward was. One moment, she thought. One moment of madness could alter the world forever.

"No one will look askance if you ask merchants to bring their wares here so that you can look at them. Have you given thought to a nursery?"

"Mrs. Smythe showed me the room that had been used as one, but I did not care for it." Georgiana put her hand over the child growing within her. "I want my baby surrounded by sunlight."

"When will the babe arrive?" Mrs. Thomas asked. Taking advantage of Georgiana's unaccustomed talka-tiveness, she planned to gain answers to questions that had been gnawing at her since they met.

"At the beginning of the new year," Georgiana whis-pered. Her face was red. Talking about the birth made her think of the babe's father and her own wanton be-havior. She picked up a fan lying on a table nearby and began fanning furiously.

"Then there will be plenty of time."

"For what?"

"To redecorate a room and complete the babe's cloth-ing. We will need material for several gowns and caps."

"And napkins. My sister's children always have dozens and dozens of napkins," Georgiana added, feel-ing excitement beginning to rise within her.

"Have you arranged for a lying-in nurse? Or do you prefer a doctor?" Mrs. Thomas inspected Georgiana carefully. "With your build, I do not foresee any compli-cations."

Although she had been banned from her sister's bed-room during the birth of her children, Georgiana was not ignorant of the process. But she still blushed. Her chap-eron's question made her consider her options carefully. During her years on her own estate, she had helped two of the farmers' wives through the birth of their babies.

Their doctor, a kindly man who treated each new baby he helped into life as gently as though it were his own, had made the women feel much more secure. "A doctor. In her letter my sister reminded me of my promise to seek one out. I must send for one soon."

"Ask Mrs. Smythe to suggest one. She is certain to know the most reputable," Mrs. Thomas suggested. "Do you want me to visit the merchants and ask them to call or arrange for the ride into the country."

"The doctor must come first. Then I will decide."

Over the next few weeks, Georgiana endured a visit from the doctor, a gruff man much unlike the doctor she was accustomed to. Even with Mrs. Thomas and her maid present, his examination was an agony for her. After he had finished and she was dressed once more, he led her to a chair and then sat down beside her, his face serious.

"What is wrong?" Georgiana asked, clenching her hands together in her lap until her knuckles turned white. She looked wildly from the doctor to her companion. Mrs. Thomas crossed the room to stand behind her, her hands resting soothingly on Georgiana's shoulders.

"These problems you have been having worry me," Dr. Mackensie told her. Mrs. Thomas felt Georgiana's shoulders tighten under her hands. "I recommend that you spend part of every afternoon, two hours at the least, in bed. If that does not improve your condition, we will try something else."

"What is wrong? Will I lose the baby?" Georgiana said in a voice that cracked with her pain and despair. She wrapped her arms around herself as if to shield the child she carried.

"If I knew, I should be famous," the doctor said sharply. "For now, you must rest and try not to worry. Call me if you have any further problems. Otherwise, I will see you next month."

Both Georgiana and Mrs. Thomas stared at him, willing him to give them more information. He simply picked up his bag and left.

As soon as the door closed behind him, Georgiana dissolved into tears. "My baby," she moaned. "My baby."

Soothing her the best way they could, Mrs. Thomas and her maid put her to bed. Sending the maid to the kitchen for a tea tray, Mrs. Thomas pulled a chair beside the bed and talked soothingly to her mistress. Georgiana, too caught up in her own fears, did not hear what she said, but the sound comforted her.

When the maid left the room, Mrs. Smythe was waiting. "Daisy, what has happened?" she demanded. The girl burst into tears. "Pull yourself together, girl, and give me the news," the housekeeper demanded.

"He said she might lose the baby," Daisy mumbled.

"What? If that is not like a man," Mrs. Smythe complained. "Scared the lady to death, I suppose?" The maid nodded. "Well, we shall have to prove him wrong."

"How can we do that?" the girl asked, scrubbing her tears from her face with a hand.

"What did he tell her to do?"

"Rest. Every afternoon for at least two hours."

"Sensible. Leave everything to me. I'll have a talk with Mrs. Thomas. We will arrange everything. Now, be off with you." She watched the girl hurry toward the back staircase. Then she walked slowly back to her office.

As soon as Georgiana fell asleep, Mrs. Thomas made her way downstairs. Mrs. Smythe was waiting. "You've heard, I suppose?" the companion asked, certain of the answer.

The housekeeper nodded. "We will have to work together to keep Mrs. Carrington in good spirits.

"Too bad she has no friends or family nearby to support her now," the housekeeper said quietly.

"Men, they only think of themselves. If it had not been for her husband's dislike of her family, she would be safe with her sister now."

Mrs. Smythe, who had often wondered what had brought her mistress to the north of England, nodded.

"Well, we shall have to see that she has not time to worry," she said.

"She can finish redecorating," Mrs. Thomas said thoughtfully.

"No painting, though. We would not want to take a chance with fumes affecting her," Mrs. Smythe added. "And I will have a word with Cook about the food. Mrs. Carrington has lost weight since she arrived. Her dresses hang on her. That cannot be good for the babe."

"And I will urge her to spend more time in the garden. Until it grows colder, she should be outside more," Mrs. Thomas said. The two women looked at each other and nodded.

That very day they put their plan into effect. As soon as Georgiana awoke, Mrs. Thomas was ready. Refusing to allow her mistress to rise, she spread samples of wall-coverings and fabrics over the bed, almost covering Georgiana in them.

"This has all the colors you told me you liked," she said as she held out a piece of fabric for Georgiana's approval.

"The design is too bold. I am looking for something simple," Georgiana replied, intrigued in spite of herself. The next two hours passed quickly as she inspected fabric for her new bedroom. Although she had already finished one bedroom, she had decided that she wanted the one next to hers to be the nursery. She did not intend to leave her child in the hands of its nurse.

Following the regime concocted by her companion, housekeeper, and doctor, Georgiana was busy. She spent her mornings in the garden with her sketch pad or sewing in her newly refurbished sitting room. Afternoons she rested or read. At the end of each day when she walked through the changing rooms, she held her hand over her growing child and described what she saw.

While Georgiana found things in her household to occupy her time, her companion became a regular feature around town. From the merchant who supplied the lace and skeins of thread for the baby's clothing to those ladies who gathered every morning to take the waters, she became an accustomed sight. Because she was naturally friendly and loved to talk, everyone she met soon learned the sad tale of her mistress, recently widowed and expecting a child.

The morning Georgiana appeared in gray, Mrs. Thomas smiled. "Are you ready to take the waters, Mrs. Carrington?" she asked.

"Take the waters?" Georgiana wrinkled her nose. "I had not planned to do so."

Her companion laughed merrily. "My dear, you do not have to drink them, although some are not as bad as the others. I meant that today you may visit one of the springs in person."

The drives in the country and her time in the garden had whetted Georgiana's desire for being outdoors. Accustomed to coming and going as she pleased, she had not enjoyed being so confined. Therefore, she had been planning the resumption of her activities very carefully. "I had thought to visit the shops first," she admitted. "But if you disagree?"

"Not disagree. But how much better it will be to make the acquaintance of those people of quality in the town. Despite your circumstances, no one would think it wrong if you entertained callers now. But first you must become acquainted with people," her chaperon explained. "Shall I call for our bonnets?"

Although people at first stared at the tall lady in gray who accompanied Mrs. Thomas that morning, soon she was an accepted figure, remarked on only by newcomers. As fall progressed, most of the visitors disappeared, leaving only the residents of the town, who welcomed the newcomer with sympathy and understanding, so much sympathy and understanding that her guilt at her deception made Georgiana uncomfortable. That did not, however, keep her at home.

One morning, a crisp, golden morning of late fall, Georgiana and Mrs. Thomas were sitting and talking to two of their acquaintances when a group of gentlemen dressed in riding clothes entered. Although they continued their own conversation, all the ladies could hear the gentlemen's remarks. "You lost. Now it is time to pay up," one of them told another. They all laughed heartily.

Georgiana could not tell who was talking. Her eyes had been caught by a gentleman who stood taller than the rest. Telling herself that she was simply dreaming once again, she forced herself to concentrate on the conversation in her own group.

"Why could you not ask for something simple, Stokley? Three full glasses?" the loser complained. Once again interest in the gentlemen consumed the ladies.

"Three full glasses of our choice," his friend reminded him. "I wonder which of the springs tastes truly vile?"

"You are wicked, Stokley!" the loser proclaimed.

"Let us ask the ladies." Before the four ladies sitting nearby could register their surprise, they were surrounded. The gentlemen removed their hats and began introducing themselves, asking pardon for their familiarity. Georgiana glanced up curiously. Then her face went white.

"Mrs. Carrington?" she heard a familiar voice ask.

She could feel herself drifting away, but could not stop it. She could only stare helplessly into the brown eyes above her. Then she slumped and slid from her chair.

# 5

"MRS. CARRINGTON!" Her companion bent over her, waving the vinaigrette she carried under Georgiana's nose.

"We cannot leave her there," the oldest lady, who had been sitting with her, protested. "Someone must do something."

"Where shall I put her?" Charles Harcourt asked as he picked Georgiana up and stood there holding her. He resisted the impulse to walk out the door with her in his arms and find the closest bed. He frowned as he wondered if seeing him again had caused her to faint. Then he looked down at her and was quick to notice the changes in her figure. A question ran through his mind and then was quickly discarded. He tightened his arms around her and wished that he did not have to put her down.

"Over there," Mrs. Thomas said quickly, pointing to a bench beside the wall. The other ladies on his heels and his friends staring at him curiously, he walked across the room and laid her gently down.

"Will she be all right?" he asked, noting the pallor of her cheeks.

"I am certain there is nothing to worry about," one of the ladies, a Mrs. Wykcombe, assured him. She blushed and whispered, "Ladies in her condition often faint, Mr. Harcourt." Then she raised her fan and waved it furiously, trying to dispel the heat in her cheeks.

"I can manage now, Mr. Harcourt." Mrs. Thomas paused and looked at him expectantly. He did not disappoint her.

"And you are?"

"Mrs. Thomas, her companion."

"Where is her aunt?" Harcourt asked, wondering if Georgiana were in mourning for the elderly lady. He also wondered if she had known she was with child the night they were together, but covered his concern under an air of general interest.

"With Mrs. Carrington's sister. Apparently she is indispensable with children." Although she wished to pursue their conversation, she turned her attention back to her mistress. "Thank you, sir," she said firmly when she looked and discovered that he had not moved a step. "If I need you again, I will call on you."

Realizing that he had been dismissed, Harcourt retreated. Soon he was surrounded once more by his friends.

"Who is she?" Stokley asked.

"And why did she faint?" added the man whom they had planned to force to drink the water. He was a slight man. "She is a tall one, isn't she," he said with a sigh as he looked once more at the bench where Georgiana lay. The chance he had to look at her had given him a tantalizing view of russet curls and creamy skin.

"Too tall for you, Elmore," Stokley told him. "Too tall for any of us except Harcourt. Now do not fob us off, Harcourt. Who is she?"

"Georgiana Carrington. That is all I know."

"And where did you meet her?" Elmore demanded, looking up at his friend. "And when may I be introduced?"

"She was staying at the same inn as I the night I was robbed," Harcourt said quietly. He looked at the bench where Georgiana lay and frowned. "We both had to talk to the magistrate. And I do not plan to introduce anyone to her. At least not today."

"Trying to keep her all to yourself, are you. It is not working. You must have frightened the life out of her that night. She looked at you and fainted," Elmore said with a laugh.

"Nonsense. Not like that at all," one of the other gentlemen, somewhat older than the rest, said firmly. "I once knew a lady who fainted when the wind changed."

"Mrs. Carrington is not one of those," Harcourt said indignantly. "In spite of the general confusion at the inn, she managed to rescue herself, an elderly aunt, and a maid that night. There must be another explanation." Not willing to let his friends see that he would rather be near Georgiana, he turned back to Elmore. "Which of these waters shall we have him drink, gentleman?" he asked. Quickly, their attention was back on their amusement.

Across the room, the ladies hovered around Georgiana. "Is she coming around, Mrs. Thomas?" asked Mrs. Wykcombe in a soft voice. "Shall I send for Dr. Mackensie?" All the ladies had heard the story of Georgiana's difficulties. She waved her fan around Georgiana's face as though the breeze it raised would bring her back to herself again.

Trying to evade the fan that the lady was waving furiously, Mrs. Thomas waved the vinaigrette under her mistress's nose once again. This time she was pleased when Georgiana moaned and brushed it away. "She is coming around."

Stepping back, the ladies watched as Georgiana opened her eyes and, realizing that she was lying down, tried to sit up. "Do not try to rise, Mrs. Carrington. Nothing could be more disastrous after a faint. You must take care," Mrs. Wykcombe said in a fluttery voice.

"Just rest here for a few more minutes, my dear," Mrs. Thomas added. "You gave us a scare."

Then Georgiana remembered. Her face lost the color it had only recently regained. She looked around the room frantically, but her view was blocked by the ladies who surrounded her. "Charles? Mr. Harcourt?" she asked weakly, hoping that his appearance had been just a dream.

"He carried you over here, Mrs. Carrington. So much of a gentleman," Mrs. Wykcombe said with a sigh, her cheeks growing warm. She waved her fan furiously. "So tall. We were very fortunate that someone was here to help us. Tell me, Mrs. Carrington, what is his background?"

Both her older sister, Mrs. Bishop, and Mrs. Thomas stared at her as though they could not believe what she had just said. "I always knew you had an empty cockloft, Betsy, but I thought you had more sense than to tell the world it was so," her sister said. Her face wore an amused smile, but her words were stern. "Will you need us any longer, Mrs. Thomas?" When Georgiana's companion shook her head, she put her hand on her sister's arm and pulled her away.

"But I do not want to leave yet, Isabelle," Mrs. Wykcombe said as they walked away. She glanced at the gentlemen as though she wished to join them, but they were counting as Elmore swallowed his punishment. Her sister said something very low. Finally giving up with at least a show of acceptance, Mrs. Wykcombe left.

Across the room, Harcourt watched his friend drink the second of three glasses of the water filled with minerals. He had managed to turn so that he could also see the bench on which Mrs. Carrington lay. His eyes narrowed as he watched carefully.

When their companions had left, Georgiana swung her legs to the floor and sat up cautiously. For a moment everything swam alarmingly. She closed her eyes. When she opened them again, the room was steady once more. But when she tried to rise, her companion put her hands on her shoulder and held her down. "Wait just a few moments more, my dear. There is no sense rushing about. Far better to take this slowly." Georgiana nodded. Mrs. Thomas stepped back, relieved.

Glancing around to see who had been watching as she fainted, Georgiana was relieved to note that, except for the party of gentlemen, her companion, and herself, the room was deserted. "How did I get over here?"

"Mr. Harcourt carried you," Mrs. Thomas said quietly.

She noted with interest that Georgiana blushed. "He asked after your aunt, also."

"My aunt?" Georgiana asked in confusion. Conflicting emotions of desire, anger, and regret poured through her, keeping her from thinking clearly. He had held her closely, and she had not been awake to enjoy it. Her eyes fell. The small mound that was her constant reminder of their night together was evident. Her cheeks flamed red. He must know, she thought. Looking up under her lashes, she tried to measure his reaction. He still was standing with his friends, watching the youngest drink his third glass of foul-tasting water. Nothing in his bearing revealed his thoughts. Georgiana watched him for a while. He must not know. She took a deep breath and then another.

"Good. That is just what you must do. Let me fetch you a glass of water, Mrs. Carrington," the older lady suggested.

"Not if it is from the springs. The one I had last time was so salty it almost turned my stomach," Georgiana protested. "I will sit here for a few minutes more. Then I will be fine." She took another deep breath. Mrs. Thomas sat down beside her on the bench, satisfied for the moment.

When Georgiana stood up a few minutes later, Mrs. Thomas hovered by her elbow. Charles Harcourt said a few words to his friends and then walked across the room toward them. "Shall I order a chair for you, Mrs. Carrington?" he asked, not at all satisfied with the way the color in her cheeks came and went.

"Nonsense. A walk is just what I need," she said firmly, brushing aside both Mrs. Thomas's and his objections. "It is a beautiful day."

"Then I insist on being your escort," the tall man said, his face set in stern lines. He slipped his arm through hers and stared down at her, daring her to deny him. Unwilling to confront him and bemused by the touch of his hand, Georgiana walked from the room on his arm, her companion only steps behind them.

Hoping to keep him from asking her questions she would rather not answer, Georgiana asked, "Did you recover your money?"

"Not a pony. After you left that morning . . ." He paused and stared at her as if willing her to give him an explanation. She kept her eyes on the ground in front of her, and her mouth closed. "The magistrate as good as told me that he did not intend to search for the thief. He did, however, promise to keep an eye on Tindle."

"That man! He probably stole your money himself. He has shifty eyes. And he was so worried about himself he did not see to the safety of his guests." Remembering the fear she had felt that night sent color into her cheeks and eliminated the listlessness that had been present in her voice. She frowned. "The magistrate should have locked him away," she said. "He is probably using Aunt Flora's chair covers right now."

"You do him too much credit, Mrs. Carrington. I fear he was only a pawn in the hands of someone far wiser than he. I cannot believe that he had enough in his cockloft to plan the deed."

"If he did not plan, he at least went along with it."

Consumed by curiosity, Mrs. Thomas, who was walking behind them, caught up with them and asked, "Of whom are you speaking?"

"The innkeeper in the inn where my aunt and I were robbed," Georgiana explained.

"You were robbed!" Mrs. Thomas's eyes grew wide. "You must tell me about it."

Pleased that her indignation over the robbery and fire had restored her animation, Harcourt encouraged Georgiana to continue her explanation. He stepped back and allowed Mrs. Thomas to walk beside her mistress. As soon as there was room enough for them to walk abreast, he took his place between them, tucking Georgiana's hand back into his arm.

She was still explaining when they reached the house she had rented. Before Georgiana could smile and say good-bye to Harcourt, Mrs. Thomas had invited him inside for a cup of tea. "I simply must hear the rest of the story."

Harcourt looked down at the lady whose hand he still held. She glanced up. He wanted to run his finger around his neck to make his cravat looser; she felt a shiver of desire run through her. Their eyes locked. Even Mrs. Thomas paused for a moment and took a deep breath as she looked from one to the other. She hid a smile. Then Georgiana dropped his arm and stepped back, her face frozen into a false smile. "Please join us, Mr. Harcourt, unless you feel you must return to your friends immediately."

"They will do well enough without me," he said as though he were not the host of the party. After six months of remembering this lady at unexpected times, he did not intend to have her disappear on him again.

Soon they were in Georgiana's sitting room with a tea tray on the table. Allowing Mrs. Thomas to dispense the tea, Georgiana took a chair opposite their guest but kept her eyes fixed on her clasped hands. She yearned to gaze at him but was afraid of giving her feelings away.

"What brings you to Harrogate, Mr. Harcourt?" Mrs. Thomas asked as she handed him his cup of tea. He took it and smiled at her. Georgiana looked up at that moment and caught her breath.

"I have an estate nearby," he explained. "Every year about this time I visit it."

"For the hunting?" Mrs. Thomas asked, a knowing smile on her face.

"You are a wise woman," he replied. "My friends and I have enjoyed the sport for years." He paused and sighed.

"What is wrong?" Georgiana asked before her common sense told her to be quiet.

"Some problems on the estate," he said quietly. "I find I will have to spend more time here than I expected." Mrs. Thomas hid her smile, wondering to herself if the problem had existed until a moment ago, and held out a plate of cakes. He took one. "How long do you plan to be here?"

"Until spring," Mrs. Thomas said, not realizing what agonies her remarks were causing her mistress. "Until Mrs. Carrington is out of mourning." Georgiana tensed and then gasped. She clutched her midriff as a pain shot through her. Mrs. Thomas was out of her chair and at her side immediately. "Are you unwell? Shall I call the doctor? She has not been in the best of health," she explained as their guest looked worried. "I think you must excuse us. I should have insisted on her going right to bed as soon as we returned home."

Georgiana, too frightened by the pains racking her to say anything, gasped again. "Let me help you get her to bed," Harcourt suggested. "I can carry her. Show me the way." He swung her up into his arms as easily as he had the night at the inn.

Nodding her agreement, Mrs. Thomas hurried from the room. Seeing the footman on duty in the hallway, she called, "Tell Mrs. Smythe to call the doctor at once." He disappeared on the run. "This way, sir."

Charles Harcourt let his arms tighten around his burden. Georgiana, feeling warm and secure, relaxed and nestled against him. She could hear his heart pounding under her head. She sighed. Then she tensed as another pain ripped through her. "Relax," she heard him whisper. "Relax. Everything will be all right." His breath caressed her cheek.

"No. Something is wrong," she said with a sob. "I cannot do anything right." Big tears began to trickle down her face in spite of her efforts to stem them.

"Do not be foolish, Georgiana," he whispered suggestively. "I know something you do very well." She blushed and hid her face against his shoulder.

Mrs. Thomas opened the door to Georgiana's bedroom. "Put her down over here, Mr. Harcourt," she told him as she rushed to turn back the covers. Daisy, Georgiana's maid, hurried in after them, her eyes wide as she saw the tall man carefully putting her mistress down on the bed. "Daisy, you get her settled. I will see Mr. Harcourt out," Mrs. Thomas said firmly, taking his arm. Georgiana, her eyes full of anguish, watched them go.

The door swung closed behind him. Harcourt turned to the older lady. "What is wrong?" he demanded.

"She has had difficulty with the child for months," Mrs. Thomas said, surprising even herself. Although Mr. Harcourt was acquainted with her mistress, she was not certain it was proper to answer his questions.

"Difficulties? What kind of difficulties?" he asked anxiously. "She will be all right?"

"We are doing all that we can to insure that she will be," the older lady said calmly. "Any further questions I suggest you address to Mrs. Carrington."

"I will." Before he could say anything more, the door swung open and the doctor hurried in.

"Good day, Mr. Harcourt. Doctor, thank you for coming so promptly. Mrs. Carrington is upstairs." A few seconds later, Charles Harcourt was outside looking at a closed door, not certain how he had gotten there.

He walked down the steps and then turned to look back at the house. "I will be back," he whispered to himself and set off to find his friends.

# 6

ALONE except for her maid, Georgiana began to relax. As the tension slipped from her, the pains that had been racking her began to subside. Taking deep breaths, she willed herself to rest. Carefully, she suppressed memories and she kept her mind a blank and her eyes shut. By the time the doctor arrived, most of the pain had disappeared, although her face was set in lines that had not been there before.

Mrs. Thomas followed the doctor into the room and crossed to stand by the bed. "Are you better, my dear?" she asked anxiously.

Georgiana smiled at her weakly and nodded. The doctor frowned and picked up her hand. "Hmmm. If this is better, you must not have been following my instructions very well," he said in a voice that was more gruff than he intended.

"We only went for a walk to one of the wells, Dr. Mackensie," Mrs. Thomas explained. "We were just talking when she fainted."

"Has this happened before, this fainting I mean?" he asked sternly.

"Not since I arrived in Harrogate," Georgiana said quietly. "I fainted once or twice when I was at home."

"How far did you fall?"

"What do you mean?" Mrs. Thomas asked. "She said she fainted, not fell down."

"Then someone caught her today when she lost consciousness?"

"No. She simply slid from her chair. Before we knew

what had happened, she was on the floor. Then Mr. Harcourt picked her up and carried her to a bench." Mrs. Thomas tried to read the doctor's face but could not. Georgiana had closed her eyes at the mention of Charles's name, the lines beside her mouth growing more pronounced. Once more she tried to clear her mind, but this time the memories rolled over her. "He's here!" kept echoing through her mind, sending fire racing through her veins.

"Hmmm." The doctor inspected his patient again, noting that the pulse in her neck was pounding as though she had been running. "And was it the pain that caused you to faint?"

"No. The pains came later," Georgiana said quietly, her voice almost emotionless. Only the tiniest quiver on the last word revealed her uneasiness. Deliberately, she tried to put the thought of Charles Harcourt from her mind, hoping to relax once more, fearing if she did not that harm might come to the babe.

"Hmmm. How are you feeling now?" The doctor picked up her hand once more, his fingers on her wrist. Georgiana tried to answer but could not force a sound out of a throat that had frozen. What if Charles finds out that this is his child, she wondered. "Are you still having pains?" he asked. He put her hand on the bed and stepped back. Once more she tried to speak and could not. "Bring a glass of water," he told her maid. When she rushed to give it to him, he put his arms under Georgiana and lifted her up, holding the glass to her lips until she took a sip or two. "Now perhaps you can answer my questions."

"Tired," Georgiana whispered, wishing that everyone would go away and leave her alone with the fears and joy that filled her.

"And the pains?" the doctor asked relentlessly.

"Gone." She closed her eyes, trying once more to push everything but the baby from her mind. Once again she was unsuccessful. When the baby kicked her, she smiled and put her hand over the spot. "Our baby," she whispered, wondering if the child was a boy or a girl. Then her face, which had for a moment worn a look of serenity, crumpled. She drew a shuddering breath. "What am I to do? What am I to do?" she asked hopelessly.

"Stay in bed," the doctor ordered, his face stern. "Do not let her get up for more than a half hour." Georgiana's maid and Mrs. Thomas nodded. But Georgiana did not react. The doctor, recognizing her retreat into herself, took her hands once more and gave them a shake. "Mrs. Carrington," he said sternly. She did not open her eyes. "Mrs. Carrington!"

This time she could not avoid an answer. "Yes," she said, wishing that everyone would go away and leave her so she could sleep.

"Did you hear what I said?"

"My name."

"Before that." She shook her head, closing her eyes once more. "Look at me," he demanded. She looked up into his face. "Do you want this baby?"

Georgiana's eyes opened wide. She put her hand protectively over where her child rested within her. Had she been given the choice six months earlier she knew what she would have said, but now, after feeling the baby move inside her, the thought of losing it terrified her. Despite her efforts not to weep, tears welled up in her eyes. She nodded, afraid to speak.

"Then you must do as I say," her doctor said sternly. She stared at him anxiously. "No walking up and down the stairs." She nodded. "No walks to the wells. Just bed." Again Georgiana nodded. "I have given Mrs. Thomas and your maid my instructions. If the pains should return or you have any other problems, send for me at once." All three of the women nodded then. Georgiana, her face a pale mask, closed her eyes again and tried to still her racing mind.

Mrs. Thomas followed the doctor from the room. "I feel you will have a difficult task, Mrs. Thomas," he said quietly, smiling at the older lady, whose charms he had noted the first time he visited the house.

"Why?"

"It will be your task to keep her occupied. Mrs. Carrington does not impress me as a lady who is used to being idle."

Mrs. Thomas smiled and agreed. "Can she have visitors?" she asked, holding up the skirts of her gray walking dress just a bit as she walked down the stairs.

"As long as they do not stay too long or agitate her. If the child is to survive, she must rest. And do not let some of the older ladies tell her any horror stories of childbirth. She is nervous already."

"Yes, Doctor," Mrs. Thomas said quietly. She watched him leave and then hurried into the sitting room. A short time later, she handed a footman the notes she had written and sent him on his way.

Exhausted and more frightened then she was willing to admit, Georgiana sank into sleep. But it was a sleep punctuated by bad dreams. In one she was at a ball, dancing with Charles even though she was as large as though she were in the last month of her pregnancy. The other couples on the floor stopped dancing as soon as they got on the dance floor and began to whisper and point at them. Georgiana wanted to run, but Charles would not let her go. "We can do as we want," he told her, holding her tight. The music around them grew louder.

"No! Let me go!" Georgiana twisted and turned, trying to get free of him, away from the other people. She turned to the people around them, hoping they would help. They turned away.

"Mrs. Carrington, are you all right? Should I send for the doctor again?" her maid asked, shaking her awake.

Her heart racing, Georgiana took a deep breath. "No. It was just a silly dream," she said with a shaky smile. "Bring me a cloth so that I may wipe my face."

Relieved to have something so simple to do, the maid hurried about her task, returning only moment later with a cloth dampened with lavender water. She stayed beside the bed. After taking the discarded cloth, she asked, "Would you like some tea? Cook said to tell you that she will send up something special as soon as you are ready."

Although only a short time earlier she would have denied that she was hungry, Georgiana agreed. When the tea tray returned to the kitchen, both she and Cook were surprised that it was empty. As soon as she had finished, Georgiana slipped back into sleep again, this time peacefully.

Later that evening, the memories that Georgiana had been trying to suppress refused to be denied. Charles Harcourt was in Harrogate; he had smiled at her, his eyes reminding her of the pleasures they had found in each other's arms. The thought of his arms holding her tenderly sent her pulse pounding once more. Georgiana closed her eyes and smiled, remembering the way he had lifted her into his arms, his shoulders broad beneath her clutching palms.

Then her smile disappeared. If he found out . . . The thought made her go cold with fear. She could imagine his warm brown eyes going cold with anger and dismay. He must not find out. She twisted her coverlet, creating permanent wrinkles in the silk. Then she sighed in relief. Her doctor's orders would protect her. Isolated in her bedroom, she did not run any risk of seeing him again. That thought brought her pain. Though she realized that seeing him would lead her into danger, the knowledge that he was so close and she could not see him sent Georgiana first into melancholy and then into painful self-recriminations. Why had she made love with him? Why had she given in to temptation? Facing her questions honestly made her laugh ruefully. "I did not give in. I reached out and grabbed what I wanted. Now I am paying for it," she whispered. Then remembering that night, she shivered and smiled wistfully. "And if I had another chance, I would probably make the same choice," she admitted. She hugged herself, wrapping her arms protectively over the child she carried. Lost in seductive memories, she drifted off to sleep.

The next day, Mrs. Thomas's notes began to have an effect. As soon as it was time for visits, the knocker on their door sounded. "Mrs. Wycombe and Mrs. Bishop, I knew I could count on your support," Mrs. Thomas said as the older ladies were ushered into the drawing room. Her smile welcomed them as though they were her friends from childhood.

"We simply could not allow the poor child to suffer alone," Mrs. Wycombe said in a fluttery voice. "Sister and I worried so all last evening. I finally had to retire with a tisane that my maid makes for me when I am agitated. The poor child."

"Has she had any further difficulty? I remember when I was expecting my son I fainted regularly. He was such a healthy baby. I had to hire two wet nurses to keep him satisfied," Mrs. Bishop confided in a soft voice.

"And look at him today. He is as bad as the Prince with his creaking corsets. I told you that indulging him would only bring him harm," her sister said cuttingly. Mrs. Thomas tried to intervene, but the sisters ignored her.

"Well, you were no better. As I recall, your daughter screamed every night of her life until she was six or seven. My nursemaids used to hate to hear that you were coming and bringing her with you."

Mrs. Thomas could bear their bickering no longer. "Ladies, I beg you to remember our goal. I am hoping that you will agree to help me keep Mrs. Carrington occupied. The physician has said she must stay in bed," Mrs. Thomas interjected before the quarrel could escalate any further. "I am at your mercy. What do you suggest?"

"The poor dear," Mrs. Bishop said. She took one of Mrs. Thomas's hands and patted it. "It is our Christian duty to help, is that not true, Sister?"

"Without a doubt. How fortunate that we decided to spend the fall as well as the summer here. Usually, the

town is quite empty of company this late in the year,"
Mrs. Wycombe replied, her face beaming. "Amuse-
ments, hmmm."

"She has to stay in bed?" Mrs. Bishop asked. Her
brow creased for a moment.

"Almost all the time."

"We could supply her with books from our library,"
Mrs. Wycombe suggested. Mrs. Thomas nodded pleasantly, but she was disappointed. She had been hoping for
more active involvement from the two. "I recently read
the most delightful novel. So exciting. The heroine had
to fight off the advances of her uncle. He kept her im-
prisoned in a dark castle away from everyone."

"I am certain anything you send her she will like,"
Mrs. Thomas said. "The poor child is so alone."

"Will you send for her sister?" Mrs. Bishop asked.
During their recent visit Georgiana had admitted that she
had only one relative, a sister. Her face showed her curiosity. She looked at Mrs. Wycombe and smiled. "My
sister has been my support since my husband died. I do
not know what I would have done without her."

"You would have managed, Sister," Mrs. Wycombe
said. "But you are right. It is much more comfortable to
have your own family near at hand. Is there no hope that
Mrs. Carrington's sister will come?"

Mrs. Thomas sighed and smoothed the blue-gray
gown that she wore. "I am afraid to ask. When I was
hired, Mrs. Carrington's sister explained that Mr. Carrington had insisted in his will that his wife be separated
from her family and that she had to live here at least
until she was out of mourning. He could not have known
what hardships that would cause." She closed her eyes
and sighed again. "I dare not suggest that we break the
conditions of the will. I simply do not know what might
happen if I were to do so." She looked at the other two
ladies, hoping they would respond as she thought they
might. According to local gossip, neither had fared well
under their husbands' wills.

"Then you must do nothing," Mrs. Wycombe said

forcefully. "Men! If they are not out gambling away a fortune or spending time with mistresses, they are creating difficult situations for their families. Humph!" She scrubbed her hands together as if she were throwing away an unhappy thought. "We will keep her entertained."

"If she will let us," Mrs. Bishop added in a hesitant voice. "Perhaps we could visit her."

"Tell her what is happening in town. Keep her abreast of the news," Mrs. Wycombe added. "Does she enjoy silver loo? We could play that with her."

"I do not know." The faces of the older ladies that had grown so bright fell. "I could ask her. I do know that she will be delighted to see you," Mrs. Thomas added hurriedly, afraid she would lose the help she so desperately needed. "Let me go up and tell her you are here." Quickly, she made her way up the stairs to Georgiana's room.

As soon as her door opened, Georgiana looked up from the book she had been reading and laid it to one side. "You have visitors, Mrs. Carrington," her companion told her. Georgiana's heart began to race, and her cheeks grew flushed. "Mrs. Wycombe and Mrs. Bishop hope that you will allow them to come up."

Taking a deep breath and trying to hide her disappointment, Georgiana nodded. "Dolt!" she whispered to herself as soon as Mrs. Thomas had left the room. "He will not come. He is not interested in a pregnant woman." A sadness overwhelmed her. Even the efforts of her acquaintances, more Mrs. Thomas's age than her own, could not overcome her melancholy.

She would have been delighted to know that her opinions were unfounded. Charles could not get Georgiana out of his mind. He had rejoined his party and taken them back to his estate, but his thoughts remained with her.

"Who was she, Charles?" his closest friend, John Wentworth, asked. "She seemed familiar." He spurred his horse to keep up with his friend who had galloped ahead.

"A Mrs. Carrington."

"Carrington? Hmmm." To the amazement of his friends, who forgot the new crop of ladies as soon as hunting season began, John Wentworth never forgot a face. It might take him several weeks or a moment, but he would remember.

"I met her several months ago. Remember. I told you about the faked fire and the robbery," his friend said, trying to deflect him. Although Georgiana had called him by name, Charles had never been able to remember their first meeting. And he was not certain he wanted to do so. The night they had shared was still vivid in his memory, so bright he did not want to risk spoiling his visions of it.

"Maybe I am wrong," John said. His voice said he doubted the statement. "Come. I will race you to that curve." With a cry, both of them were on their way with their friends following.

For the rest of the evening, Charles was too busy entertaining his friends to do more than think of Georgiana occasionally. When he was alone and undressing for bed, she filled his mind. He could see once again her russet hair tumbling over her bare shoulders, her lips slightly parted. His breathing began to speed up. He shifted uncomfortably. Then the memory of Georgiana as she had looked earlier that very day cooled his ardor. Although the night they had shared had been very special, what had happened once was not likely to happen again. He drifted off to sleep.

Once again he was in the inn surrounded by smoke, his arms full of an elderly lady. He tossed and turned restlessly. Once again Georgiana was in front of him swathed in her cloak and dressing gown, her braid trailing over her shoulder. He followed her down the stairs, holding his burden carefully in his arms, but the stairs did not end. They descended endlessly. As he grew weary, he called to Georgiana to stop, but she did not hear him. He hurried to catch up with her. She, however, was always just out of his reach. He looked down at the burden he carried, wondering that the old lady was so light. His eyes widened. He was carrying a baby, a baby with his brown eyes, a baby that stared at him accusingly. "Georgiana," he screamed, waking himself up.

Sitting up in bed, he reached for a candle and lit it. He put it on the table beside him and drew a deep, shuddering breath. It had been so real. His heart slowed to its normal pace. He forced himself to breathe slowly. As the dream faded, he leaned back on his pillows, his face a mixture of confusion and regret. A baby with his eyes. He closed his eyes for a moment and could see the child again. It had been a boy; he was certain of that. Then he laughed ruefully. He had not missed the changes in her. But just because you slept with her, it does not mean the child is yours, he reminded himself. She did have a husband. Remembering the way many married ladies of his acquaintance dispersed their favors freely, he frowned. "But she is not like those others," he whispered to himself, wishing that he truly believed what he was saying. She had welcomed his advances; he had to face that fact. Still uneasy, he closed his eyes and eventually went back to sleep.

The uneasiness of the evening before was still with him when he awoke the next morning. Pushing it to one side, he dressed in riding clothes and hurried to the breakfast room. "We were about to come looking for you," John told him. "You promised to take us hunting today."

"And I will. Let me get a bit to eat, and we will be off. I told my estate manager to have beaters ready," Charles said. From that moment on, he was too busy to think about Georgiana. After an excellent hunt when everyone got some birds, they turned to billiards and then to gambling. By the time the footmen had helped the last of his guests up the stairs to bed, he was so tired he had to concentrate to get up the stairs by himself. He crawled into bed and closed his eyes.

Once more the dream returned. Once more Charles sat upright in bed, his heart racing. Then refusing to give in to what he firmly believed was merely a bad dream, he closed his eyes and willed himself back to dreamless sleep.

When he awoke the next morning, Charles decided to return to Harrogate even if it meant leaving his guests alone. To his surprise, they decided to accompany him. "Noticed a store that stocks my snuff," one man explained. "Almost out." Confused, Charles nodded and waited for them to get ready. He would have been less startled had he known that some of his friends had noticed his interest in Georgiana and had placed bets on how long he would be able to stay away from her. One or two had declared that he would never notice a lady in her condition, but those who had watched their meeting soon convinced them they were wrong.

When they arrived in Harrogate, Charles requested a parlor at the Granby Arms and ordered their meal. As soon as the meal was over and his friends had started gambling, he slipped from the room. The moment the door closed behind him his friends looked at each other and laughed. "Well, which of us is going to follow him?" John asked.

"Well, he said he needed some snuff," another friend said, pointing to the youngest.

"That is probably the weakest excuse I ever heard," another claimed.

"You did not say anything. What were we to do, let him go off by himself. We would never be able to settle the bet then," the youngest said scornfully.

"If someone does not follow him soon, the question will be moot," John said. He looked at the youngest pointedly.

"I will go," the man agreed.

"And do not forget to buy snuff," the others told him as he was walking out the door. He turned and glared at them but did not stop. The others smiled and turned back to their game.

Charles, his mind fixed on Georgiana, would not have noticed if the French Army had been following him down the street. He walked quickly to the house where he had taken her. Standing in front of the door, he hesitated for a moment and then raised the knocker. His friend watched for a moment to make certain he did not immediately reappear and then hurried back to the inn with the news.

A short time later a maid slipped into Georgiana's bedroom and whispered her message to Mrs. Thomas. "I wish they would not do that," Georgiana complained when the girl had left the room.

Mrs. Thomas folded her needlework and stood up. "Do what, my dear?" she asked.

"Act as though I were dying," the younger lady explained. "Why did she tiptoe in and whisper?"

"I suppose she did not want to disturb you."

"She did. Please tell everyone that although I need to rest I am not ill," Georgiana said. Her usually pleasant face wore a grim frown. Unused to spending her days in bed, she was restless. Her needlework and her books did little to occupy her thoughts. All too often she found herself thinking about Charles Harcourt. She needed to be busy, she told herself. She should be working on the nursery.

"I will speak with them," Mrs. Thomas said. She had grown increasingly aware of her mistress's agitation. "I will return in just a few minutes."

"You do not have to go at this moment," Georgiana protested. But her companion was already out the door. Had Georgiana realized who waited below she would have protested more loudly.

As she entered the sitting room where Charles Harcourt waited, Mrs. Thomas consciously smoothed the frown from her face. "What a nice surprise, Mr. Harcourt." He took her hand in his and bowed. "What may I do for you today?"

"I, ah, I had hoped to see Mrs. Carrington," he stammered as though he were a schoolboy. "Will she be joining us?"

The older lady was taken aback by his directness. For a moment, she was not certain what to say. Then she said in a low voice. "The doctor has confined Mrs. Carrington to bed." She took a seat and waved him to another, keeping her eyes focused on his face. His reaction did not disappoint her.

A frown creased his brow, and his eyes reflected his worry. "I knew Georgiana was not telling me the truth the other day when she said that her fainting was nothing. How serious is it?" he demanded. He rose and crossed the room to stare down at Mrs. Thomas, who shrank back in her chair as he loomed over her.

Rising to her feet, Mrs. Thomas drew herself up to her full height, a considerable distance beneath his. "Did I miss something the other day?" she asked imperiously. "Are you a relative of Mrs. Carrington's?" She raised her chin and glared at him.

"No." Charles stared at the older lady, refusing to be intimidated.

"Then you must ask the lady herself."

"And how am I to do that while she is shut up in her bedroom?" he demanded. The word echoed in his mind. A thought he would have ruthlessly suppressed at any other time flickered through his mind. He stood frozen for a moment. Then a smile played about his lips.

Mrs. Thomas, recognizing the determined look on his face, moved closer to him. He was too swift for her. Before she could get between him and the door, he was in the hall. She watched him hurry toward the stairs. "You cannot do that. It would not be proper," she called after him as he ran up the stairs. She turned to the servant, who stared at the gentleman ascending the stairs as

though he were Napoleon bent on raping the country-
side. "If anyone else calls, inform them we are not re-
ceiving today. Especially Mrs. Wycombe and Mrs.
Bishop! Do you understand?" she asked sternly, hoping
to avert disaster. When he nodded, she ran up the stairs
after Charles.

# 7

STANDING in front of the door to the room where he had brought Georgiana only a few days before, Charles stopped. He was breathing heavily, more heavily than running up the stairs should have caused. He squared his shoulders and pulled himself to his full height. Taking a deep breath and closing his eyes for a moment, he put his hand on the latch and opened the door.

"Well, what crisis did you have to solve this time?"' Georgiana called, her eyes still fixed on her needlework. She was in the middle of a French knot and did not want to misplace it. Charles closed the door behind him and stood there, enjoying the sight of her. Georgiana was dressed in a soft muslin night rail with a blue shawl about her shoulders which made her eyes gleam brightly. Her hair was pulled to one side with a blue ribbon and fell over her shoulders. He took a deep breath and leaned back against the door, effectively blocking Mrs. Thomas's entrance into the room even though he was not aware of it. For now, it was enough simply to watch Georgiana.

She looked up to see why she had not received an answer. Shocked, she continued her stitch and jabbed her finger. "Ow!" She stuck her finger in her mouth.

"What's wrong? Should I get the doctor?" He rushed across the room and started to take her in his arms. "Are you ill?"

The door now open, Mrs. Thomas rushed in. "Mr. Harcourt!" she exclaimed as she watched him put his arms around her mistress. He swore softly under his breath and jumped back.

It was all Georgiana could do to keep from screaming at her companion. His hands had felt so good.

"She was in pain," Charles explained sheepishly.

"I stuck my finger," Georgiana said simultaneously. She held up her hand, and he could see where blood still welled. Reacting instinctively, he picked up her hand and kissed the spot of blood away. Georgiana gasped and smiled up at him.

"Mr. Harcourt, you should not be here," Mrs. Thomas protested. "It is not right." She glanced at her mistress only to see her looking up at the gentleman as if he were the sun and she a flower drinking in his warmth. The other words she had planned to say died on her lips. She looked from one to the other. Gradually, the disapproval that had been evident on her face disappeared.

Still holding Georgiana's hand as though it were a lifeline and he were drowning, Charles looked at the older lady and smiled ruefully. "I had to see her, see that she was all right," he explained. He looked down at Georgiana, who could hardly breathe because her heart was pounding so quickly. His hand tightened on her. "Mrs. Thomas said the doctor insisted that you remain in bed. What is wrong?"

Georgiana pulled her hand free and struggled to sit up, letting the shawl that wrapped her shoulders fall open. Mrs. Thomas noticed how Charles's eyes fell to the deep neckline of the nightrail and the riches it did little to conceal. She hurried to the bed and pulled the coverlet up under Georgiana's chin. Her mistress blushed. Pushed to one side by Georgiana's companion, Charles moved to the foot of the bed directly in front of Georgiana.

"You cannot avoid answering me, Georgiana," he said firmly, his face serious. "I do not plan to leave until you explain why you are in bed."

Mrs. Thomas shrugged her shoulders. "Then tell him, Mrs. Carrington." As if she could force him to leave by the weight of her stare alone, she glared at the tall man who stared at his mistress. "If anyone should call and find him here," she began. Then she realized neither of them were paying any attention to her. She sighed and began to wring her hands.

Georgiana looked from her companion to her visitor. She took a deep breath. Steeling herself for the disapproval she knew would follow, she said, "Leave us, Mrs. Thomas."

Shocked, her companion protested. "Mrs. Carrington, do you know what you are saying?" She put her hand on Georgiana's forehead as if to feel for a fever. Georgiana brushed her hand away. Knowing when to hold his silence, Charles stood by silently.

"Mrs. Thomas, I am not some young maiden about to sacrifice her virtue to an aging libertine. I am a widow," Georgiana told her. She felt her cheeks redden with the blush her lie created. "And Mr. Harcourt is a friend I have not seen in some months. Because of his help at the wells, he deserves an explanation." Although Georgiana's words were quiet, she could not keep her voice from shaking with emotion. "In private," she added.

Glancing from one to the other and noting the determined look on her mistress's face, Mrs. Thomas retreated. She stood by the door for a moment, observing the way Charles Harcourt looked at Georgiana. She could not tell how her mistress felt. For the moment, Georgiana had her eyes fixed firmly on her hands.

As soon as the door closed behind Mrs. Thomas, Charles moved back to the side of the bed and sat on the edge. He took Georgiana's hand into his once more. "Well?" he asked.

Although the desire to gaze up into his brown eyes was stronger than she had dreamed it would be, Georgiana kept her eyes fixed on her hands. He put a hand over hers. She took a deep, shuddering breath. Then she looked up. He was almost as close as he had been that night. She wanted to lean forward and rest her head on his shoulder but knew she could not. She fought with her desires and won. She closed her eyes. Then she felt his hand on her cheek.

"Georgiana, what is wrong? Are you dying?" His voice cracked on the last word.

Her eyes flew open. "No!" she said firmly and pushed his hand away.

"Then what is wrong?" He sat back in order to see her better.

"I did not think I would ever see you again," she said, surprising even herself. He sat up straighter.

"And what does that have to do with your being in bed?" he asked, jumping to conclusions. His voice was sharp as he waited for her accusations that he was the father of her child.

"Nothing. I suppose I have had more time to think lately and have been worried about what happened," she said hastily. He relaxed. "I should not have given in to you." Her voice was so low that he was not sure whether she was talking to him or to herself.

"Georgiana, that night is over. Do not keep blaming yourself," he said gently, relieved that he had misread her words. She bit her lip to keep from disagreeing with him, reminding herself that he thought she was a widow expecting her dead husband's child. "Now, before your companion comes bursting in the door again, tell me why you have to stay in bed?" His voice was low and soothing and urged her to look at him, to trust him as she had trusted him once before.

She raised her eyes to his, drinking in the sight of a handsome gentleman seated on her bed. Dressed in a blue coat with fawn pantaloons, he looked almost as young as he had ten years earlier when she had first developed a *tendre* for him. But now her love was mixed with a desire that ten years earlier would have frightened her. "My child," she whispered and waited to see his reaction. He smiled encouragingly. She began to breathe easier. "My doctor says I must stay in bed if I want to have a healthy babe." She blushed, ashamed of discussing such a delicate subject with a gentleman, no matter how intimate they had been.

Relieved, Charles smiled at her. "That is all?" he asked. She nodded. "And you cannot go downstairs?" he asked, wondering how he would manage to see her again. Storming into her room once had worked. Her companion would be prepared if he tried it again.

"I cannot walk up or down stairs, my doctor said." Her face was somber. She sighed. Accepting his advice did not mean she had to like what the doctor had said, she reminded herself.

"How boring," Charles said, patting her hand. "Did the man offer no suggestions?"

"He was only concerned with the health of the child," she reminded him. "And so am I. I can survive a few months of boredom."

"If you have to do so, you can. But perhaps there is an alternative."

"What?"

Deliberately avoiding her question, he asked, "When do you see your doctor again?"

"Whenever I call him, I suppose."

"Hmmm." Charles rose. Almost without thinking, he bent and kissed her on the cheek. Her face flushed. "I will talk to Mrs. Thomas. Do your needlework. Do not think I am abandoning you. I will be back," he said as he walked to the door.

"Charles? Charles!" she called after him. The door closed behind him. Feeling as frustrated as a cat tangled in a ball of yarn, she threw her needlework at the door and watched it fall to the floor far from its mark. "Men!" she said angrily. Then she slid down in bed and pulled the covers over her head.

Downstairs, Charles asked a servant to find Mrs. Thomas. As he waited for her, he considered his situation. Only a week earlier, Georgiana had been a pleasant dream. When he had seen her again at the wells, even though she was *enciente,* something inside had told him that he must not lose sight of her again. His dreams the last two nights had added weight to his feelings. Even though their relationship might come to nothing, Charles knew he must not pass up this opportunity.

The door opened. He stood up politely. "You wished to see me, Mr. Harcourt?" she asked. Mrs. Thomas's face reflected her disapproval.

"Have a seat, Mrs. Thomas," he suggested, forgetting for a moment that he was not in his own home. She frowned but did as he suggested. He sat down across from her. "I am worried about Georgiana, Mrs. Carrington," he said, stumbling over the last name.

"And so am I, Mr. Harcourt. I am certain that your actions today have done much to upset her. I only hope they have not brought on more problems." She glared at him and settled herself more primly in her chair.

"When I left her, Georg—Mrs. Carrington did not seem to be having any difficulties," he assured her. He rose and began to move around the room.

"You might as well call her Georgiana, Mr. Harcourt. She obviously does not object," Mrs. Thomas said. Her crisp voice told him she did not approve.

To his surprise, he turned red. "Yes, well, perhaps you are right," he said, stumbling once more. He turned to the window and stared out for a moment.

When the silence had grown thick, Mrs. Thomas shifted restlessly. "Why did you . . . ," she began.

"I have an idea to suggest," he said at the same time. Both of them fell silent again. Charles walked across the room and took his seat once more. He leaned forward, willing her to look at him. As soon as she did, he smiled at her. She caught her breath and then laughed to herself. No wonder her mistress had been willing to see him again. His smile was dangerous. "Mrs. Thomas, I need your help," he said confidentially.

"Indeed, sir."

"Hear me out. I am worried about Georgiana."

"As you should be. The doctor says she must be very careful if she expects to have a healthy baby," Mrs.

Thomas said. She looked him in the eyes, daring him to contradict her. He did not look away.

"So Georgiana told me. She also said that she is not allowed downstairs because she is not allowed to climb or descend the stairs themselves. Is this true?" he asked, his face serious.

"Yes."

"Then the only place she can receive guests is in her bedroom."

"Well, I suppose . . ."

"Mrs. Thomas, you and I know I cannot visit her there unless I am willing to destroy her. And I refuse to give her up again. I cannot go days, weeks, months without seeing her," he said. His determination rang in his voice.

Mrs. Thomas's tender heart was wrenched. Tears welled up in her eyes. "Oh, Mr. Harcourt, I had no idea. What you must have gone through." In her mind, Mrs. Thomas pictured Charles going through life with a burning love for Georgiana even though she had rejected him. Charles, not above using the concern he saw on her face, buried his face in his hands. "Of course, you must be beside yourself with worry," she said, hurrying to his side and patting his shoulder.

"Then you will help me?" he asked, raising his head and staring at her with a pitiful look on his face.

"Tell me what I must do," she begged. If he had been her son, she would not have been more concerned. She was simply delighted that she would have the opportunity to help him win her mistress.

He smiled. "I knew you could not turn me away. Your kind heart can be read in your face." He stood up once more. Mrs. Thomas looked up at him and felt even shorter than usual. As tall as her mistress was, he was taller. He definitely was the man for Georgiana. "I need to talk to the doctor," he explained.

"The doctor? Mr. Harcourt, that would not be right. I am not even certain the doctor would be willing to discuss Mrs. Carrington with you," she said with a frown. "He is a most proper man."

"Propriety be hanged!" Charles said angrily. At her gasp, he turned to look at Mrs. Thomas again. "Forgive me," he said in a soft voice. "You must see that being up there in her bedroom all alone . . ."

"She is not alone. I am with her," the older lady protested.

"But she feels she is alone, isolated. You must know how much she dislikes being shut away from the life in this house," Charles said. Georgiana's first words to him that day had struck that message home. And he knew what it was like to have to stay in bed when the rest of the world proceeded without you. When he was much younger, he had broken his leg falling out of an apple tree. While everyone else had run and played outside during the summer, he had been forced to stay inside. Had he been truly ill he would not have minded staying in bed, but after the first few days, his leg had barely ached. His mind, however, could not adjust. Only when his tutor had taken pity on him and carried him outside had he felt truly alive.

Explaining his experiences to Mrs. Thomas, he tried to make her understand what Georgiana was feeling. "If she could only come down for a little while. Ask the doctor."

"And what about the stairs?" Mrs. Thomas asked sharply. "He was most insistent that she not go up and down."

"Ask him if she can come down if someone carries her," he insisted.

"If someone carries her? Mr. Harcourt, there is no one in this household who could do that. Had you not carried her to her room the other afternoon I do not know how we would have managed." Mrs. Thomas walked across the room to the door. "The idea is absurd." She put her hand on the latch. "Good day, Mr. Harcourt."

Before she had time to leave the room, Charles had crossed to her side. He put his hand on the door and held it shut. Mrs. Thomas looked up at him, surprise and dismay written on her face. "You must hear me out," he explained.

"Well?"

Charles ran his hand through his hair, wishing that he had more of the skill of an orator. Now that it was time to make his suggestion he was hesitant. "Perhaps," he began. Then he stopped to clear his throat. The older lady stared at him in amazement. She raised her eyebrow and began to tap her foot. "I could do it," he said in a rush.

"Do what?"

"Carry her downstairs," he said eagerly. "If the doctor says it will be all right, I could visit in the afternoons and bring her down at least for a short time. No one would have to know that I did it." He shifted uncomfortably as Mrs. Thomas stared at him.

Her eyes narrowed. He ran his finger around the neck of the shirt that had suddenly grown too small for him. Minutes that seemed like hours marched by, and still she stared at him. Finally, when Charles had given up hope, she cleared her throat. "Hmmm. If you think that the servants will not talk, you are mistaken." She glared at him. Then she softened toward him. "So you are willing to spend your afternoon here, are you?" she asked, her eyes fixed on his. He nodded. "I suppose I could ask what he thinks."

"If there is any danger to her, to the child, I will forget about my idea immediately," Charles assured her. "When will you talk to him?" The hope that he would be able to spend time with Georgiana gave his voice a lilt. "Shall I come tomorrow?"

"Not so fast. Let me talk to the doctor. Then I will send you word. How may I get in touch with you?"

"I will send my groom. He can carry messages between us," Charles suggested.

"Nonsense. I will send someone from our household. Simply give me your direction," she said, holding out her hand for his card. He put it in her hand. "There is nothing more for you to do here. I will send for you when I have an answer," she said, dismissing him. To his surprise, Charles soon found himself in the street in front of a closed door.

When the door closed behind him, Mrs. Thomas sank to a chair, her face wearing a satisfied expression. "It may be too soon," she murmured to herself. "But she is a widow, and it is obvious she did not care for her husband. We shall see." For the first time in her life, Mrs. Thomas saw herself as a matchmaker; it was a role in which she planned to succeed. She walked across to the small desk and pulled out a sheet of paper.

When the doctor arrived some time later, Mrs. Thomas smiled at him. "I hope we did not pull you away from some emergency," she said softly.

"Nonsense. Your letter made it very clear I was to come at my convenience," Dr. Mackensie said. He had been pleased to have an excuse to visit the household again. Had he not thought it undignified, he would have visited every day. He smiled at the lady who welcomed him, wishing he knew her better.

Totally absorbed in the affairs of her mistress, Mrs. Thomas completely missed his interest in her. "Would you care for some tea?" she asked, leading him to the settee. When he agreed, she took her seat and poured him a cup from the heavy silver pot on the tray in front of her. When he had a selection of delicious treats on his plate, she leaned back.

He took a sip of tea and then put his cup on the table beside him. "How may I help you, Mrs. Thomas?" he asked. He smiled at her.

She settled the skirts of her deep blue gown, which made her eyes much darker than they really were. When she had chosen it, she had told herself that it was for warmth, but she knew she was making an excuse. "It is Mrs. Carrington." She stopped and took a deep breath. "She is so restless. Apparently, she cannot bear being confined. I am worried about her. She does not seem to rest as she should."

Forgetting his own interest in the lady at his side, the

doctor became a total professional. "Have there been any more pains?"

"No. Oh, no. As soon as she relaxed, they stopped," Mrs. Thomas assured him. She sighed. "She seems so unhappy."

"How long ago did her husband die?"

"I am not certain." He looked at her in surprise. "I joined Mrs. Carrington in London. Her sister hired me to be her companion during her sister's mourning."

"What is she doing in Harrogate? She does not need to drink the waters, although some medical men of my acquaintance would disown me to hear me saying it."

"She needs to be with her family," Mrs. Thomas said firmly, her lips firmly pursed together. "But that cannot be." Dr. Mackensie looked at her, his confusion evident. Realizing that she had already said more than was wise, Mrs. Thomas explained. "She is here because of her husband's will. Apparently he did not trust her family."

"Did he know of the child?"

"I doubt it." Mrs. Thomas drew herself up, squaring her shoulders. "And from what little she says about him, I doubt if that would have changed his mind."

"Not a happy marriage, then?" the doctor asked.

Embarrassed by what she had said, Mrs. Thomas blushed. "I have said too much already," she whispered, wishing she could call back the words.

"Nonsense. I am the lady's doctor. Her emotions are as much my concern as her physical health," he said soothingly. "But I do not understand why you sent for me today?"

"A friend of hers came to see her today, and he wanted to know if you would allow her to come downstairs if someone carried her," Mrs. Thomas said in a rush. Then she waited for his response, holding her breath.

"Hmmm. A friend you say?" She nodded. "A good friend, I suppose?" She nodded again, this time more hesitantly. "And do you have a strong footman who could do this?"

"No. But Mr. Harcourt, he is the one who called today, said that he would do it if you let her come down," she said in a rush.

"What size man is he? Your mistress is not tiny."

"Doctor Mackensie!"

"I mean no disrespect, Mrs. Thomas. I am only being honest. A small man could never carry Mrs. Carrington down the stairs without dropping her," he said quickly, trying to soothe her.

"Well, Mr. Harcourt could. He is tall and well-built. He carried her upstairs the other day when she became ill," Mrs. Thomas said. Her indignation gave her face a sharp look.

"He did?" She nodded. "And how long do you propose to have her down here?" he asked.

"Ah, well, ah," she stammered. "We did not discuss that. What would you suggest?"

"If I allow it, I could not permit her to come down for more than two hours a day. And she would have to recline. No getting up and running around," he said in a thoughtful voice.

"A chaise? Could she lie on a chaise?" Mrs. Thomas asked. In her explorations to find a perfect site for the nursery, she thought she had seen one. If not, they would order one.

"With pillows around her," he said firmly. He cleared his throat. Mrs. Thomas smiled at him. He cleared his throat again. "We can try this. I will monitor her closely to see there are not adverse effects. I will want to be present the first time she comes down in order to ensure that the excitement does not harm her."

Mrs. Thomas clasped her hands in excitement. "Oh, Doctor, I cannot tell you how much this will mean to her." And to Mr. Harcourt, she added to herself. She beamed at him.

"Remember. Even though she will be allowed to come down here, she must remain in bed until she is carried down."

"But, but, what about her clothing? She cannot appear downstairs in her dressing gown.'"

"I do not see why not. Perhaps you could wrap a cloak about her," he suggested, uneasy at the unfamiliar topic of women's dress. "For no reason, however, is she to exert herself more than she already is doing. Do you understand?" he asked sternly. Mrs. Thomas, her mind exploring possibilities, said yes. "Be certain to let me know when you plan this experiment. Send me word." After making his farewells, he left.

Mrs. Thomas, her mind racing, walked him to the door. Then she turned. "Send for Mrs. Smythe," she told a servant standing nearby.

# 8

TWO days later Mrs. Thomas was still trying to convince her mistress that allowing Charles Harcourt to carry her to the small drawing room would not be wrong. "Mrs. Wycombe and Mrs. Bishop will be here at any moment. They were delighted to hear that you may receive guests again."

"They did not consult me," Georgiana said. She turned her back to Mrs. Thomas and stared at the opposite wall, her face set. Even though she longed to be released from the prison of the four walls of her bedroom, she did not want to be obligated to Charles. Over the last two days, she had convinced herself that he was the author of all her problems. It was his fault she was separated from her family, his fault she had to stay in bed. The longer her list grew the angrier she became.

That morning as her maid had helped her dress, a feat that required more help than Georgiana was willing to allow, Mrs. Thomas had told her the news. At first, Georgiana had been excited. Then as she realized that the agent of her release was the man she had spent the last two days resenting, she had refused. Now she lay still, her arms crossed on her breast as though she were a medieval lady posing for her tomb.

"Doctor Mackensie is waiting to see you," Mrs. Thomas pleaded. She crossed to stand in front of Georgiana. Her mistress simply turned to her other side.

"Tell him to come up here."

"No, he wants you to come down."

At that Georgiana sat up straight in bed. "Leave me. I

do not want to see you or him until I ring." Mrs. Thomas stared at her aghast. In the months she had spent with Georgiana, she had never heard the lady raise her voice, not even with the maid she had dismissed. Now Georgiana was shouting.

"I will tell them of your decision," she said, walking out of the room with her nose stuck in the air. She gave the door an extra tug, and it slammed behind her.

Her reception in the morning room was as cool as she had expected. "What do you mean she refused to come down here?" Charles demanded. He towered over Mrs. Thomas, who felt as though she were a pygmy staring at a giant.

"Just what I said." Her mistress's last words had finally made an impression on her. Tears welled up in her eyes. "She told me that she did not want to see me until she rang for me," Mrs. Thomas said, a quaver in her voice. She took out her handkerchief and dabbed at her eyes. "She yelled at me."

The doctor came to her side and took her hand. "Remember that she is increasing, my dear Mrs. Thomas. I am certain that shortly she will regret what she has said." He led her to a seat. "She will recognize that you had her best interests in mind."

"I had the chaise brought down and re-covered just so she could rest comfortably," Mrs. Thomas said, looking up at the doctor as if he could solve the problem. Charles, his face stormy, walked out of the room with a purposeful step. "Stop him, Doctor," Mrs. Thomas cried. "If we give her time, she will change her mind; I know she will. He must not confront her now."

The doctor hurried to the door. Then he looked at her. "I think we will see Mrs. Carrington before long," he said in an amused voice.

"What do you mean?"

A short time later her question was answered as the door swung open with a bang. "Put me down," Georgiana said angrily. "I told you I did not want to come down here." Charles lowered her to the chaise and stood back. "Not here. I want to go back upstairs," she demanded.

"Well, I do not want to carry you up there right now," Charles told her.

"And what you want you get. I should know," she said, forgetting they were no longer alone.

"I do not remember your complaining before," he said.

"Mr. Harcourt. Mrs. Carrington. Here is Dr. Mackensie, who has come to see how you are doing," Mrs. Thomas said hastily, trying to forestall any unwelcome revelations. No matter what her suspicions were, she did not want anyone else talking about them. The couple, who had been glaring at each other as though they were the only people in the world, looked around in embarrassment.

Charles was the first to recover. "Dr. Mackensie, I am Charles Harcourt." He held out his hand, trying to remember exactly what they had said.

"The man who had this ingenious suggestion," the doctor said, returning his handshake.

"I might have known it was your idea," Georgiana said in a tone that was louder than she had intended. She had the grace to blush when she realized that everyone had heard her remark. "Well, Doctor, do I pass inspection?" she asked. Her voice was as crisp as a fresh-picked apple.

"Your cheeks are rosy. Your spirits seem high. Have you had any more pains?" he asked as he picked up her hand.

"None."

As he said good-bye, Charles stood up. "I will walk out with you, Doctor," he said. "Please forgive me for a few moments, ladies."

In the hall with the door firmly closed behind them, Charles confronted the doctor. "Just how serious is Mrs. Carrington's problem?" he asked.

"And what is your relationship with the lady, sir? Are you a relative?"

"No."

"Then I may not discuss my patient with you," the doctor said. He took his hat and bag from the waiting servant.

"I have to know something," Charles demanded. Since he had visited Georgiana in her bedroom, he had been plagued with the fear that Mrs. Thomas had lied to him. Even the doctor's agreement that they could bring Georgiana to the drawing room had not made him feel better. He had been able to think of several reasons why the doctor might agree even if Georgiana were dying.

"Then ask the lady."

"I have. She says there is nothing seriously wrong."

"She is right."

"Then why does she have to stay in bed?" Charles asked, wishing he could grab the doctor by his lapels and shake him until the man told him everything he wanted to know.

Finally the doctor took pity on him. "Some ladies have difficulty carrying a child," he said quietly. "Bed rest helps. Since the lady is a recent widow, we would not want anything to happen to the baby."

"That is all?"

"It is enough. Mrs. Carrington needs rest and freedom from anxiety if she is to have a healthy babe," the doctor told him, wondering at this tall man who made no claim on the lady yet showed more worry than most of the fathers he normally dealt with. "If there is any difficulty, Mrs. Thomas knows to send for me."

Charles watched him leave and then turned back to the door of the drawing room. Georgiana, who had been trying to carry on a conversation with her other two visitors, had kept her eyes on the door. When he walked back in, she relaxed but pointedly kept her attention on what Mrs. Bishop was saying. He took his seat near her and gave his attention to Mrs. Thomas.

Later that afternoon when Charles had returned her to her room, Georgiana lay there staring at the bed hanging above her, wondering at the way her heart raced when he picked her up, holding her as effortlessly as though she were a china figurine. Although she would never have admitted it out loud, she admitted to herself that the reason she had not wanted him to carry her to the drawing room was that she was afraid of the power he had over her. She had not been certain of her own reactions. She had tried to be indifferent to him, but his touch woke a fire in her blood that even the knowledge of the child that she carried could not erase. She had to avoid him. If she did not, she might give something away.

The afternoon had been a revelation for Charles too. He had thought that carrying her downstairs would be simple, would give them a chance to talk. But all he had wanted to do was bundle her back up to bed, shutting them away from the outside world. And she was increasing. It was not right, he reminded himself. She was a recent widow with a difficult pregnancy. The least he could do was leave her alone. But he could not. He had promised that he would return.

Using his visiting friends as an excuse, he delayed his return to town until the end of the week. In the meantime, he threw himself into the usual pursuits of gentlemen removed from the company of ladies: hunting, fishing, gambling, and billiards. But no matter how involved he was, no matter how many bottles he drank, Georgiana crept into his thoughts.

Although the others had decided that the reason for his poor spirits was the fact that the lady Charles wanted had refused him, John was not so certain. Charles had changed, grown more serious, more interested in the affairs of the estate. One night as they sat together finishing off a bottle, John said, "Tomorrow I leave for Scotland. Are you coming with me?"

"No."

"Thought not. That lady in town? Mrs. Carrington?" he asked. He picked up his glass and stared at the brandy that lay within.

"Yes."

"Wish I could remember where I've seen her before,"

John said quietly. He took another drink. "Want me to take the others with me when I go?"

His friend looked at him to see if he was serious. "Can you?" Charles asked.

"You have made it easy, Charles. You have not been the ideal host. Your mind has not been with us," John reminded him. "Hunting should be good on my uncle's estate, and he don't mind the company. Probably be glad of it. And most of the company will like Scotland better than going home."

"Appreciate it." For a moment silence grew between them. Charles stared into the fire.

Then John asked, "Are you going to offer for her?"

Charles got up and ran his hand through his already disheveled hair. "How can I? She is a recent widow. From what her companion says, she may never want to be married again."

"A little opposition never kept you from the prize before," his friend reminded him. "Be better if she was not happy before. She will have something to look forward to with you."

"If she will have me. Did I tell you she refused to have me carry her downstairs?"

"And you let that stop you?"

"No. She railed at first, but when she saw it would gain her nothing, she was quiet. Did not talk to me all afternoon though."

"Not good. Must keep her talking," his friend told him. "Can't win her if she will not talk to you." He yawned and drained his glass. "Never saw you like this before, not even when you were engaged to . . . to . . . what's her name. Oh yes, Celeste." He stood up, weaving slightly. "Wish you luck, Charles," he said, holding out his hand. Charles took his hand and shook it. Then he threw his arm around John's shoulders and walked upstairs with him.

As he watched his friends leave the next day, Charles was filled with nostalgia. He could be leaving with them.

Then he smiled. He had a larger fish than a Scottish salmon to catch.

After several days of her watching the four walls of her bedroom, Georgiana was pleased when Mrs. Thomas entered with a letter from Charles. "He will be here this afternoon," the older lady said, not quite certain how her mistress would react. She glanced at her and hoped that she would not have to endure another tantrum.

Georgiana stretched. She covered a yawn with her hand. Then, as though her heart were not pounding with excitement, she asked, "Does he say what time he will be here?"

"Just this afternoon."

"Well, you had better tell Cook that we are expecting visitors. We cannot allow him to leave without offering him some refreshment," Georgiana said. She yawned again to show that she had no interest in the proceedings. But as soon as Mrs. Thomas had hurried out, Georgiana lay back against her pillows, her face dreamy. Then a look of horror crossed her face. What was she going to wear?

When Charles walked into Georgiana's bedroom that afternoon, she lay propped up, her russet hair carefully coiled at the back of her head and soft curls around her face. Instead of the dressing gown she usually wore, she had bullied her maid into helping her into one of her afternoon dresses. After inspecting her wardrobe for something to wear, Georgiana had made the best of what she saw as a bad situation. She had chosen a black gown trimmed in white. Even the excitement she felt about seeing Charles again could not counteract the stark colors she was forced to wear. She had wanted to change, but Charles had arrived before she could do so. And, as she admitted to herself, she had nothing better to wear.

Biting her lip in frustration, she greeted him pleasantly. Surprised and pleased by her reaction after her temper storm the last time he had tried this, he bowed. Then, asking her permission, he picked her up as though she weighed no more than a feather. Although she was taken aback by his stiff correctness, Georgiana gave in to temptation and put her head on his shoulder, listening to the steady beat of his heart. Charles stiffened and then walked quickly down the stairs. Even though he longed to clasp her to him, to sweep her from her home and take her to his, he simply carried her into the drawing room and put her on the chaise.

As soon as he was certain she was comfortable, he turned to Mrs. Thomas. "If Mrs. Carrington wishes to go back to her room before I return, here is my direction," he said quietly. Georgiana stared at him in dismay. Before she could utter the protest that formed on her lips, he had bowed to her and her companion and was gone.

"Well," she said weakly. She leaned back into her nest of pillows. Georgiana stared at the door as if willing Charles to reappear immediately.

"Such a gentleman. Not many men would take time from their busy schedules to be of assistance to an acquaintance," Mrs. Thomas said. She smiled at Georgiana and took a seat.

"He did not stay long," Georgiana said in a disgruntled voice. She picked up a china figure from a table beside her and stared at it so long that Mrs. Thomas began to wonder if something was wrong.

"Is it cracked, my dear?" she asked.

"What?"

"The Meissen figure you are holding. Is it cracked?"

"No." Georgiana replaced it on the table. She glanced around the room, which suddenly felt very empty. She sighed, this time not pretending. "Are we to have any company this afternoon?" she asked wistfully.

"Mrs. Wycombe and Mrs. Bishop mentioned that they would be here. They are such kind ladies, do you not agree?" Mrs. Thomas glanced at Georgiana. Although Charles had not asked her help in gaining Georgiana's support, the older lady was delighted with his actions that afternoon. Since forcing her to pay attention to him had not worked, this was the perfect plan to capture

Georgiana's interest. At least she hoped it was a plan. Her mistress did not need any more disappointments.

The two hours before Charles returned seemed to crawl by. Georgiana smiled at the ladies who had come to see her but had no idea what they had discussed. When the door opened and Charles walked in, she sat up straighter, and the smile that she had carefully maintained became real.

"You are just in time to join us for tea, Mr. Harcourt," she said, hoping that he would not insist on taking her back upstairs immediately.

"How could I refuse with the promise of such delightful company?" he replied. He greeted the older sisters as though they were girls in their first Season, taking their hands and bowing. They giggled girlishly. Then he took a seat on the settee beside Mrs. Thomas.

"Cook made macaroons this afternoon. Would you care for one?" Mrs. Thomas asked, holding out the plate.

Smiling at her, he took one from the plate. "Now what have you ladies been discussing this afternoon?"

During the next half hour, Georgiana was more of a spectator than a participant. She could not keep her eyes away from Charles, who avoided looking at her. Finally giving in to her frustration, she sank back on the pillows that surrounded her and closed her eyes.

"I believe it is time for someone to return to her bed," Charles said firmly. He had been watching Georgiana even though she had not noticed his attention on her. The other ladies looked at Georgiana and nodded solemnly. Ignoring Georgiana's protests, he picked her up and walked out of the room. "Hold on," he said as he took the first step up the staircase. She wrapped her arms around his neck, and he smiled in satisfaction. He glanced down at her and was startled to see her eyes wide and her hand over the child she carried. "What's wrong?" he demanded.

Georgiana smiled mysteriously. "Nothing."

"Are you having pains?" He began to walk faster.

"No. I am all right," she tried to reassure him. "This happens frequently."

"What? What happens?" he asked anxiously. Although several of his friends had children, he personally had never had anything to do with a pregnant lady and was worried he would do something to hurt her. He pushed open the bedroom door and hurried toward the bed. "Shall I call the doctor or Mrs. Thomas?"

"Nonsense. I am fine." Moved by some force she truly did not understand, she let him put her on her bed. Then, before he could hurry away, she took his hand and put it on the growing child.

Startled by her action, he stood for a moment. Then he stepped back, his face worried. "What was that?"

Georgiana wanted to tell him the truth. Ever since he had appeared at the wells, she was longing to share her news with him. She opened her mouth. Then she smiled ruefully. "It is the child," she whispered. She longed to say *your* child but was afraid of his reaction.

"Does that happen very often?" Charles asked. He came closer to the bed and put his hand on her again. "I cannot feel anything now. Is something wrong?"

"No. The babe turns and stretches. When it does, I feel it," she explained, using the words the doctor had used with her.

"Does it hurt?" He sat on the edge of the bed. He longed to undress her, to see the changes in her body for himself. Her skin had a faint luminescent quality about it that fascinated him. He leaned forward.

The door to the bed chamber opened. "Shall I help you out of that dress, Mrs. Carrington?" her maid asked, her arms full of fresh linens. She looked up. "Oh! I am sorry! Shall I return later?" Her shock and confusion were evident.

As soon as he had heard the first word, Charles had jumped up. "Not on my account," he said quietly. "I am leaving. I will send you word when I can return."

Georgiana watched him leave, her eyes dark with disappointment. "Help me out of my dress. I think I want to sleep," she said in a voice that held no emotion. Freed of her confining garment, she slid down in bed and closed her eyes, lost in memories of Charles's arms holding her tight, driving away her loneliness and fear.

While Charles was carrying Georgiana to her room, Mrs. Thomas and the sisters were still talking. "Well, do you still think my hopes are unfounded?" Mrs. Thomas asked.

"He was more attentive to us than to her," Mrs. Bishop said. She took another macaroon from the plate.

"But he was definitely aware of her. Look how quickly he noticed when she tired," Mrs. Wycombe added. "Hmmm. I believe that you should continue as you are doing. She has several more months of mourning left. If the attraction continues, then we shall see."

"It is so exciting," Mrs. Bishop said with a giggle.

"And so improper. I wonder what her family is going to think," Mrs. Thomas said. "I only hope I am doing the right thing."

"He may only care for her as a friend," Mrs. Wycombe reminded her.

"A friend never looked at me that way," her sister retorted. "When he thinks no one is looking at him, he watches her. It is a match as sure as I am sitting here."

"He will be returning soon. Let us talk of something else," Mrs. Thomas suggested. Although they preferred to discuss the exciting events happening in the household, the ladies turned their attention to the actions of the people of the town.

When Charles returned to take his leave of them, they looked up with smiles. "She is resting in her own bed once again, Mrs. Thomas," he said quietly. "And now I must go." More shaken by the experience he had just gone through than he wanted to admit, he bowed and left. As soon as the door had shut behind him, the ladies looked at one another and smiled.

On his ride home that afternoon, Charles replayed the memory of that movement under his hand. Although he had known that Georgiana was with child, he had been able to discount the fact until that afternoon. With covers drawn up to her chin when she was in bed or swathed in shawls or a coverlet on her chaise, Georgiana looked as radiant as she had that night in his arms. But that movement under his hand had reminded him that she carried another life. And the thought of her in someone else's arms had him raging with jealousy. He wanted to scream in rage, but bit his lip so hard that he drew blood instead. Another man's child. He closed his eyes. When he did, the memory of Georgiana in his arms returned. He groaned. Another man's child. He spurred his horse into a gallop.

For the next few days he was distant but polite as he carried Georgiana from her bedroom to the drawing room and back. Using estate business as an excuse, he left as soon as he had deposited Georgiana on her chaise, returned only to carry her upstairs, and hurried off.

The older ladies tried to engage him in conversation. He was polite but refused their offers. "We obviously were wrong about him, Mrs. Thomas," Mrs. Wycombe said one afternoon after he had made his escape.

"You may be right. And I had such high hopes," Mrs. Thomas said with a sigh.

Georgiana, too, had begun to feel hopeless once more. She cried more easily and had begun to sink into lethargy. The only time she showed any animation was when Charles arrived and picked her up. She would smile up at him, ask him questions, and wilt when he answered politely without looking at her. Had she known how difficult that attitude was for him to maintain she would have been happier.

As it was, her general condition deteriorated so much that Mrs. Thomas felt compelled to call the doctor. He inspected her mistress, his face impassive. Then he called Mrs. Thomas out into the hallway. "How long has she been like this?"

"Only a few days," she assured him.

"Do you have any idea what caused it?"

She blushed. "I would prefer not to say," she whispered.

He frowned at her. "That attitude will not help your mistress. I need to know as much as you can tell me."

She hung her head. Then she took a deep breath and looked at him. "I think she is attracted to Mr. Harcourt."

"The gentleman who carries her down to the drawing room?" he asked. "You think it is he rather than her husband's death?"

She nodded vigorously. "During the last few days, there has been a strained atmosphere between them. And Mrs. Carrington is more listless after he leaves."

"Hmmm. I am afraid that I can do nothing to improve that situation. But we must do something for your mistress." He thought for a moment, his eyes on her. Dressed in a purple bombazine with black braid trim, she was a fine figure of a woman, a woman who should have her own household rather than depending on an employer's whims. He knew her birth was better than his, but that did not stop his hopes. "Has she had any more of those pains?" he asked.

"No. And I am not sure that they were the type of pains we thought they were."

"What do you mean?" he asked, not certain he enjoyed having his diagnosis challenged.

"Mrs. Carrington told me that when she was a child she often had stomach pains, usually because she was too excited," Mrs. Thomas said hurriedly. She glanced up at him and saw with relief that the faint frown that had appeared at her last statement had disappeared from his face.

"And you think she might have had those pains again? What could have caused them?"

"That I am sure I cannot say," Mrs. Thomas told him. She had her suspicions though.

"If that is true, then keeping her in bed is doing her more harm than good. She should be up and keep active," the doctor said thoughtfully. Mrs. Thomas waited while he thought the situation out. "Perhaps we should modify her treatment," he finally said. He turned and went back into the bedroom. Mrs. Thomas hurried to keep up.

"I think we shall try an experiment," he told Georgiana. She sat up further in bed. "I will permit you out of bed for an additional two hours a day." He was surprised when she frowned. "You may move around as you want during that time."

"Can she go up and down stairs, Doctor?" Mrs. Thomas asked, afraid that if Georgiana could, Mr. Harcourt would stop coming to the house. Georgiana, too, recognized the threat. Her face grew even sadder. She knew she would not see him again when that happened.

The doctor looked from one to the other. Then he changed what he was about to say. "I think stairs are still too risky. If you wish to go downstairs, you must depend on Mr. Harcourt." Georgiana smiled weakly and drew a deep breath. "If after a week or so you have no further problems, then we will discuss other changes. I encourage you to walk, to build up your strength," he told her. "This time in bed has weakened you more than I like."

"There is nothing wrong with the babe, is there?" Georgiana asked, her face a pasty white.

"No. The child is growing nicely. It is you I am worried about," he said heartily. "Remember. Use your two hours out of bed to walk, to move around. Do whatever you usually do. I do not want you to think of yourself as an invalid."

"May I go outside?" Georgiana asked wistfully. Through a window near her bed she had watched the sky, longing to breathe fresh air.

"A walk in the garden could not hurt," he said kindly, noting the fresh color in her cheeks.

"When Mr. Harcourt arrives, I am certain he will be happy to take you there," Mrs. Thomas said encouragingly.

Georgiana's color faded. "Perhaps. May I get up now, Dr. Mackensie?" she asked.

"If you plan to go for a walk later, I must insist that you rest now," he told her.

Georgiana closed her eyes to hide the tears that welled up within them. She sighed. The doctor's words marked the end; she was sure of it. A few more days and she was sure she would not need Charles to carry her to the drawing room. The doctor would allow her to climb any stairs she wanted, and Charles would be free of her once more.

# 9

LATER that afternoon as she dressed to go down, Georgiana was still in the depth of despair. She was determined not to let her emotions show, to project an air of serenity when Charles arrived. Never one to wear her feelings so that everyone could see them, she was determined that no one would know how deeply she felt about him.

To give herself courage, she had dressed in her newest afternoon gown. "You look very elegant, Mrs. Carrington," her maid assured her as she tied the ribbons that threaded through her braided hair.

"Like one of the nameless birds of the forest. All gray and colorless," Georgiana said in a discouraged tone.

"I will admit that gray is not your best color. But you look very nice," her maid said quietly. Like Mrs. Thomas she was worried about her mistress and had been working ceaselessly to build her spirits.

Georgiana turned sideways in front of the mirror looking at her stomach. "I suppose even the brightest colors would not make me look good. I look like, like an elephant." One of the books she had been reading was about India. "At least I will not have to carry this child for eighteen months," she said putting her hands over the large mound.

"Eighteen months? Mrs. Carrington, are you feeling all right?" her maid asked, hurrying to her side. Her eyes were wide.

"Elephants carry their young for eighteen months,"

Georgiana explained. "I wonder how they stand it. I have not seen my feet in months."

"Strange. And where do these creatures live?"

"In India."

"I thought it must be some foreign land. You sit down here and let me fix that strand of hair that has come free." Quickly, the maid loosened her mistress's braids and began to brush her hair.

The door to the hallway opened. "Georgiana, Mr. Harcourt has arrived," Mrs. Thomas called. Her face wore a beaming smile. Then she caught sight of her mistress. "Oh my. Perhaps we should wait in the hall until the maid has finished. I apologize, Mr. Harcourt."

Charles allowed her to usher him back into the hallway. Seeing Georgiana with her hair streaming down her back had taken him aback. For days he had had himself under stern control, had gotten to the point that he was certain that he visited every day simply because he said he would, had begun to consider rejoining his friends. That moment had destroyed all his careful control. He took deep breaths, trying to regain his composure.

"I did not want to tell you, Mr. Harcourt. Were you surprised?" Mrs. Thomas asked. She smiled up at him, willing him to agree with her.

"Ah . . . yes . . . yes I was," he stammered. The sight of Georgiana seated in front of that mirror, her hair unbound, had robbed him of his ability to think. Georgiana, in front of the mirror. "What is she doing up?" he demanded. His brown eyes bored into Mrs. Thomas's.

"The doctor said that she can get up a few hours a day," she said with a smile. "I think it is wonderful."

"Wonderful," he said. His excuse for holding Georgiana was fast disappearing. Even though he had longed to be free of his promise, now that he was he was not pleased. "When did this happen?"

"This morning. Naturally, there are still restrictions." He turned to look at her, his heart beginning to beat faster. He raised an eyebrow. "She still may not walk up or down stairs, but she can go for a walk in the garden and is determined to do so this very afternoon. I think the doctor is just being cautious. Or he could be afraid she might trip and fall. I am glad you will be with her," she said, smiling up at him.

"Has she been dizzy?" he asked.

Before she could answer, the door opened, and Georgiana came out. "I apologize for keeping you waiting," she said, keeping her eyes fixed on the floor. She held a cloak in her hands. Charles took it from her and wrapped it around her shoulders, letting his hands linger there for a moment.

"It was nothing. Mrs. Thomas told me the happy news. Are you ready for your walk?" he asked. Lying down or even when he was carrying her, she seemed so small. Now her head came above his shoulder. Slowly they walked to the head of the stairs. "Here we go!" he said. She nodded, and he swept her up in his arms.

"Are you coming with us, Mrs. Thomas?" Georgiana called.

"I am expecting guests. You enjoy the day. It is beautiful outside," her companion said. She watched as they disappeared from view and sighed. Then she hurried down the stairs to the drawing room.

As the footman opened the door to the garden, Charles could not keep his arms from tightening around her. He stood on the path for just a moment while Georgiana lifted her face to the sun, drinking in its warmth like a flower. Then he carefully set her on her feet. "Are you dressed warmly enough?" he asked, taking her hand in his. He drew it through his arm and led her down the path.

"I am fine. Just fine," Georgiana said with a laugh. "Everything looks wonderful."

"Wonderful? The garden has begun to die," he teased her. "What is so wonderful about that?"

"If you had been shut up within the house for weeks, you would understand," she said with a smile. "Look, there is a late-blooming rose."

"Let me get it for you. You sit here. I will be right

back." Using his penknife, he cut the crimson rose and brought it back to her. She smiled at him. He tightened his hand around the stem and then yelped in pain.

"What is wrong? Are you ill?" Georgiana asked, hurrying to his side.

"No. I simply forgot that lovely roses have thorns," he said. Breaking them off, he handed the rose to her. She took his hand in hers, wincing as she saw the blood welling up from the thorn prick. Before she had time to think that what she was doing was wrong, she took his hand and raised it to her lips, much as he had done when she had pricked her finger.

Dropping a kiss on the spot, she glanced up mischievously. "My mother always said a kiss made it better," she told him. Her blue eyes reflected the blue sky of the autumn day.

He swept her into his arms and kissed her, intending at first just to brush her lips with his. Then the kiss deepened. Her lips parted. He pulled her closer and kissed her again. She returned his caresses. Hungry for his lips, his arms, she wrapped her arms around his neck. Then he stepped back, his face confused. "Was that what I think it was?" he asked, putting his hand over her stomach.

"Yes." A faint blush tinted her cheeks. She took several steps back. Feeling the stone bench behind her, she sank down. Although she longed to stare at him, to entrance him with her eyes as she had seen others do during her Season, she could not. Her hands came up to cover her hot cheeks. "You must think me without shame," she whispered.

He grinned, feeling more himself than he had for days. "And what does that make me?" he asked, sitting beside her and taking her hands in his. "I completely forgot where we were," he admitted. "Do you think Mrs. Thomas and the sisters saw us?" he asked.

"Ohh!" Georgiana pulled her hands free and covered her face. "Ohh!"

He leaned close to her and whispered in her ear. "And

if the babe had not reminded me, I might have made the same sort of advances that I made at the inn." A wicked smile played about his mouth.

"Ohh!" How could any lady with child respond the way she had, Georgiana wondered. And why would any gentleman be interested in a lady in her condition? She glanced up at him from the corner of her eye and saw him wink at her. She lowered her eyes again and blushed.

Charles, thoroughly confused by his own emotions, stood up and took her hand. "We had better continue our walk, or Mrs. Thomas will join us." He helped her stand.

"You forget. I am a widow. The rules that young girls must follow do not concern me," she reminded him. In spite of the problems she had to face, she did enjoy the freedom from restrictions her assumed position provided.

"Rules. Yes," he sighed. "And if a gentleman forgets just one, he may find himself betrothed to someone he never intended to marry."

"How cynical. One would think that had happened to you. And I know you offered for Celeste. Why did you never marry? Your engagement was announced." She stopped and put her hand over her mouth. "You will think me a Polly Pry. Forget I ever said anything," she said, trying to look anywhere but him.

"It was over long ago. There's no need to be embarrassed. Everyone in the ton knows, and I came to terms with it long ago," he said easily, surprising even himself. Although he knew that he no longer cared for his former fiancée, he had not realized that the memory no longer had the power to wound him.

"Then what happened?" Georgiana demanded. She turned to look up at him.

"She threw me over."

"What?"

"Don't be so indignant. It was for the best. Even my mother said that. If she could not be happy with a plain mister, then it was better that I discover it before we were married."

"Whom did she marry?"

"A baronet from Derbyshire. Someone no one ever heard of before. They rarely come to town," he said, grinning at the memory of the last time he had seen Celeste. "She has three brats and has gained a stone or two. Alas, the sylph is sylphlike no longer."

To his surprise, Georgiana did not share his humor. She glanced down at her own waistline. "Like me?" she asked. The tone of her voice told him that he needed to choose his words carefully.

"You are infinitely more lovely than she," he said in a soothing voice. His answer surprised even him. Searching his memory, he realized that he could not think of a more beautiful woman. "You are a giver. She merely took."

"Gentlemen did not realize that ten years ago," she said angrily.

"Ten years ago. Was that your Season?" he asked.

Just then Mrs. Thomas opened the door to the garden. "There you are. Your two hours are almost up, Georgiana. And I was certain you would want to have a cup of tea with Mrs. Wycombe and Mrs. Bishop before you go back upstairs," she said. Both Georgiana and Charles bit back angry remarks. They nodded and walked toward the house.

Riding home later that afternoon, Charles tried to remember the details of that Season ten years earlier. But he had been so deeply infatuated with Celeste that he had paid little attention to anyone else. "I wish John were here," he muttered. "He would remember."

The question of who Georgiana truly was haunted him all evening. After he had finished his meal and drunk more port than was his usual habit, he wandered into his library, a rather dark room. After looking at one book after another—most were rather dull religious treatises purchased by an ancestor almost a century earlier, he sat down at the desk. He searched through the desk drawer until he had found what he wanted. Sharpening the quill with his pen knife, he pulled the piece of paper closer. "Dear John," he began.

As he waited impatiently for a reply, he proceeded cautiously with Georgiana. Still ambivalent about the child when he was away from her, his doubts seemed to disappear when he was in her presence. And Georgiana was as mysterious as she had ever been. After their discussions that one afternoon, she had avoided his questions, taking care never to be alone with him.

Released from the captivity of her bed and from her fears that she would never bring the child she carried to term, Georgiana slowly regained her natural good spirits. The slight puffiness that had filled her face disappeared when she began to exercise regularly. Even though many days it was too cold or wet to walk in the gardens, she always walked, often wandering from room to room.

Once again she was deeply involved in planning the nursery. Under Mrs. Thomas's direction, the room had been cleaned and stripped of its former wall hangings and curtains. Georgiana made her selections carefully. In the north the days were short in the winter, but she wanted the babe surrounded by light. To the horror of the painters and of Mrs. Thomas, who tried to persuade her to change her mind, she selected a soft yellow for the walls and white for the trim.

"It will be dirty in a week," Mrs. Thomas said with a frown. "As soon as a fire is lit in the grate, the walls will be dingy."

"And until then, my babe will be surrounded with color," Georgiana declared, setting her chin stubbornly.

"I thought we had decided that we would do nothing to the walls," Mrs. Thomas said, trying a different approach.

"That was before I asked the doctor if there was any harm in having the room painted," her mistress said. The set of Georgiana's chin told Mrs. Thomas not to question her further.

"Well, it does brighten the room," the older lady said.

"No matter what the doctor says, however, you are not to go near there until the painting is complete and the room has been aired."

Having learned something herself in the time she had spent in bed, Georgiana agreed. She picked up her book and tried to find her place, seeing instead her child comfortable and warm inside the clean nursery. No stern nursery for her child, she thought, remembering the blank walls of the room in which she had grown up. And no nurse who had known her mother either. A few tears welled up in her eyes, but she brushed them away angrily. She should have thought about the consequences months earlier, she reminded herself. Despite her occasional moments of sadness, the closer she got to the birth of the child the more excited she grew.

Autumn gradually gave way to colder temperatures. Snow flurries began in earnest. One morning Charles woke up to find the ground covered. He rose slowly at first; then the frost in the room chilled him. Hurrying into his clothes, he made his way downstairs where a huge fire roared in the breakfast room. He shivered and longed for the milder temperatures of the south.

"Post just arrived for you, sir," his butler said, handing him a letter.

John, he thought. Then he recognized the handwriting. Tearing it open, he quickly glanced through its lines. As usual his mother had written more in haste than in elegance. But the main idea of her letter was clear. He was to finish whatever he was doing and hurry home for Christmas. He accepted a cup of chocolate and crossed to look out of the window. Already the snow was melting. If he left soon, he should have no problem traveling.

Although he had been claiming estate business as his motive for staying, he knew it was a weak excuse. Days or weeks ago, he and his manager had finished discussing the problems of the estate. Not for years, in fact, had he been as scrupulous about tending to its affairs. Usually, he came to hunt or fish and left quickly.

He thought of the reason he had stayed—Georgiana.

He had acknowledged her importance weeks ago. But he still did not know what to do. He wanted her, wanted her more than he had ever wanted a woman before. But the child she carried made him hesitate. More than once he had been poised, ready to ask her to be his wife. Each time he had stopped, drawn back. If only he could return to the careless determination he had felt that day before John had left.

Perhaps it would be better for him to do as his mother suggested and return home for the holiday. Lately even Mrs. Thomas, his staunchest supporter, had hinted that he did not need to visit every day. Now that the doctor had given Georgiana permission to climb the stairs he was not really needed.

The longer he considered the dilemma, the stronger his desire to escape became. Maybe if he were away from her, he could make up his mind. And maybe he would forget her, forget the kisses they had shared. Finally making up his mind, he sat down and wrote both Georgiana and his mother notes.

Although her child had become the center of her world, Georgiana never forgot about Charles. In spite of constant lectures to herself, somehow he had become necessary to her. Where once she had lived a quiet but relatively happy life, now she was alive only when she felt the babe move or had Charles nearby. The infatuation that girlish dreams had kept alive for ten years had changed into love, a love that caused her to burn for him, made her want to confess that she carried his child. Only her fear kept her silent.

What would he say when he found out? She admitted to herself that she would eventually tell him, no matter how afraid she was. The thought of his reaction worried her greatly. Charles was not known for his gentle nature. Would he believe her? Would he turn on her in anger, declaring that she was a liar? She felt like a button on a string that is twirled by a child, never in the same place twice.

When she received Charles's letter telling her that he would be gone until the first of the New Year, she wanted to cry, partly in despair, partly in relief. Pulling herself together, she hid her unhappiness from her companion, who had ranted and raved enough for both of them. When Mrs. Thomas had finished her tirade, Georgiana said, "We should have expected this." Her companion looked up the bough of greenery she was stitching together. "We knew that Mr. Harcourt had come to Yorkshire for the sport and stayed because he thought we needed him. Now that I am better he can return to his usual pursuits."

"Well, I think it is unhandsome of him not to come for one last visit," Mrs. Thomas said with a sniff. She held up the greenery she was working on. "Is this long enough?"

"We want it to drape down. Maybe you should add some more," Georgiana said after she had inspected it.

"Why you want a kissing bough is more than I can imagine." Georgiana, who was working on her own bundle, did not say anything. "Well, this is not my home. I suppose you can decorate it any way you want."

As Christmas grew closer and she had had no word from her son, Mrs. Thomas's usual good spirits had deserted her. Each day she waited for the post. Each day she was disappointed.

Georgiana, too, felt out of tune with the holiday season. For the first time in her life, she would not be sharing the time with her family. As cheerful as her sister's letters had been, Georgiana had discovered an undercurrent of unhappiness, an unhappiness she was certain had something to do with her. Maybe it would have been better had they broken completely, she thought. She closed her eyes, trying to banish the desolation that thought brought.

The two ladies continued working in silence. Then a footman entered. "Are you at home for Dr. Mackensie?" he asked his mistress.

"Of course," Georgiana said with a smile. She had

gotten used to the brusque doctor and welcomed his practical advice. And even in her own state of confusion, she had realized that he was courting her companion. She wondered, however, if Mrs. Thomas was aware of the fact.

"Have you come to tell us you are leaving us alone for Christmas, too?" Mrs. Thomas asked, looking up over the pile of green in her lap.

"Me? My dear ladies," the doctor smiled at Mrs. Thomas, "I shall probably be so busy on Christmas that the season will have come and gone and I shall not have noticed."

"That is terrible. Do you mean that you will not have a Christmas dinner?" Georgiana asked, glancing at her companion. Mrs. Thomas was frowning.

"Usually I am gone most of the day. I send my housekeeper to visit her family rather than wait on me. She always leaves me a meal," he said.

"Cold, I imagine. How can you be expected to work well when you do not have a hot meal? And people should let you have some peace on the holiday," Mrs. Thomas said indignantly.

"Babies are born on Christmas just as on any other day," he reminded her. "Would you have me turn them away? What would I do with my time?"

"Have you no family to share the day with?" Georgiana asked. He shook his head. "Then you must share it with us. No, I do not want to hear excuses. If you are called away, we will understand. You will have to pardon us; our numbers may be rather uneven; Mrs. Wycombe and Mrs. Bishop will also be here," Georgiana said firmly. Then she smiled at him. Intrigued by her and hoping for a chance to be alone with Mrs. Thomas, he allowed himself to be persuaded.

"Do you go to evening services on Christmas Eve?" he asked. Both ladies nodded. "Then perhaps you will dine with me that evening and allow me to escort you." They looked at each other and smiled.

"It would be our pleasure, Dr. Mackensie," Mrs.

Thomas murmured. She picked up her fan and waved it vigorously, hoping to cool the warmth in her cheeks. He smiled back.

By the time Christmas Eve came, the house was filled with greenery and the smells of Christmas baking. The night was crisp, cold, and clear. As they walked into Georgiana's home after the service, large flakes of snow had begun to fall.

They paused in the hallway to remove their outer garments and brush the few snowflakes from their hair. "A gentleman is waiting to see you," the servant said.

"Charles?" Georgiana practically ran down the hall to the drawing room door. "Charles?" All her love and hope were clear for her companions to read. They followed along behind her, ready to add their greetings. Then all the joy disappeared from her face.

"What is wrong?" Mrs. Thomas asked, hurrying to her side. She crossed the threshold of the room and into the circle of light shed by a branch of candles.

"Mother!" A young man almost exactly the height of Georgiana rushed forward, grabbed her, and swung her about.

"Richard? Richard? How did you get here? Why did you not let me know you were coming?" Mrs. Thomas babbled. She held him still and stared at him as though she could not see enough.

Dr. Mackensie noted the laugh lines by the man's mouth and his resemblance to his mother and quickly made his excuses.

"Remember. You are expected for dinner tomorrow as we planned," Georgiana said firmly as she walked him to the door, leaving the other two alone.

When she returned a few moments later, Mrs. Thomas and her son were seated in front of the fire. "Georgiana, my shatterbrained son did not think about a place to stay. May he stay with us?"

"I insist on it," Georgiana said. Hiding a yawn, she allowed Mrs. Thomas to present him to her formally.

"You are most kind," Richard Thomas said in a low

voice. When his mother's letter telling him about her job as a companion had reached him, he had not been happy. As soon as his ship had docked and he had been given leave, he had rushed to find her, determined to carry her away with him and set her up in her own small house wherever she chose. But his mother, despite the few tears she had shed on seeing him, seemed happier than she had been since his father's death. Used to making quick decisions at sea, Richard accepted the offer of a bed and decided to study the situation for himself. "I promise that I will be gone before long."

"But you cannot. You just arrived," his mother said, taking his hand in hers.

"I do not plan to rush away immediately," he told her with a smile that reminded Georgiana of her companion's. "The ship needs repairs. I have leave until the captain sends for me."

"Good. Now tell me everything you have done since last I saw you," Mrs. Thomas said. She pulled him down beside her.

Georgiana yawned, this time too broadly to hide behind her hand. "And I will bid you good night. Someone will be here to show you to your room when you are ready to go up."

"Send the servants to bed, Georgiana. I will see my son to his room," Mrs. Thomas suggested. "Tomorrow is a holiday."

"As you wish." Once again Georgiana yawned. She nodded to Richard, who stood as she left the room. As she slowly walked up the stairs, she wished that she had someone to share Christmas with. "Next year, little one. Next year," she whispered.

# *10*

MILES away, Charles was feeling the same isolation that Georgiana was experiencing. As he had expected, his mother had filled his house with a horde of relatives. What he had not expected was the young lady and her family that his mother had invited to share their celebration.

As soon as he could do so without offending their guests, he slipped his arm around his mother's waist and led her from the room. Their guests smiled as the handsome couple walked out. The door to the small office that his mother claimed as her own had scarcely closed when he turned to face her. "What do you think you are doing, Mother?" he demanded. His mother hesitated, startled by his fierce frown. Her brown eyes, so much like his own, were wide with surprise.

"I was only trying to help," she said, her voice artfully breaking on the last word.

"I have told you before that I can find my own bride."

"That is what you say, but you have done nothing about it," she said. She frowned at him, but then she reached up a hand and stroked his cheek. "I just want you to be happy."

"I am," he said through clenched teeth. He squared his shoulders and glared at her.

"If you are, you are the strangest person I have ever known. Ever since you arrived, you have been going around the house with a frown."

"Do not try to change the subject. Really, Mother, did

you seriously expect me to offer for that child. She is hardly out of leading strings."

"Do not exaggerate," his mother said sternly. Then she sighed and collapsed in a nearby chair. She clasped her hands together and studied them intently. "The moment I saw her, I knew she would not do," she admitted.

"You invited her here without meeting her?"

"Her mother and I were at school together. I assumed she would be like her mother."

"She is. They are both lovely wigeons without two thoughts in their heads."

"You do them an injustice, Charles," his mother said, trying to maintain a calm expression. "They frequently worry about many things."

"What dress to wear or what flowers to carry. Any more than that, and their minds would rebel."

His mother looked at him sternly and then permitted her rueful amusement to show. "I should have known that an empty-headed chit would produce a daughter as much like herself as was humanly possible. But the child does have pleasant manners and a wonderful disposition."

"For once you admitted the truth. She is a child," he said.

"A child who will no doubt be married within the year. You could do worse," his mother told him. For once her voice was completely serious.

Charles looked around the small room with its small desk and chairs that seemed only a little too small to hold his frame completely. "She is so young," he whispered. He took a seat across from her.

"No one who will be presented this year will be any older," she reminded him. She stood and walked behind him, putting her arms around him. "All I want is for you to be as happy as your father and I were," she whispered, stroking his hair.

He captured her hand and brought it to his lips. "I want that, too, Mother," he said, thinking about Georgiana. "I think I have met someone special," he said a moment later. A carefully expurgated story of Georgiana came pouring forth.

His mother heard the word "widow" and decided that her son had been snared by a conniving woman, but she hid her horror, not wanting to stem the tide of his confidences; however, when he told her about forcing his way into Georgiana's bedroom, her eyebrows shot up. "You did what?" she asked weakly, sinking into a chair opposite him.

"I did not intend any disrespect," he insisted, thankful that she did not know about the first time he and Georgiana had met earlier that year. "That companion of hers was determined not to let me see her. I was equally determined I would." His face was as set as it had been when he was a child and someone had told him no.

"And was Mrs. Carrington happy to see you?" his mother asked, wondering what sort of person this woman was.

"No."

"Well?"

"Well, what?" he asked in an irritated voice. He pulled the sleeves of his corbeau-colored evening coat further down over his wrists, his eyes fixed on a string that he had just pulled from the lace on his sleeves.

"You cannot stop there," his mother told him. "What happened next?" His face showed his anger and hurt, and she longed to smooth the cares from him with a kiss and a hug. She knew, however, that this time they would not be enough.

Feeling as though he were caught in a maze and did not know the key, he nodded, wishing his path was clear. He closed his eyes and saw Georgiana propped up in bed, a blue shawl around her shoulders. A burst of longing so strong that he had to bite the inside of his lip to control it shot through him. Georgiana was his. He had put his brand on her the night of the fire. He laughed ruefully to himself. The only fire that night had been caused by desire, and he was still burning.

"Charles? Charles!"

Startled, he sat up straight and looked at his mother. "Yes?"

"Where is Mrs. Carrington now?" his mother asked. She controlled her impatience with difficulty.

"In Harrogate," he said. Then he sighed.

"You could have brought her with you, Charles. I would have been happy to meet her," she said, smiling up at him. Only to herself was she willing to admit she was glad to have her son to herself.

He got up and began to prowl around the small room. "No. To have done so would have been the same as making a declaration. I'm not certain I'm ready for that."

"Why not?" his mother asked, a fiercely protective tone in her voice. She rose and stood next to him, her hand on his arm. "What is wrong?"

He bent his head and kissed her cheek. "We have left our guests to themselves far too long," he said quietly, determined to bring this interview to an end.

His mother glanced at him, noting the fixed line of his mouth. Biting back the questions she longed to ask, she nodded and took his arm. Taking her cue from him, she asked, "What do you have planned for tomorrow?"

Even though he kept busy entertaining their guests by leading expeditions to find greenery and mistletoe or to lead his guests into the field for a hunt, Charles discovered he could not hide from his memories of Georgiana. He would be involved in his activities; then, suddenly, he would hear a laugh. Forgetting what he was doing, he would twist around searching for Georgiana.

After an evening when he had been particularly distracted and everyone had begun to notice, his mother invited him to share her breakfast in her room. She handed him a cup of chocolate and waited until he took a drink. For a moment the only sound was of the wind whistling around the window. Leaning back on her lacy pillows, Mrs. Harcourt inspected her only son, trying to see him with impartial eyes. She put her cup down with a clatter she would have thought reprehensible in anyone else. Charles looked up, startled. "Is something wrong,

Mother?" he asked, finally realizing that she was not her usually bubbly self.

"So you have joined me again, have you?" she asked.

"I apologize. I have been distracted occasionally."

"Occasionally? Charles, last evening you pointedly ignored our guests for the entire evening, ignored their questions, and behaved like an uncouth bore." She sank back against her pillows and put a hand over her face. "Why would you think something is wrong?"

"You must be exaggerating," he said, wondering what had come over his usually calm and happy mother.

"Even if I tried, I could not exaggerate how rude you were," she told him, sitting up in bed and glaring at him. "What is wrong with you?"

"Wrong?"

"Do not try to fob me off with a question, Charles. Is it that woman?" Her tone of voice was both sharp and brittle.

He stood up and squared his shoulders. "Are you talking about Georgiana, Mother?" he asked quietly. The set of his shoulders and the tone of voice he used told her more than his words.

Quickly, she tried to backtrack. "My dear, you have not been yourself lately. I merely wondered what was disturbing you. You yourself told me about Mrs. Carrington. Naturally, I assumed that only a problem with her could cause my son to act this way."

The tension in his body disappeared. Charles sat back down in his chair and put his head in his hands. "Oh, Mother," he said with a sigh.

"What can I do?" she asked, leaning forward so that she could run a hand through his hair.

"I am afraid I have grown past the stage where you can solve every one of my problems," he said. He sighed again. "I must solve this one myself."

"Talking about it can help. At least I can listen. Then if I can see a solution, I will tell you," she urged. "Remember. A shared burden becomes lighter."

He rolled his head back and closed his eyes. After a

few minutes in which his mother had to force herself to keep from biting her nails, he said, "I cannot make up my mind."

"If you are not certain that she is the one you want, you are wise not to make a commitment," she said with a smile, relieved that she would not have to accept a woman she had never met as a daughter-in-law.

"Oh, I want her."

"I do not understand." Mrs. Harcourt kept her disappointment from showing in her voice, but only by being very careful.

"She is not only a widow. She is a pregnant widow," he said quietly, opening his eyes to stare into her face, watching for the horrified reaction he knew would follow.

He was not disappointed. A look of dismay that she quickly hid crossed her face. "Pregnant?" she asked in a whisper. "Charles, what have you done?"

"Mother! This is not my child." He glared at her and then got up and began pacing around the room. "That is the problem."

"What are you saying?" she asked in a voice that was carefully controlled.

"If the child were mine, I would ask Georgiana to be my wife today," he said, squaring his shoulders and turning to face her. Then he realized the implications of what he had said. He noticed the shock on his mother's face and hurried to the side of the bed. "Wipe those thoughts from your mind, Mother. Georgiana is not that type of woman." As soon as he said the words, he realized that somewhere within himself he, too, had had doubts. Georgiana's response to him that night at the inn had been so passionate, so exciting that he had wondered if she had been unfaithful to her husband before. His memories of the night were still vivid in spite of the amount of wine he had drunk. He knew Georgiana's response had been passionate but unskilled. The thought made him smile. "You would like her, Mother."

His mother wisely held her tongue. She looked up at

her only son, her concern evident upon her face. The silence in the room grew. She shifted, pulling herself higher on her pillows. "If she is important to you, Charles, you should bring her here," she suggested.

"After her mourning is over and after the babe arrives?"

"Whenever you choose. Asking her to travel now may not be the best course. When is the child expected?"

"Mother, I can scarcely get her to talk to me about ordinary things. She would never tell me anything specific about the baby," he said with a rueful laugh, wishing that what he had said was not true. Georgiana had kissed him, had held him tightly, but had never allowed him into her mind. If the memories of the night in the inn had not been so clear, he would think they had happened to two other people. He bent and kissed his mother's cheek. "I need to think. I will see you later," he muttered. He walked toward the door.

"Charles," she called after him.

"Yes?"

"Please remember to be considerate of our guests. They did not cause this problem," she said sternly. "I have made all the apologies I care to."

"Yes, Mother," he said in the same tone he used when he was a boy and she had to reprimand him. He smiled sweetly and then quickly left the room.

She closed her eyes and took a deep breath. "I will pray that you make the right decision, my dear," she whispered.

During the days that followed, Mrs. Harcourt tried unsuccessfully to reopen their conversation about the woman in her son's life, but he evaded her, preferring to spend his days on the estate. He visited his closest tenants, making careful mental notes of who needed help and which families had had a leaner year than the rest. Although he usually left the managing of his estates to his estate steward, he, as his father before him, prided himself in knowing what was going on with his tenants.

To his dismay, Charles discovered that he did not

know his estate as well as he once did. He no longer
knew the names of all of the people living on his land.
"You have not spent much time on the estate in the last
two years, sir," the steward reminded him in a voice that
was carefully bland. In spite of the lack of blame in his
steward's voice, Charles's first reaction was anger. Before he let loose a salvo that would have destroyed his
relationship with an excellent employee, he paused, trying to get a grasp on his temper. When he did, the truth
of what the man was saying was an impenetrable wall.
Shaken, he merely nodded, resolving to himself that he
would do better.

Glad that he now had a project that would keep his
mind occupied, Charles rode over every acre of his
home estate until he once more knew the names of every
child and had a firm grasp of the condition of the property. Every once in a while he found himself wondering
what Georgiana would think of a project he had suggested or whether she would laugh quietly as he had
when one of the little children had said something surprising. Although he had hoped that working on the estate would keep her out of his mind, he could not forget
her. As time went on, he thought more and more about
her, not just at night lying alone in his bed but every moment of the day.

The holiday passed. Members of the house party
began to take their leave, reminding each other that they
would meet again in London in a few short weeks.
Charles, too, was restless. As the company grew fewer
in number, it was harder to evade his mother.

Finally, Mrs. Harcourt found her son alone in the
small room that served as estate office. "You have been
hiding from me, Charles," she said accusingly. "No, do
not try to fob me off with some kind of excuse. You and
I both know what has been going on." She smiled at him
and sat down in the chair in front of the desk, her cor-
beau kerseymere skirts falling about her in graceful
folds. Her eyes so much like her son's held the faintest
hint of sadness.

"What can I do for you, Mother?" Charles asked, wondering as he had so many times before why his mother had never remarried. He knew it was not from opportunity. She always had some gentleman around to escort her to parties or to the opera. He leaned forward, resting his elbows on the desk.

She cleared her throat, finding the words harder to say than she had dreamed they would be. "You can tell me what you have decided," she said quietly. She clasped her hands tightly as though she wanted to say more but was afraid to do so. He flinched. "Whatever you decide I will support. You can bring the lady here whenever you want, or I will go to Yorkshire to meet her," she said quietly. "If she is your choice, I will receive her happily." The words were not easy for her to say. Since their earlier conversation, she had had many talks with herself. At last, however, she had realized that she trusted her son. If she did not want to drive a wedge between them, she was the one who would have to give in. She looked across the desk at him and smiled.

To her surprise, he did not smile back at her. He frowned. He shifted in his chair. "Mother," he began. Then he stopped.

"Yes?" she prompted.

The emotions rolling around inside him made him want to jump up and leave the room, to get outside where he did not feel so confined. "Would you believe me if I told you that I still do not know what to do?" he asked, his voice so low that she could barely hear it.

She sat back in her chair and stared at him in surprise. The last few days Georgiana's name had been on his lips often. Mrs. Harcourt's eyes narrowed. Was he unaware of how much he had talked about her? Several of their guests, especially her closest friends, had asked her for information about the widow since Charles had mentioned her so often. Although she had tried to deflect their questions, she had been certain that she would soon be welcoming Georgiana as her son's bride. Wishing that he were younger and she could solve the problems that perplexed him as she had when he was a child, she shook her head. Then she asked, "Charles, do you love her?" The words seemed to echo in the small room.

"Yes. At least I think I do. But . . ."

"But what? If you care for her, what are you waiting for?" she asked.

"Mama." Her heart melted as she heard the name he used to call her before he went off to school and grew so formal. She smiled at him. He got up from his chair, pushing it back violently so that it fell over. He picked it up, put it back in place, and then stood there looking like a lost child.

"This is one decision you must make alone, Charles. But if you need someone to talk to, I am here and ready to listen," she said in a soothing voice. "Sometimes talking about a problem makes it appear smaller."

"This is a small problem all right," he said almost angrily. "But it will not get any smaller. It will only grow."

She sat back in her chair and stared up at him, her face reflecting her dismay. "Then you must forget her," she said in a voice that was as calm and gentle as she could make it. Not even ten years earlier when Celeste had called their wedding off had he appeared so upset. It had taken him ten years to think of marriage again. How long would it take this time, she wondered.

"I cannot. I have tried." He began to pace, but the room was too small to allow him to go very far. He finally came around the desk and sat on the edge. "What am I to do, Mama? What am I to do?"

She rose and put her arms around him, patting him as she had so many times before when he was much smaller. She sighed. Then she stepped back. "Tell me once more about this problem that will only grow larger."

He sat up straight as if he could force himself to look at the problem squarely. Then he closed his eyes, and his shoulders slumped once more. "The babe," he whispered. His mother sat down, startled. "She is mine," he said angrily. "I do not want to share her with anyone.

Whenever I look at her and see the child growing within her, I cannot forget that she married someone else."

"But you did not know her then."

"I know her now, and the thought of her belonging to someone else tears me apart." He got up and walked behind the desk again. His shoulders sagging, he sat back down and put his face in his hands. His mother longed to soothe him to tell him it would be all right, but this time his problem was larger than she could handle. "If only . . ." He stopped.

"If only what?" she urged.

"There were no babe."

"But there is. Charles, if you cannot accept the child, you will have to give up the mother," she said, wishing there were an easier answer.

"I am not certain I can do that," he told her. His face was set in harsh lines.

"You cannot punish the child for your own jealousy," his mother told him. "It would be far better never to see her again than destroy all three of your lives with your anger."

"I know. I have told myself that many times. But I want her." He thought of Georgiana and smiled. "Mama, you would like her. She is tall, taller than you are. When she smiles at me, I feel I can do anything. She is shy, and I can make her blush easily." For the next half hour, Mrs. Harcourt sat and listened to her son extol the virtues of Georgiana Carrington. She nodded occasionally and added a word now and then. More than his words, her son's excitement in talking about this lady made her realize how much he loved Georgiana.

As soon as Charles began repeating himself, his mother broke in. "Charles," she said quietly. He looked at her, seeing her once more. "I cannot tell you what to do. But as you are making your decision, ask yourself if you would rather have Georgiana and the babe or not have Georgiana at all. Whatever you decide, I will support you. Let me know what you want me to do." She stood up and came around the desk to kiss him on the cheek. "Let me know," she repeated.

The question his mother had proposed haunted Charles. One moment he would decide to ask Georgiana to marry him; the next he had decided to forget her. As he struggled to come to a definite decision, he received a letter from John Wentworth, inviting him to London for a few days. Bidding his mother good-bye, he eagerly set off in hopes of finding something to distract him.

Even bare of company, London offered more entertainment than a country estate. After joining his friend, Charles plunged into a series of activities designed to make him forget Georgiana. Rejecting the safer gambling establishments, he began to visit the halls on Jermyn Street in spite of the protests of his friends. "Charles, are you daft?" John asked him, only a day or two after his arrival. "You know the games are not honest there. Why do you persist in returning?"

"If you do not want to go with me, I will go alone," Charles replied. The fast pace and the need to keep a steady head drove thoughts of Georgiana from his mind. And he had not lost enough to matter. That evening, however, things began to change.

"Have another drink, sir?" asked a servant. To John's dismay, Charles took another glass of brandy. He turned back to the cards. His eyes narrowed dangerously. In spite of the brandy he had been drinking, he was not disguised, at least not as much as his partner thought he was. The cards showing on the table were slightly different from what they had been when he had turned away. His mouth set in a narrow line. He felt John's hands on his shoulders, warning him to be alert. He nodded and turned back to the game, his vigilance turning the change to his advantage. As he had not done earlier in the evening, he collected his winnings. His smile grew more dangerous.

Soon a man in the dress of a gentleman strolled by the table where Charles played and his friend watched. "Care for a game?" he asked Wentworth.

John smiled sardonically. "I am waiting for a friend," he said quietly. "Perhaps later."

When the newcomer began to protest, Charles shoved back his chair. "Are you ready to go?" he asked, clearing the table of his winnings, much to the dismay of the man playing opposite him. Wentworth nodded. Cautiously, the two made their way to the door.

"Have you had your fill of this place, Charles?" Wentworth asked as they walked down the dark street, their eyes searching the night for the thieves they knew lurked in the gloomy streets.

"More than enough," his friend said. "I wonder if our 'friends' will follow us?"

"If they do not, I will be surprised," John told him, his attention focused on the furtive movement he had spied up ahead. "Get ready."

Having taken the precaution of bringing their pistols and swords, Charles and John easily overcame the three men who lay in wait for them. When the injured men had been turned over to the watch, the two friends hailed a hackney. "Brooke's," Charles said, leaning back against the squabs.

"Haven't you had enough gambling for tonight?" his friend asked.

"Never thought you would turn Methodist on me, John."

"And I never thought that I had a friend who was a fool. What are you trying to do? Give money away? I know several charities that need money more than the people you have been playing with."

"Have I lost more than I can afford?"

"No. But you will. What are you trying to do, beggar yourself?"

Although Charles could have answered the question, he ignored it. But he could not ignore the lady who crept once more into his mind. "Faster, driver," he urged. His friend leaned back, his lips set in a straight line.

Despite his efforts to the contrary, Charles did not forget Georgiana. One afternoon as they sat perusing the papers, John came across a mention of Harrogate. He read the item to his friend and then lowered the paper so that he could look over the top edge. "Thought I might see your announcement in *The Times*, Charles. What happened after I left? Did you decide you two would not suit?"

His nerves already on edge because of the article in the paper, Charles threw down his paper and stood up. "I do not want to talk about it," he said angrily.

"Your business. As you like," John said, raising his paper in front of his eyes. "By the way, I finally remembered who your widow is."

"Who?"

"Remember the Maypole?"

"Who?"

"You know. You always felt sorry for her and danced with her. The only one of us who did not feel dwarfed," his friend told him. "The year you got engaged."

"Georgiana? That was she?"

"Only Georgiana Carrington I can remember. Must say she has improved with age," his friend said. He lowered his paper to peer over the edge again. "Rather strange about the last name though."

"She said she married a cousin," Charles told him. He tried to remember what she had looked like ten years before, but he only had a vague impression of a tall, thin girl who was painfully shy.

"Oh, that explains it," John Wentworth said. He raised his paper again and turned a page. "What do you want to do tonight?" he asked.

"I thought we accepted Moore's invitation to dine," Charles said. He had not picked up his paper again and was staring off into space. Georgiana? The Maypole? She was no straight stick any longer. His memory of the way her soft curves had fit his hands caused him to stiffen. He shifted uncomfortably, trying to regain control of his emotions.

"That's right. Surprised to see him in town so soon. He usually spends January at home with his family."

"He told me that they have some disease, measles maybe."

"No wonder then. Have you ever noticed that the lads with children spend more time in town than those of us without?" Wentworth asked.

"Except for Denby," Charles reminded him. "We can hardly entice him away."

"What can you expect? Since his wife died in child-birth, he has to care for his son alone. I expect that he will remarry soon as he can to provide the son a mother."

"I thought Denby's mother was living with him to help with the child," Charles said. His voice was quiet and thoughtful. The thought that he might lose Georgiana in childbirth terrified him.

"Not the same. A child needs someone of his own. And Denby himself mentioned that his mother was growing older. He was the youngest child and the only boy. Heard his father had given up hope when he was born. I suppose his family is pleased that he has a son to carry on their name."

"I suppose he will be looking at the young ladies who will be presented this Season?"

"Not according to his last letter. He said he was looking for a widow, someone more of his own age."

Georgiana. Denby would like Georgiana. No sooner had the thought crossed his mind than a white hot rage followed. Denby could not have her, he thought angrily. She was his. And nothing would come between them. He got up and walked purposefully toward the door.

"Charles? Charles? Where are you going?" John called after him.

"To Yorkshire to find me a wife." He turned to look down at his friend, who was at the foot of the stairs. "And this time nothing is going to stop me."

"Do you want me to go with you?" John asked. He shifted from one foot to another hoping Charles would not accept his offer.

"This I must do myself," his friend said firmly. He ran

further up the stairs and then stopped again. "Do you have a groom I can borrow. I need to send my mother a message?"

"He will be ready whenever you choose." Charles nodded and hurried on up the stairs. "And I wish you happiness, my friend," John whispered.

# 11

FOR Georgiana the holiday was both better and worse than she had expected. As soon as she went down to breakfast on Christmas morning, she was greeted with smiles and happy voices. Mrs. Thomas could hardly contain her joy at having her son with her once more. Richard, although he still did not approve of his mother's occupation, found Georgiana interesting. Without neglecting his mother, he found time to become better acquainted with her employer.

"Last Christmas we were in the islands. The air was warm; the sun shone brightly." Richard leaned closer to Georgiana. "Some of the crew went for a swim. You cannot do that in England," he said with a smile.

"At least not unless the person planned to freeze," Georgiana returned.

"You cannot imagine how strange it was. All we talked about that day was returning to England for a proper Christmas with snow and crisp weather," he said with a satisfied sigh.

His mother had overheard his last remark. "Now that you have arrived I am certain you would like to return to those pleasant breezes once more," she said with a twinkle. She turned to glance in the pier mirror, noting with satisfaction the way the ruffle at the edge of her new red dress moved gracefully.

"You would be wrong," Richard said quietly, his face serious for once. "Any man of us would rather have been in England with loved ones rather than in the sunshine.

Knowing you are so far away from those you care about can blight the brightest day."

Some of the laughter drained out of Georgiana's day as she thought of the truth of his words. She missed her sister, her aunt, and the rest of the brood. If she had been with them, she would now be surrounded by children in all stages of excitement. Carols would fill the hall. Servants she had known all her life would be bustling around, finishing the preparations for the day. Undoubtedly, someone would be asking her a question or pulling at her trying to get her to go see some wonderful surprise. And then the family pageant would begin. As she thought of that Christmas tradition, Georgiana's eyes began to fill with tears. Hastily, she brushed them away and turned back to her own company.

In spite of the pleasant company of Mrs. Wycombe, Mrs. Bishop, and the doctor, Georgiana could not keep loneliness at bay. She would think of her sister and wonder if the goose they were serving this year would be larger than last year's. In moments when she did not keep up her guard, thoughts of Charles slipped in. What was he doing? Was he at home? Why had he left? She allowed her peaceful facade to slip for a moment, and her loneliness was evident to all around her.

"Mrs. Carrington, you must tell us what name you have chosen for the child," Mrs. Wycombe demanded. "Come. Put away your sadness. Your husband would want you to be happy. You owe it to your child." She patted the seat beside her, and Georgiana sank down beside her, a more cheerful look plastered on her face.

"Mother, what is wrong?" Richard Thomas asked, his eyes following his hostess as she talked with her guests. He kept his voice so low no one else could hear him.

His mother merely frowned and shook her head. In the months she had shared Georgiana's home, she had learned little more than she had known when she took the job. "Her husband must have been a brute," she whispered, almost to herself.

"Tell me what you know," her son demanded.

"He is dead."

At this her son turned and stared at her. "She is known as the Widow Carrington," he reminded her. "I did not expect to meet him."

She shrugged and continued. "His will states she must live in seclusion away from her family." She paused and looked toward the other group. The doctor looked up and smiled at her. She could feel herself blushing. She turned away hastily, wishing she could put her hands over her hot cheeks.

"And?" her son asked.

"That is all I know. Come let us rejoin the party." She led the way back across the room, taking the seat the doctor suggested. Her son followed slowly, his face carefully arranged in a smile, but his mind teeming. Georgiana fascinated him. Then he happened to intercept one of the glances that his mother and the doctor were exchanging. Georgiana and her problems were forgotten. He leaned forward. "Have you no family in these parts, Doctor?" he asked, his voice rather stern.

The doctor, who expected at any moment to be interrupted by a call for a physician, leaned back in his chair and smiled at him. "None at all. If these lovely ladies had not taken pity on me, I would have been all alone today."

"Are you a Yorkshire native, Dr. Mackensie?" the sailor asked. Georgiana smiled at him warmly; she had longed to know more about the doctor but had had no opportunity to ask.

"With a name like Mackensie? No, lad, I am a Scot. My father came to England to make his fortune."

"And did he?" Mrs. Bishop asked, her voice hushed and excited. She leaned forward in her chair, much like a child who tries to get closer to the storyteller spinning the tale.

"Enough to allow me to choose my own career. Thanks to him I will never starve," the doctor said quietly, talking more to Mrs. Thomas than to the other members of the group. She smiled at him.

"Let us drink a toast to families that let us follow our dreams," Richard Thomas said, picking up his cup of hot punch. His mother looked at him, wondering if he was being sarcastic. But his face was serious. He looked at her and smiled. Then as though he could not be separated from her for another moment, he crossed to her and gave her a hug. "Mama let me go to sea even though she wanted to refuse, even though my father had been lost on a voyage when I was younger. It must have been a difficult decision for her." He hugged her again and kissed her cheek.

Mrs. Thomas blushed and tried to pull away. "Hush. You are embarrassing me," she said. The others heard but merely smiled.

Turning the attention on their seafaring guest, the doctor asked, "And have you no one but your mother to pine for you when you once more go to sea?"

The young man shifted nervously. "My mother is enough for me," he said quietly. He pulled his sleeves down over the bands of his shirt. "Unless one or more of you ladies would care to join her?" he asked mischievously. He winked at Georgiana, who tried to stifle her laughter.

The rest of the afternoon was spent in laughter and song. Only when she was once more alone in her bedroom, the embers of the fire glowing, did Georgiana's loneliness return. She looked down at the burden she carried and wrapped her arms as far around herself as she could get. "We will have each other," she promised. And perhaps next year her brother-in-law might take pity on her and allow her to join his family's Christmas festivities.

The next few days were busy ones. With the babe's arrival only a few weeks away, Georgiana was busily finishing baby clothes. Mrs. Thomas supervised the final decorations for the baby's room, telling Georgiana that she must spend more time with her feet up. In spite of her longing to do as much as she could for her child herself, Georgiana gratefully allowed the older lady to take care of much of the details. One reason she did so was that her feet had begun to swell alarmingly. Even her softest shoes felt as though they were cutting off her circulation.

Growing worried about the size of her mistress's ankles, Mrs. Thomas sought the advice of the doctor, who, since Christmas, had found one excuse or another to visit every day.

"Hold out your foot, Mrs. Carrington," he demanded as he walked into the drawing room. Georgiana glared at her companion, who simply ignored her, but she did as he said. He frowned as he looked at them. Then he picked up her foot and pressed his finger against her ankle. His frown grew heavier as he noted the depth of depression his finger had made. "It is too bad that Mr. Harcourt is no longer here to amuse you, Mrs. Carrington." Mrs. Thomas glared at him, hoping he would simply be quiet. But he went right on. "Once again it is time for bed. And unless this swelling goes down, there will be no reprieve this time."

Georgiana's eyes grew wide with fear. "What is wrong?" she asked. "Is the babe in danger?"

"Nonsense. This is a precaution only. And I will give Mrs. Thomas some suggestions for your cook. Until the child arrives, I want you to stop using salt in your food."

"I never salt my food," Georgiana complained.

"Maybe not, but your cook does. For the next few weeks tell her she must leave it out of everything she cooks for you." Georgiana made a face. "You can survive a few weeks of bland taste," he assured her.

"If I must," she said grudgingly.

"You must. Now off to bed. And no lying about on the top of the covers either. You get into bed right now." He smiled at Georgiana, but she could tell he was serious. She sighed and then nodded.

As the New Year began, Georgiana was beginning to find her confinement more than she could bear. She could not find a comfortable position to lie in. Her sleeping patterns became erratic. As soon as she was settled, a muscle in her leg might begin to cramp or the baby would begin to kick. She twisted from one side to another restlessly.

Mrs. Thomas was a tower of strength through all the discomfort. "This is just a phase. You will be through this before long. As soon as you see the babe, you will forget all about these problems," she told Georgiana every day.

The doctor, too, added his encouragement. After examining her after she had been in bed for about a week, he stood up and smiled at her. "Your ankles have almost returned to normal," he said in a pleased voice.

Georgiana, who had begun to feel somewhat sorry for herself, sniffed. "I would not know. I have not seen my feet in weeks."

"This will all be over before long," Mrs. Thomas assured her once again. The doctor merely nodded.

"May I get up?" Georgiana asked. When Dr. Mackensie nodded, she heaved a sigh of relief. "Get me my dressing gown," she told her maid, who stood at the foot of her bed.

"If your feet and ankles start swelling as they did before, go back to bed," the doctor said firmly as he opened the door into the hallway. She nodded and moved toward the edge of the bed.

Even though she still was uncomfortable and could not rest easily, Georgiana did not complain. She spent much of her time in the room she had decorated as a nursery, dreaming of the not-too distant day when she would have someone of her own to love and care for.

During the days when Georgiana had been in bed, Richard and his mother had come to an understanding. The son now knew that his mother would not desert her employer, at least not until the child had been born. And when she did leave, it would not be to return to live with him. Richard and the doctor had spent much time together while Georgiana was in bed, discovering strengths in each other. When Richard was finally recalled to his ship, he had given the match between his mother and the doctor his approval. Although he planned to return for the wedding sometime in the spring, both he and his mother knew that if he was at sea it would be impossible.

The day before he was to leave, Georgiana, his mother, and he were in the drawing room talking quietly when a guest was announced. Georgiana's eyes widened as she saw the tall figure in the doorway. Mrs. Thomas started to smile and then remembered the way he had deserted them during the last few weeks. Only Richard could be said to be impartial. When Charles saw another man, a man almost as tall as he, sitting with Georgiana as though he had the right to be with her, he had to fight to control his temper.

Mrs. Thomas's introductions soothed him somewhat, but when Georgiana smiled at the stranger and ignored him, Charles seethed. "I must talk to you," he told Georgiana in a cold voice, daring her to refuse him.

"I am listening," she said quietly. Her heart was beating like a drum. As soon as he had entered the room, she had had difficulty in breathing. She longed to put her hand in his and allow him to draw her from the room to some place where they could be alone, where she could run her hand through his hair. Then the babe moved. She looked down and smiled ruefully. Even if she had the opportunity, she did not think she could get very close to him.

Charles stood in front of her, absorbing the differences in her looks. Unaccustomed to spending time with ladies who were increasing, he was surprised at the change in her in such a short time. Her face was fuller as was her body. "Please," he said as he held out a hand to help her up. Mrs. Thomas exchanged a significant look with her son.

Georgiana nodded and let him help her to her feet, all the time wishing she were not so ungainly. "Follow me," she said quietly, leading the way down the hall to her small office. The soft gray wool dress that she wore swung around her like a bell. Charles longed to stop her, to pull her into his arms, but there were servants around.

When the door to the office closed behind them, Charles took a deep breath. Before he could speak, Georgiana asked, "Have you returned for more hunting?"

"No." Usually, words came easily to him. This time his voice froze in his throat. He shifted nervously. Georgiana kept her eyes fixed on him. The way he disappeared and reappeared in her life had her confused. Just when she was growing uncomfortable in the silence, he reached out and pulled her close to him, proving her fears groundless. Tilting her face up, Charles kissed her, not the burning kisses filled with desire as he had the night at the inn but a kiss that was tender, that promised more than it demanded. His arms held her tenderly.

"Charles?" she asked, her face flushed and happy. Her thoughts filled with unspoken confidence.

"Shush. I just want to hold you." He put his lips over hers once more. Georgiana relaxed, letting her body sink into his. His arms tightened around her as if he would never let her go. Finally, his desire beginning to get out of his control, he stepped back. He took a deep, shuddering breath.

"Georgiana," he began. Once more he stopped. The words did not want to leave his mouth. Then he thought of the man he had just met. His face grew stern. "When did Thomas arrive?" he asked, surprising even himself. His voice was full of suspicion.

"Christmas Eve," Georgiana said, still caught up in the emotions of the moment. "Mrs. Thomas was so happy to see him. Having him here has made her Christmas brighter. She has been so worried about him. He has been sailing in dangerous waters." The words bubbled forth from her as though they were waters from a spring. She smiled at the man standing so close to her, willing him to put his arms around her once more.

He took a step back. "Did he stay here?" he asked.

Georgiana, finally recognizing the tone of his voice, frowned. "Of course. He wanted to be with his mother."

"And when does he plan to leave?"

"Tomorrow. Though I cannot see what concern it is of yours. He is my guest." She stood as straight as she could and glared at him. Her heart was pounding with anger and with hurt.

"Have you forgotten that you are a widow. What will the people of Harrogate think of you for inviting him in?"

"Well, I can tell you what three of them thought. The ladies Wycombe and Bishop thought he was a pleasant addition to our Christmas dinner. And Dr. Mackensie said he was an excellent chess player. Their opinions are enough for me. How dare you insult me in this way." By now she had allowed her anger over his absence to fuel her rage. Her face was flushed, and her heart was beating rapidly. She took another step back from him. "If you cannot control your vicious mind, sir, I do not care to see you again. Good day. I trust you can find your own way out!" Before he could stop her, she flew through the door and slammed it behind her.

For a few moments he was frozen. Then he slumped. "You certainly know how to win a lady, Harcourt," he said to himself. He pulled the special license he had purchased from his pocket and looked at it for a moment. He reached up to tear the document in two. Then he stopped. A stubborn look came over his face. He straightened his shoulders and walked out the door and to the stairs, shoving the heavy paper back in his pocket.

Out of breath when she reached her room, Georgiana longed for nothing more than to throw herself on her bed facedown and cry. But she knew the position would be uncomfortable. She headed for the chaise instead. Putting her feet up, she tried to calm herself by taking deep breaths. The baby gave a kick or two as if to remind her she was not alone. The calming breaths did nothing to stop the tears that ran down her face. "How could he?" she whispered. She covered her face with her hands, sobbing bitterly.

The sobbing covered the sound of the door opening. Charles stood there for a moment, his face sober, his eyes anguished. He took a deep breath and walked softly across the room. Before she knew that he was even close, he sat down on the chaise beside her and took her hand. "Forgive me?" he whispered. He leaned forward to kiss her, but she turned her head away from him so that his kiss just brushed her cheek. She tried to ignore him, but he took her face in his hands and turned her to face him.

"Let me go," she demanded angrily, moving her head from side to side to make him release her. "Go away." She pulled back and broke his hold. "If you do not leave immediately, I will call for help." She glared at him, her eyes flashing angrily. Her breasts were heaving.

He leaned forward and captured her lips with his. In spite of herself, she responded. "I will never go away again," he said.

Georgiana gasped. She began to shiver as if with the cold. "Stop this," she begged. "I cannot take any more." He tried to put his arms around her to comfort her, but she pulled away. "Go away, Charles. Please go away."

"But I love you," he whispered. "I want you."

"You proved that the night at the inn. That was over long ago. You ask too much of me," she said through chattering teeth. "Please leave me alone."

"You cannot mean that," he said, holding her by her arms. "I will not believe that you do not care for me. You must. You could not have responded as you did a few minutes ago if you did not care." Never in his wildest imagination had he dreamed that she would not fall in his arms. What other man would offer for a pregnant lady? He smiled at her, willing her to agree with him.

She pulled back as far from him as their closeness would allow. Her face was filled with anger. "Care for you? Of course, I care for a man who caresses me and then leaves me alone for weeks. A man who absents himself from my company and then takes exception to another man who has spent time with me."

"You said he was here to see his mother." Charles leaned forward and grabbed her by the shoulders, his face alive with anger.

"He was. But he was also a kind guest. Where were you, Charles?"

"With my mother." She pulled away once more. This time he did not try to recapture her. "Georgiana, I had to be sure. I had to know my own mind."

"I hope you do. You have certainly been playing havoc with mine," she said angrily. She tried to turn on her side away from him, but he had sat on her dress, holding her prisoner. "Get up," she demanded.

"Not until you listen to me."

"Well, if that is what it takes." She turned to face him, her shoulders squared and her jaw set.

Charles looked at her fixed expression and wanted to reach up and wipe the frown from her face. But he did not dare. He took a deep breath. "I might have been a coward before," he said quietly. Then he stopped. She kept her eyes fixed on him. A wary look played in her eyes. "But I had to be sure."

"Sure? Sure of what? That you would be welcomed back into my life and my bed once this babe is born?" Georgiana asked bitterly.

He drew back. "Have I ever suggested such a thing to you?" he asked angrily.

"What else was I to think?"

"If you would let me finish, you would know what I was planning." Georgiana gave an unladylike snort. Charles had held his temper under control as long as he could. He grabbed her shoulders again and gave her a shake. She fell back, her eyes opened wide. He dropped his hands and got up, embarrassed by his lack of control. As she began to struggle to get up, he sat back down by her side. "I never lose my temper. Never," he said. He shook his head and sighed. "If you can do this now, what will it be like when we are married?"

"Married? What are you talking about?" Georgiana began to struggle to get up once more. Tired of resisting her efforts, Charles got up and reached down to help her rise. As soon as she was once more standing, Georgiana turned to face him. "Charles, this is what I was talking about. One moment you are making outrageous suggestions or kissing me and the next I do not know where I am with you. I cannot take these abrupt changes of emotion."

"My emotion has not changed." He pulled her close to him. His face was only an inch or two away from hers. "Marry me," he begged.

Georgiana's face went white. She took a step or two back, her arms clasped around her child. "What are you saying?" she asked. Her heart was pounding so hard she could hardly hear his words.

"Marry me," Charles said again. He took a step toward Georgiana. Before he could put his arms around her again, she gave a little sigh and sank to the floor. He reached for her, but she slid out of his grasp. Quickly, he picked her up and laid her on the bed. Then he crossed to the bell to summon help.

By the time the maid appeared, Georgiana was beginning to show signs of recovery. Her eyes fluttered open. The first thing she saw was Charles hovering over her. She closed her eyes again. "Go away," she whispered.

Acknowledging defeat, he bent down and brushed her lips with his. Once more in spite of her determination not to do so, she responded to him. "I will return tomorrow for your answer," he told her. He turned to Georgiana's scandalized maid. "If you have any influence with your mistress, convince her to accept my suit," he said. The maid's face turned pink with excitement, and her eyes grew wide. She nodded.

When the door had closed firmly behind him, the maid gave all her attention to her mistress. "How romantic," she said with a smile.

"Do not believe a word that he says. By tomorrow he may have changed his mind," Georgiana said bitterly. The up and down emotions of the afternoon had exhausted her. She yawned, wishing she could find a comfortable spot in which to rest.

"Oh, Mrs. Carrington, I am certain he meant what he said. He is so determined." The maid sighed. "And so handsome." She sighed once more.

Georgiana closed her eyes, trying to forget the way he had loomed over her. She also tried to forget the words he had said. He had been amusing himself at her expense, she told herself. But she wanted to believe. How she wanted to believe him.

All the way down the stairs and out the door, Charles had been cursing his rash manner. He had planned everything so carefully. But nothing had gone as he had intended. Why had she not accepted him? He was certain she cared for him. Her kisses that afternoon had told him so. If only he had controlled himself. The road back to his hunting box was both cold and lonely. What if she never accepted him, he thought? Ten years earlier when his fiancée had broken their engagement, after his immediate feeling of loss, he had been relieved. But now all he could think about was what would he do if she did not accept him. How would he manage to go on with his life?

For both Charles and Georgiana, the night was long and sleepless. Toward morning Georgiana did drift off to sleep, her last thoughts of Charles. Had he meant what he said, she wondered?

When morning came, Charles had not slept at all. For most of the night, he had planned his strategy. At first light he rose and pulled on the clothes he usually wore to go hunting. Then he hurried to the forcing rooms. As small as the estate was, its gardener was excellent. Gathering flowers himself, he tried to select only perfect blooms. His haste and his inexperience frequently led him astray, but soon he had a small bouquet of flowers even he was satisfied with. Leaving them in a basket on the table in the front hall, he ran up the stairs to his room, taking them two at a time.

By the time he was dressed for a morning call, his valet was ready to find a new master. Only Charles's words as he inspected himself in the mirror kept the man from despair. "Wish me luck, Digby," he said hopefully. He had a smile plastered on his face, but his stomach was quivering with fear.

The valet sighed in relief. "Good luck, sir," he said. Then before Charles could change positions, he reached up to pull an errant curl into place. "There. That is better." He stood back and inspected his master one more time. Charles had chosen a coat as dark brown as his eyes and buff pantaloons. The tops of his boots were a crisp white, and the boots themselves shone so that he could see himself in them. Charles donned a sixteen-cape greatcoat and picked up his beaver hat. Then he took a deep breath and walked through the door. "And God help me if she refuses," said the valet with a sigh.

As tired as she was, Georgiana had not been able to sleep late. Although not up as early as Charles, she was up before either Mrs. Thomas or her maid wanted her to be. She had refused to stay in bed. "I cannot let Richard leave without wishing him good-bye," she said firmly. The other two women exchanged a look and sighed.

"I will tell him good-bye for you," his mother suggested. "He will understand."

"Nonsense. I have but to choose a gown for today, and I will be ready," Georgiana said. She looked at the selection of dresses and sighed. "I am so tired of black and gray," she whispered. Then she pointed to one of her dresses and allowed her maid to help her put it on. As soon as the tapes had been tied and her hair dressed to her satisfaction, she hurried down the stairs. Richard was waiting in the hallway near the front door.

"You must come back," she told him.

"As soon as I am given leave," he promised her. "I am entrusting you with my mother . . ." He looked around to make sure his mother was nowhere in sight. He knew his mother had kept her news to herself. "At least until her marriage."

Georgiana's eyes grew wide. "Marriage?"

"To your doctor. He asked me permission to pay his respects to my mother." He smiled at Georgiana, willing her to see the absurdity of the situation. "If I cannot get leave to return for the wedding or if I am at sea, I expect you to represent me."

"Wedding?" Georgiana repeated. She had known of the doctor's feelings but had not expected that he would speak so soon. What was she going to do without her companion, she wondered. Then she felt guilty for not being happier for her friend.

"Sometime this spring. That is why I am not sure I will be able to return." He looked up to see his mother enter the hall, a basket on her arm. "Remember. Not a word to anyone else until after the announcement appears," he whispered. Then he said louder, "I expect to be notified as soon as the child is born. If it is a boy, I shall claim him for the sea."

"We have enough sailors in this family already," his mother said. "Mrs. Carrington will not want to see as little of her son as I do of mine." She laughed to ease the sharpness of her words.

"Mother, you always said you did not mind my going to sea," Richard protested.

"And I do not. What I do not like is not seeing you more often," she assured him. "But I do want you to be happy. Now be off with you before I drown you with my tears." Although her words were light, her face was serious. Georgiana pulled back into the shadows of the hall in order to give them a few moments of privacy. Then as they stepped back from one another, she walked toward the door. They stood there for a moment, a sailor with a lady on either side. Then she bid him good-bye, letting his mother accompany him outside to the waiting chaise.

She had just turned to go into the drawing room when the front door opened. Hoping to lift her companion's spirits, she told her, "Come. A cup of hot tea is what you need to lift your spirits."

A voice behind her made her stop. She turned slowly. There standing beside her companion was the man who had haunted her dreams and her mind. "What I need to lift my spirits is your promise to be my wife," he said again. The servants and Mrs. Thomas stood as if frozen, afraid to move for fear they would break the tension that connected the two as a harness connects a horse to a carriage. "Do not disappoint me," he begged.

# 12

GEORGIANA stood so still that for a moment Charles wondered if she was breathing. He walked forward slowly, hoping that she would not dismiss him without a hearing. Mrs. Thomas frowned as she watched the pair, not approving of the way Charles had pushed his way into the house much as he had pushed his way into Georgiana's bedroom earlier, but acknowledging that he was good for her mistress's spirits. Looking into Georgiana's face, she tried to decide whether to interfere or not.

Instead of retreating in front of his advance, Georgiana held her ground. "It is very early for morning calls, Mr. Harcourt." Charles winced at the formality of her tone. "I had not thought to see you again," she added, wondering at his brash behavior. He had always pursued whatever he wanted, no matter the cost, she reminded herself. At the sight of him, her heart had begun to beat faster. She longed to check her looks in a mirror to make certain the tears she had shed during the night had not left indelible marks on her cheeks.

Now that he had gained entrance into her house, Charles was less certain of himself. She had ignored his plea; he admitted to himself that she had not even acknowledged what he had said. What if she refused to listen? Instead of giving in to his worries, he squared his shoulders and came so close to her that only inches separated them. "Good morning, Georgiana," he whispered as he lifted her limp hand and carried it to his lips.

She took a step or two back from him, her face still

unreadable. The gray dress that she wore did little to add
color to an already pale face that had grown whiter as he
grew closer. A flush had tinted her cheeks when he
kissed her hand, but it soon disappeared. Georgiana
turned and walked toward the drawing room. Mrs.
Thomas took a deep breath and started forward. When
Charles followed her mistress into the room and closed
the door behind him, she stopped. Then she walked toward the stairs.

The servants who had been in the hallway when
Charles walked in hurried down to the kitchen full of
news for the other members of the household. "You
should have seen him," Georgiana's maid declared. "He
walked in as bold as brass as though he owned the
place."

"Why should you be surprised?" the housekeeper
asked. "He has acted that way for weeks, carrying her
down the stairs against her wishes, forcing her to go into
the garden."

"What do you think will happen?" the maid asked,
wondering about her job.

"He said he wanted to marry her," the footman who
had carried Richard's things to the waiting coach told
everyone.

"And she less than a year a widow," the Cook said,
scandalized. "What do you think he is saying to her
now?"

"You can be certain it is not good-bye," the housekeeper said. She frowned, looking at the small group as-
sembled there in the kitchen. "Now off with you. There
are jobs aplenty for all of you. And keep your ears and
eyes open." Sheepishly, they all nodded and hurried
away.

In the drawing room, her prediction was coming true.
As soon as they were alone, Georgiana had whirled to
face Charles, her skirts swirling about her. "What are
you doing here?" she demanded.

"Marry me, Georgiana," he begged, recapturing her
hand and holding it close to his chest. She pulled free

and walked further away from him. He pursued her, deliberately stalking her. She retreated to a small window enclosure and sank down on the seat, the pale wintery sun creating flames in her russet hair. A fixed look about his mouth, he moved to sit beside her. She moved to the center of the seat, eliminating his opportunity. He stood before her, looming over her. She kept her eyes on her clasped hands. "Georgiana," he whispered. She refused to look up. "Georgiana," he said just a little louder. Each time she ignored him.

Finally losing control of his patience, he grabbed her shoulders. When she looked up, her lips parted in surprise, he bent down and kissed her. Georgiana jerked her head backward. In her efforts to get away, she knocked her head against his chin, pushing him off balance. She grabbed for him, trying to keep him from falling over their feet. Refusing to let go of her, Charles tightened his hands around her shoulders, pulling her forward. Before long, Georgiana was lying on the floor on top of him.

"Ohhh," she whispered, feeling the old remembered fire pulsing through her veins.

"Are you all right? Do you want me to call the doctor?" Charles asked anxiously. He pulled himself up from the floor even though he longed to stay there and capture her in his arms. He reached down a hand and helped her up.

Awkwardly, she got to her feet, trying to smooth her crumpled skirts. She tried to pull away again, but he held her fast. "Georgiana, are you never going to talk to me again?" he asked, the hurt in his eyes evident in his voice. "I am sorry I left you. I will never leave you again. I want to be with you always."

"Now you want to be with me," she muttered, looking up at him and hoping that her child had his deep brown eyes. Even the clasp of his hand made her ache for him.

He reached up and brushed back one of her curls that had drifted over her forehead. "I am sorry I made you cry," he said. His fingers smoothed the darkness under her eyes as though by his touch he could erase the pain that had caused it.

She pulled herself upright. "How do you know I cried over you?" she asked. She would have denied her tears if she had thought he would believe her.

Relieved to receive any kind of response, he sighed. He stepped closer to her and wrapped his arms around her and held her close, resting his cheek on her hair. The action was one she had been expecting. But rather than step back as she had planned to do, she lost the tension that had kept her away from him and nestled close to him once more.

"Georgiana, I love you," he whispered into her hair.

She closed her eyes, wishing she could believe him, wishing she had more determination so that she would not yield to him. She sighed, knowing that this brief interlude would soon be over and she would be alone once more.

"Will you marry me, Georgiana?" he asked. This time he did not sound as sure of himself as he had done before. Her silence frightened him. He tilted her head back and forced her to look up at him. "If you do not agree, I do not know what I will do. While I was gone, I was so lonely. I thought of you constantly. You haunted me." He stared down at her, willing her to respond to him.

His arms around her sent tingles into her fingers and toes. She wanted to yield but was afraid to. What if he changed his mind again?

"Georgiana, you cannot leave me in suspense," he begged. "I have a special license in my pocket. We can be married today."

"Today?" Once again her blue eyes widened until they dominated her face. "You want to marry me today?"

"As soon as I can talk to the minister. But we can wait for your family if you insist," he said persuasively.

"No. They cannot come," she stammered, shaken to the core of her being. For the first time she had hope that he really meant what he had said. She blinked, wondering if she was asleep. She raised her hand to touch his cheek. The sight of her arm clothed in gray reminded her of another problem. "I cannot marry you. I am still in mourning," she said, feeling her heart sink within her. She wished that she had protested harder when her sister had suggested this solution.

"Is it because you still are in love with your husband or because you think society will disapprove?" he asked, smoothing her hair back away from her flushed forehead. Once more she tried to pull free, to step back so that she could think more clearly, but he refused to release her. "Are you still in love with him?" he demanded, gritting his teeth as he waited for an answer.

"No."

"Do you love me?"

Caught off guard by his question, she answered, "Yes." Then she froze.

He smiled and closed his eyes, pulling her even closer. Then he kissed her, not the tender kisses he had been bestowing upon her as he tried to woo her, but a deeply passionate one that spoke of his hunger for her, his longing to make her his.

"Charles, we cannot do this," she began to protest.

"Why?"

"It would not be right."

"Not right to have the only woman I want as my wife?" he asked angrily. "Are you afraid of what society will say? If you wish, we can marry and stay in Yorkshire for a while. No one except our families has to know anything about the marriage until we are ready to return south."

"You are ashamed of me?" she asked, her voice quivering. Caught on the wheel of changing emotions, her reactions surprised even herself.

"Never think that. We can announce the marriage tomorrow," he said in a soothing tone.

"No." Georgiana shivered. Charles reached forward to pull her even closer. This time she broke away from him and wrapped her arms around herself. When he would have followed her, she held up her hand, keeping him where he was. She took one or two deep breaths, trying to steady her emotions.

She had reacted hastily once. She did not want to react that way again. But she wanted him. She wanted to reach out and grab him and never let him go, never let him out of her sight. She closed her eyes and took another deep breath. She owed it to him and to herself to think rather than react. "What about the babe?" she asked. "If we marry now, the child will bear your name. Is that what you want? Are you willing to chance the gossip that will follow us?" She held her breath, waiting for his reply.

The question was one that Charles had solved in the dark hours of the previous night. After weeks of indecision, he was ready. "I will love your child as though it were my own," he promised.

She winced but hid it well, her conscience screaming for her to tell him the truth. Then she nodded. "What if it is a boy?"

Somehow that idea had never presented itself to him. Giving her question the attention it deserved, he stayed quiet for some time. She watched him anxiously, knowing his answer would determine her own. Then he said quietly, "Then he will be my heir." He prayed that he had not made a commitment that he would regret. Georgiana let out the breath she had been holding. She smiled at him, her joy bursting forth like summer sunshine. She walked toward him, her arms outstretched. Never one to pass up an opportunity, he walked into them.

When his body began to demand more than kisses, more than Georgiana would be able to give him for some time to come, he stepped back. "Tell your servants to start packing. I will go and talk to a minister."

"Charles," she said hesitantly.

"Yes?"

The guilt that she was feeling threatened to overcome her. She had to tell him. But what if he changed his mind? Her fear made her cautious and cowardly. She would wait until they were married.

"Georgiana, is something wrong?"

"No, nothing." She paused, knowing that her next words should be about the child. Instead, she asked, "Why should I pack?"

"To move out to my estate. I know it is not very large. I use it as a hunting box," he explained. "We will stay there until the child comes. As soon after that as the doctor thinks it is wise, we will return to London. I will send word to my servants to prepare the house for the Season. I can hardly wait to see John Wentworth's face. He thought you would turn me down."

"Charles, wait. I am not sure I wish to leave Harrogate and go to live in the country. With my time so near, I need to be closer to Dr. Mackensie. I think we should stay here in this house." Georgiana ignored the threat of the Season and London. She would deal with one thing at a time.

"Here?" he asked, looking around the drawing room as if he were seeing it for the first time.

"I am not sure Dr. Mackensie will allow me to travel so far from him," she explained.

"Why? What is wrong?"

"Nothing." He stared at her. She shifted nervously. "Well, it is not serious," she finally added.

"What is?"

"Some swelling. Dr. Mackensie is such a worrier that he confined me to bed once more." She smiled up at him, willing him to see how healthy she looked. He frowned. Ever practical, she added, "And the rent is already paid through June."

He frowned. "If you think I will allow you to pay for our lodgings, you are mistaken," he said in a voice that told her not to argue with him.

Naturally she ignored the warning. "I do not see why not."

"I will not live on your husband's money," he said through gritted teeth.

Once more guilt ripped through her. "Charles," she began. She stopped. He raised one eyebrow as if asking a question. "Do you insist that we move then?" she finally asked.

Although he originally had suggested exactly that solution, he could now see that it would not be practical. He clasped her hand and drew her across the room to the settee. After seating her as carefully as though she were a piece of priceless Venetian glass, he took his seat beside her, her hand still in his. He ran his fingers across the pale skin on the inside of her wrist, wishing that he could see the answers to their problems as clearly as he could see the blue beneath her skin. After the tumultuous moments they had recently shared, Georgiana simply enjoyed the peaceful quiet and the clasp of his hand.

Before the silence could grow oppressive, Charles said, "We will stay in town. I will repay what you have spent on the house."

Georgiana started to protest. He frowned at her, and she hushed although she had to bite her lip. She nodded. Relieved, Charles put his arm around her. "Charles?" she asked in a quiet voice. He smiled at her. Her pulse fluttered, and she wondered if she was a fool for what she was about to say. "Charles, I will marry you."

He looked at her in some confusion. "I thought that had already been understood."

She drew back in indignation. "You simply assumed that. I had not answered." Then her common sense reasserted itself. She reached up and touched his cheek tenderly. Her finger smoothed the dark brows, brushing away the confusion that he felt at her words. "I will marry you but not until after the child is born. Can you imagine what the minister will say when you talk to him?"

"If he is sensible, he will not say a thing. We are going to be married today. I am not taking any chances of your changing your mind," he told her.

"I won't do that," she protested, trying to ignore the thrill she felt at his words.

"How do I know you are not just saying that? I want you to be mine not only by affection but also by the rituals of the Church. You escaped from me once; you will not escape again."

"Escaped?"

"You were gone when I awoke at the inn. You never even said good-bye," he reminded her.

She blushed. "But, Charles," she protested.

"You should have said good-bye to me when you left. But then I might not have let you go." He smiled. Turning more serious, he suggested, "Go upstairs and put on another dress while I talk to the minister, something brighter."

"Brighter?"

He pulled her to her feet and took her in his arms. The feel of her next to him drove all thoughts of her clothing from his mind, all thoughts except how he wanted to rid her of them. "Mine," he said happily. "Finally mine." He kissed her, his lips soft against hers in a promise. Then he stepped back. He closed his eyes but did not walk any further. "I am afraid to leave," he finally admitted.

"Why?"

"What if you change your mind?"

Georgiana smiled at him, his fear driving all her guilt from her mind. "Never," she promised. She stepped forward and put her arms around his neck, reaching up to pull his head down so she could kiss him. He took her lips hungrily. "Promise?" he asked huskily.

"I promise." Their arms around each other's waist, they walked from the room. Georgiana's head was on his shoulder. The chambermaid, who had just come up the stairs, glanced at them and quickly found an excuse to return belowstairs.

"I will not be long," he said quietly, taking his hat and coat from the waiting footman. Then he saw the basket of flowers that he had cut early that morning. "These are for you," he said as he handed them to her.

Georgiana looked down at the flowers, the first she had received from someone who was not related to her. She bent her head to smell them. Then she looked up at him, the love she felt evident in her eyes. "Where did you find them?"

"My forcing house. I wanted you to have something to carry during the ceremony today."

"You were that sure of me?" she asked.

Realizing that he had to proceed carefully, he quickly said, "I wanted to give you something lovely to remind you of how much I love you." He was rewarded with a smile that broke across her face, lighting it up with happiness. Well aware of the servant who stood nearby, Georgiana merely bent her head to sniff the blooms once more. "I will return quickly," he promised. Once again he picked up her hand. This time he turned it over and left a kiss in her palm. She tightened her fingers over the spot as if she could save the thrill that shot through her. His eyes still on hers, Charles left.

As soon as the door closed behind him, Georgiana awoke as from a spell. When she realized what she had promised to do, she called frantically, "Mrs. Thomas! Daisy!" Then she hurried up the stairs.

In the short time Charles was gone, Georgiana and her two helpers pulled every dress she had with her from the wardrobe. "Everything is so drab," Georgiana complained. The other two exchanged a rueful glance and sighed.

"That is the last of them, Mrs. Carrington," her maid said as she put the last dress on the bed. The lightest color was a light brown.

"Have you anything else packed away?" Mrs. Thomas asked, trying to remember the number of trunks and boxes that had accompanied them.

"I think I might. Where did she put them?" Georgiana tried to recall what her former maid had said.

"I could try the attic," Daisy suggested, looking at the pile of black and gray dresses on the bed.

"Quickly," Mrs. Thomas urged. "Of course, if it has been packed away all this time, it will need to be pressed. At what time are you to be ready?" she asked, wondering how her mistress could be so calm.

Georgiana was anything but calm. Her stomach was turning flips, and the baby was doing a dance on her kidneys. "He will be here as soon as he has talked to the minister," she explained. She glanced at the basket of flowers sitting on her dressing table and smiled dreamily.

"Then let me arrange your hair. We would not want to keep the gentleman waiting," Mrs. Thomas suggested. In spite of the rush and the unconventional nature of the groom, Mrs. Thomas was pleased about the wedding. Georgiana needed someone of her own. However, Mrs. Thomas was worried. What was going to happen to her, she wondered. She had hoped that the doctor would declare himself before she had to leave, but he had said nothing. She could find another post. However, that was not a solution she favored.

Before she could worry about it too much, Georgiana relieved those fears. "Charles has agreed that everything is to remain the same until after the baby arrives," she said.

"How thoughtful. I shall have to give him my thanks," Mrs. Thomas said. She drew a deep breath. "And how much better for you. I was worried about your living in the country."

The door to the hallway opened wide. The chambermaid stood to one side as Daisy put an armful of dresses on the already covered bed. "These looked to be your size, Mrs. Carrington. Are they yours?"

Georgiana held up one after another, the colors of the fabric creating a rainbow. "No more gray or black," she said exultantly.

"The only problem seems to be choosing a color," Mrs. Thomas said as she held up a pale pink muslin.

"Hmmm. I do not remember this being so small," Georgiana said, holding up one of the dresses she had worn the previous spring.

"My dear, it is not the dress. It is you. Have you forgotten? Your shape has changed," Mrs. Thomas said in a kind and sympathetic voice.

"I will never find anything to wear. Tell Charles when he calls I cannot come down."

Mrs. Thomas and Daisy exchanged glances. "If you think that will keep him away, you had best think again," Mrs. Thomas said. "Here. Try this one on. Maybe it will fit." Fortunately for Georgiana, two of the dresses had been very full and loose-fitting last spring. These, a light green sprigged with a darker green and a medium blue silk, were the only ones which Georgiana could wear.

"Choose the silk," Mrs. Thomas said. "It is much too cold for muslin."

As she considered the two, Georgiana acknowledged the validity of her companion's suggestion. "But it is so wrinkled," she protested more to have something to do than out of despair.

"The irons are already heating belowstairs. Give me a few minutes, and it will be as fresh as the day you first wore it," Daisy said as she picked up the dress once more.

Although Charles was waiting, Georgiana did not descend as soon as Daisy had slipped the gown over her head and tied the tapes. She looked at herself in the mirror, staring at her reflection as though she were seeing herself for the first time. And she was not certain she liked what she saw.

"Do you want your pearls?" Daisy asked, uneasy at the way her mistress kept staring at herself.

"No. There is a locket. Find that," Georgiana said in a low voice that was scarcely louder than a whisper. She could not do this. She would have to tell him the truth. The thought of his reaction frightened her. What if he called the marriage off? She glanced at the pile of gray and black dresses on her bed as though they were the life she might have to resume. The thought caused her throat to close. One of her hands crept up to her neck and clasped the locket her maid had just put there. She longed to open it, to stare at the miniatures of her parents that she wore. But she was afraid to look at them. They would not have approved of what she was doing. She laughed ruefully. They would have disowned her had they still been alive.

Mrs. Thomas bustled into the room once more. She wore her warmest cloak over her red dress. "Mr. Harcourt is very impatient. He said to tell you to hurry down, or he will come up." She looked at the lady who had been both employer and friend. "My dear, you look lovely," she said sincerely.

"I look like an overripe pumpkin," Georgiana said as she turned sideways to get another look.

"Nonsense. You are just nervous. Here is your cloak and bonnet. Hurry now." Still not sure of what she would do or what she would say when she saw Charles again, Georgiana let her maid wrap her in the warm fur and settle the bonnet on her bright curls. Then she closed her eyes for a moment. When she opened them again, she squared her shoulders and walked out the door.

Her courage lasted until she saw Charles waiting at the bottom of the stairs. He was so handsome. He stared up at her as if she were a vision of loveliness. She stopped for a moment, wanting to prolong the feeling of power, of admiration. He smiled at her and held out his hand. Silently, she walked down the rest of the stairs and into his arms, ignoring the small voice inside her that shouted, "Tell him! Tell him!"

# 13

THE wedding was brief. Almost before Georgiana had time to make her responses, the minister pronounced them husband and wife. Then they were back in the carriage and at home once more. She glanced down at the new ring on her finger, wondering if it were any more real than the old one had been. Her confusion did not diminish her joy. She happily accepted the congratulations of her staff and introduced Charles to the people he did not know.

As soon as she could make her excuses, Mrs. Thomas sought her own room. Georgiana and Charles stared at each other, uncertain in their new relationship. She shifted nervously. Then she crossed to the fireplace and held out her hands to its warmth. Charles followed her. Putting his arms around her, he pulled her back so that she was resting against him. For a while there was no sound other than the crackle of the fire as it licked at the coals.

Then she pulled away and straightened, her right hand behind her in the small of her back. "What is wrong?" Charles asked anxiously. "Shall I send for Dr. Mackensie?"

"No. I simply needed to stretch." She turned to face him. "Charles, there is no reason to be nervous. The doctor has assured me that all is well." She put her hand on his cheek and caressed him. He captured her hand and brought it to his lips. She smiled.

Pulling her into his arms, Charles kissed her. Then he sighed. He glanced down at her bulging middle. "I am not certain I will survive until the child is born," he said almost to himself.

She pulled back. "What do you mean?"

"One of the people I talked to today was your doctor," he admitted.

"Why?"

"To find out exactly what you are permitted to do."

"I can do whatever I want," she assured him.

"But not everything I want," he said wistfully. She frowned, trying to figure out what he meant. Then she blushed. "You would think you had never had a husband who wanted you," he teased.

"I haven't." He looked at her, his head cocked to one side and a frown on his face. She froze in fear as she realized what she had admitted.

"What do you mean?" he asked.

Realizing that her error had given her a chance to explain, Georgiana began to stammer. "Ah, ah. Charles, I, I . . ."

Her nervousness unsettled him. He stepped in quickly to soothe her. "You do not have to explain to me. I should have known. You would never have been willing to marry me today if your marriage had been a good one."

"Charles," she began again.

"Hush. You can explain later. Right now I simply want to hold you." He kissed her, stopping her words with his mouth. When he raised his head, he was breathing heavily. "Do you wish to dress for dinner or have it upstairs?" he asked.

She looked up at him and smiled. "Upstairs," she said quickly. With her limited wardrobe, she knew she had nothing becoming to change into. Then her eyes grew round. "Ohhh," she said quietly, covering her mouth with her hand.

"Are you ill? Is it time to call the doctor?" he asked anxiously. She merely shook her head and smiled at him. "Well, what is wrong?"

Georgiana merely laughed. Then she said, "You must

stop jumping whenever I make a sound. I merely forgot
something."

"What?"

"To have rooms prepared for you," she admitted
rather sheepishly.

"That is just as well. It would have been for nothing. I
plan to share your bedroom."

"Charles."

"Do not try to evade me, Madam Wife. I have made
up my mind. You cannot escape me even in sleep." Although his words were said in a humorous way, his face
was serious. He watched her, waiting for her response,
his heart banging against his chest.

She did not disappoint him. "I have not been able to
escape you for months. You have haunted my dreams,"
she admitted, wondering what he would do if she walked
up to him and put her arms around him.

"I have?" His voice was as boyishly excited as that of
any schoolboy enthralled with his first love. She nodded.
The passion in his eyes made her long for a fan to cool
her heated cheeks, but she did not lower her eyes. At
first only the hint of a smile touched his lips; then, as
though his joy could not be controlled, he grinned
broadly and swept her into his arms. "You dreamed of
me," he repeated. He lifted her up off the floor and
swung her around until the room spun around them. She
laughed and held on to his neck tightly.

When he put her down, she kept her arms around his
neck, for the room continued to spin around her. She
closed her eyes and giggled. "I see two of you," she said.
"I do not know which one to kiss."

"No more going in circles for you, my love. I do not
intend to miss any kisses you are ready to give." He
picked her up in his arms. As they had so many times
before, the servants saw him carry her upstairs. This
time the footmen exchanged knowing looks, and the
chambermaid who had been crossing the hall giggled.

When they reached her rooms, Georgiana reached
down and opened the door. Her maid, putting the last of

the clothes from the attic away, looked up in surprise. Then she blushed. "My wife will ring when she needs you, Daisy," Charles said. Georgiana hid her face against his neck, hoping her own bright cheeks could not be seen. The maid made her curtsy and hurried out of the room.

Charles put her down, holding her to be sure that her dizziness had completely worn off. He touched her hair and wrapped a lock of it around his finger. Then he smiled again. He leaned forward and took a deep breath. "You smell so good."

"So do you." He raised an eyebrow as if to contradict her. "Why do people have such individual smells?" she wondered. He shrugged. "I do not mean their perfume. I mean the smell that is different from anyone else. I think I could find you by smell even if I were blindfolded."

"Shall we try?" he asked, too happy to be serious about anything. He stepped closer to her. The baby decided to give a good kick at that moment. He jumped back. "You do not think the child is trying to separate us, do you?" he asked only half comically.

"I think it is just reminding us that it is there," Georgiana said. Before she could put a hand over her mouth or try to stop it, she yawned. Then she yawned again.

"And perhaps it is saying that its mother needs a nap," Charles suggested. "Shall I play maid for you?"

"I can call my maid," she said hesitantly, not at all sure what to do in this situation.

"Let me." She glanced up at him, noting once more the passion in his eyes. She nodded. The next few minutes were almost torture for her. Slowly, as though he were unwrapping a package, he removed her clothing. Slipping his hands into her dress, sending flickers of passion along her nerve endings, he untied the tapes that held the dress in place. Then he stripped it away until it fell in a puddle of blue at her feet.

She stood before him in her zona and her petticoats, very conscious of the way her body had changed. She looked up, hoping that he did not find her too ungainly.

His eyes were fixed on her breasts. She wanted to put her hands over them to hide them from his view, but forced herself to stand perfectly still. For a few minutes no one moved. Then he took a step closer and untied her petticoats. They joined her dress on the floor. In the dim afternoon sunlight, she stood quietly, one hand clasped to her breasts, in her zona, waiting for his next move. Moving slowly as though time had almost come to a stop, he reached out and released the ribbons that held the neck of her zona in place. The thought of him seeing her distorted body completely without clothes made her reach up and pull the ribbons tight again. Embarrassed, she moved to the wardrobe and pulled out a dressing gown and pulled it on.

He sighed. Then he reached up and closed the garment, tying the ribbons in an unwieldy bow. Taking her by the hand, he led her to the bed. While she climbed in, he shrugged out of his jacket and pulled off his boots, showing a careless disregard for their finish. Then he lay down beside her, pulling her close.

For a long while, Charles merely held Georgiana, his hand stroking her hair, her head resting on his shoulder. Exhausted from her almost sleepless evening the day before, Georgiana drifted off to sleep. Before long, Charles followed. But his sleep was light. Every once in a while he would wake, and he would pull himself up on his elbow to check to see if he had only been dreaming. When he had reassured himself that she was really there, he would go back to sleep once more.

The last time he awoke, the room was dark although the fire still burned brightly. He slid from the bed and checked the time on the clock on the mantel. He glanced over at Georgiana once more. She still slept peacefully. Then he rang for her maid.

When Georgiana awoke a short time later, she stretched. Then remembering the events of the day, she sat up and searched the room frantically. When she saw her husband sitting in front of the fireplace, she heaved a sigh of relief and relaxed, snuggling down into the pillows and pulling the covers up to her neck. She yawned and then stretched again.

"So you have decided to rejoin us," her husband teased as he came to stand beside the bed. He softened his words with a brief kiss that promised future excitement. She smiled and put her arms around his neck in an effort to bring him back to bed with her. As soon as she got into that position, she knew she had made a mistake. Her back began to ache. Gritting her teeth, she let go and slid to the floor, her hand on her back. As soon as her feet touched the floor, she stretched, trying to limber up.

From his discussion with Dr. Mackensie, Charles realized what was happening. He quickly got behind her and began massaging her back. When his fingers found the exact spot where the pain had begun, she sighed and leaned back into his hands. "Does this hurt?" Charles asked, feeling the knots along her spine.

"I would not call it hurting, just discomfort. Sometimes I feel if I could stretch far enough everything would be back to normal," she explained. He hit a particularly tight spot. "Ahhh," she sighed, relaxing more.

Charles kept his fingers moving up and down her back until he felt her relax completely. "Does that happen very often?" he asked as he wrapped his arms around her and led her into her sitting room where a pair of chairs were pulled up beside a table filled with delicacies.

"More than I would like," she admitted. "Mrs. Thomas says it is a sign the baby will soon be here." She looked at the repast laid out before her. "Did you arrange for this?" she asked. The table was brimming with special dishes.

"I merely asked for a light supper. This is what arrived," he explained. Georgiana looked in amazement at the variety of foods spread before her. Obviously, the cook had begun preparing the meal as soon as she had heard about the wedding, using her own imagination. She allowed him to seat her and fill a plate with a few of the selections.

As soon as they had eaten their fill, Georgiana once

more retreated to her bed. After ringing for the servants to have the food taken away, Charles came back into the bedroom. He stretched, causing the muscles to ripple under his thin lawn shirt. For the first time, she noticed the trunk sitting in the corner. "My clothes," Charles explained. "My valet arrived. Have you someplace where we can store them?"

Georgiana looked around the room as if searching for a new piece of furniture. "Daisy has complained that I do not have room even for my meager wardrobe," she explained. "We could have something moved in."

Both she and Charles looked around the small bedroom. "Perhaps you should arrange for rooms for me after all," he suggested. She bit her lip to keep from crying. After only one afternoon with her, he was ready to sleep apart. "Digby will be happier that way. Any room will do as long as it has adequate wardrobe space."

"There is a bedroom on the right, but it does not have a sitting room, she said in a voice that had lost all its joy.

"A sitting room? When we have a perfectly adequate one here?" he asked. "Digby will get ideas above his station."

"Digby?" she asked, her voice breaking just a bit.

He pulled his shirt over his head and put it on a chair. Then he turned to stare at her. "My valet. You did not think I was going to use it, did you?" When he realized that she was not going to answer, he crossed to the bed. She was blinking back tears she was determined not to shed. "I told you I was going to sleep with you. Did you think I had changed my mind so quickly?" She shook her head hesitantly, unwilling to admit the truth. "Good. Do you need your maid to change into a nightrail, or do you plan to sleep in that?" he asked.

"I can do it," she said, sliding from the bed. As they changed into their nightrails, each was careful not to watch the other, stealing only peeks every once in a while. Georgiana wanted to stare at him, to watch the muscles ripple in his back, but she was too shy. Charles, respecting the shyness she had exhibited that afternoon, kept his back turned most of the time.

When they were both in bed again, Georgiana snuggled close to him, expecting to put her head on his shoulder and go to sleep once more. He had other plans. Rising up on one elbow above her, he untied the ribbons at the neckline of her night dress. "Charles," she protested, pulling back from him.

"We will do nothing the doctor would not approve of," he promised her. Then he spread her neckline open, revealing her creamy white breasts. He bent his head to pay them homage, sending her into shivers of delight. "Do you like that?" he asked. Her moans gave him his answer. For a while, Georgiana surrendered to the passion. Then she could no longer be still.

She opened his nightshirt as he had opened hers. Using her lips and tongue as he had, she caressed the small, dark nipples that hardened when she breathed on them. Rubbing her cheek against the hair on his chest, she reveled in the sensations she was causing in both him and in herself.

His control slipping, Charles once more took control of the assault on her senses. He pushed her nightgown to her waist. "Charles," she said, wanting him to continue but knowing she must make him stop.

He ignored her. His cheek brushed her extended abdomen. Then he pressed a kiss against the inside of her thigh. She spread her legs farther apart. His kisses moved higher. Her eyes widened. She gasped and tried to push him away. He paused for a moment and lifted his head. "There are other ways of making love than what we did at the inn," he told her.

"What do you mean?" she asked in a voice that quivered with suppressed passion.

"Let me show you." Slowly, Charles played her, finding new spots to love. Tension built inside her. She twisted restlessly until she finally exploded into passion.

Later she lay there limp. He changed his position so that he could once more take her in his arms, cradling her head on his shoulder. As she returned to herself, Georgiana was aware of him still hard against her. Without thinking about it, she reached down to touch him. He caught his breath. She started to pull her hand away when he covered it with one of his own, teaching her what to do. When he gained his release, Charles lay there for a moment, his chest heaving. Then he took a deep breath. "Are you all right?" he asked, wishing the firelight lit the room more. Georgiana simply lay there amazed by the power they had over each other. Then she turned over on her side and kissed Charles, her mouth open and warm. "Hmmm," he whispered. Her kisses answered him again.

In the dark hours of the night as she was twisting and turning trying to find a comfortable spot, Georgiana once again remembered that she had not admitted the truth to Charles. Then he put his hand on her breast, and she forgot again.

The first five days they were married Charles and Georgiana ignored the outside world as much as they could. Although he constantly fought his desire to make her his completely, Charles could not bear to be separated from her. He wanted to be the first thing she saw in the morning and the last thing she saw at night. For Georgiana, never the center of anyone's existence since she had been a child, the attention was a heady business. Added to the new sensations he was introducing her to, she was completely lost. The only thing that mattered in her world was Charles.

Although he had resolved most of his anger over the child, during those days Charles lost most of the rest. The thought that there was a little person under his hand made him return time after time to feel her belly, to watch the movement of the child as it shifted. For Georgiana it was a bittersweet experience. Her conscience troubled her constantly. If Charles was so interested in a baby he thought was someone else's, how would he react if he knew it was his own?

Their peaceful idyll was interrupted on the sixth day of their marriage. Charles's mother arrived bearing the London papers. When the servants at his estate informed her of her son's wedding, she went white. Then pulling herself together, she went into the study and emerged a short time later. "Deliver this to my son as soon as possible," she told a footman, handing him a folded note. He nodded and hurried away.

When the note was delivered, Charles smiled. That smile vanished when he read what she had said: "Come alone. I have something important to discuss with you." Georgiana, who had been watching him carefully as he read his mail, noticed his change in expression. "Is something amiss?" she asked, crossing to stand beside him.

"It is probably nothing. But I shall have to ride out to my estate to make certain," he told her, annoyed at his mother's secrecy. What would Georgiana think if she found out his mother was nearby and had not asked to meet her? "I would ask you to go along, but Dr. Mackensie warned me this morning that the babe could come at any time," he said in a voice that was designed to soothe her. "Send for me immediately if it does." What he would do when the time came he was not certain, but he wanted to be close at hand.

The ride to the estate was a cold one. By the time Charles reached it, he was tired and hungry as well. When he walked into the room where his mother waited, his temper was not as even as it normally was. "Well, Mother, what do you want?" he demanded.

"A wonderful way to greet your mother," she said briskly. "A good day to you, too. Did you have a lovely wedding?"

"Is that why you called me out here? To complain about my hasty wedding?" He sat down opposite her, his face as dark as a storm cloud. "I told you what I planned to do."

"I wish that were the only reason," she said with a sigh. She looked up at him with sadness in her eyes.

"If you have something to say, Mother, why not come

out with it instead of being mysterious? Are you so reluctant to acknowledge Georgiana as your daughter-in-
law?"

"Have you seen the London papers recently?" she
asked, ignoring the spiteful words that ripped her heart.
He shook his head. She sighed. She glanced down at the
dull gold gown she wore, wishing that she could avoid
the coming event. Then she got up and walked to the
desk. "Read this," she suggested, handing him a newspaper.

He glanced over it, finding nothing of value. "Well?"
he asked.

"You did not think it was strange?"

"What?"

"The death notice. I think it is strange when one man
dies twice in the last year," his mother said. She sat
down again heavily.

"Whose death notice?" Charles asked, wondering if
his mother had lost her wits in the short time they had
been apart.

"Thomas Carrington. It was the first one on the page.
Did you not tell me that your lady was the widow of
Thomas Carrington?"

"Yes, but . . ." Charles grabbed the paper again,
searching for the article. He found it quickly. "He is sur-
vived by two sons and a grandson," he read. "It says
nothing about his wife, about Georgiana."

"I thought that rather strange, too," his mother added.
"Almost as strange as his dying in the spring and in De-
cember." Charles looked at her through narrowed eyes.
"And notice where he died." Charles did not look down,
but continued to stare at her. "In Jamaica," she added
when the silence had grown more than she could bear.
Charles simply looked at her, his face set in harsh lines.

"There must be a simple explanation," he finally said.
"Maybe Georgiana was married to one of this man's
sons."

"Perhaps," his mother said. She looked at him with

pity, regretting her own role in exposing his wife's duplicity.

Charles simply stood there, his mind whirling with questions. Finally he said, "I need to talk to Georgiana." He whirled and walked to the door. He had his hand on it, ready to open it when he turned back around. "Thank you for coming, Mother," he said quietly. She watched him go, her heart heavy.

In Harrogate, Georgiana discovered she could not bear to be still. She bustled around sorting linen, planning meals for the next week or so, checking the nursery once more to be sure that all was ready. It was there that Mrs. Thomas found her.

The older lady had spent much of her time that week with her friends. The doctor had been pleased to realize that she was no longer Georgiana's only support. As soon as he had a chance to see her alone, he formally asked Mrs. Thomas to be his wife. Expecting the declaration, she accepted quickly. She had not yet told her employer because she had seen little of her since the wedding. But once the baby arrived and the doctor's house was in order, they planned to marry. Mrs. Thomas wanted her son to be with her at her wedding and knew that soon his ship would be repaired and put to sea once more.

When she finally discovered Georgiana in the nursery, the older lady was serious. "This came for you by special messenger," she said and held out a letter.

"Charles!" Georgiana went white and sank into the chair behind. She looked at the letter in her hand as though it were a snake ready to strike her.

"Nonsense. If anything had happened to him, a groom would have come for you." Georgiana looked up, hope in her eyes. "Now open it so that you can stop worrying."

Georgiana followed her advice. Although Mrs. Thomas did not know how it could, her face grew even whiter, losing any semblance of color. "Oh no!" she cried. "No! No!"

"What is wrong? What has happened?"

Georgiana ignored her, looking down at her sister's letter. Their carefully concocted plan had just unraveled, and before long Charles would find out. She should have told him. She had known that. Now what was she to do? Then she remembered. He had not seen the paper. She heaved a sigh of relief. She still had time.

"Mrs. Harcourt, Georgiana, what is wrong?" Mrs. Thomas asked, wanting to shake the younger lady to make her respond.

"Nothing for you to worry about. Send the housekeeper to see me and have Daisy press the dress that I was married in," she said. As soon as Mrs. Thomas had left the room, Georgiana finished her plans. She would tell him this evening.

When Charles returned, she was in the drawing room working on the babe's christening gown. She heard the door open and looked around, a bright smile on her face and trembling in her heart. She had never seen him look so closed, so stern. "Is something wrong?" she asked.

He put the newspaper he carried on the table. "You might think so." During the ride back, he had tried to discover a simple explanation. But all that he thought of seemed so implausible. Finally, the only thought that remained was the way Georgiana had played him for a fool.

Pulling herself up from the chair, no longer an easy process, Georgiana walked up to him and leaned forward to kiss him. He pulled away. She drew back, a knot in the pit of her stomach. She glanced at the table and noticed the newspaper for the first time. She bit her lips.

"Do you have something to tell me?" he asked in a tone of voice that made Georgiana shiver. She could not open her mouth. "I have tried to think of explanations, but nothing fits. Georgiana, explain this," he demanded, holding up the paper so that she could read the story.

"I am sorry, so sorry," she said, fighting back the tears that threatened to overcome her.

"Sorry because the truth has come out?" he asked viciously. "Or sorry you were caught?"

His tone made her stiffen. She looked up at him and gained control of herself once. "Sorry to have lied to you."

"So you admit it." His last hope died. He looked at her, wondering how in spite of all that had happened, in spite of what he now knew, he could still want her. "Why did you choose me?"

"Choose you? You are the one who began this," she said angrily. "Oh, I admit that I should have told you the truth as soon as we met again, but I was afraid."

"Afraid? Afraid of what? My telling the world that you were masquerading as a widow? Who was he anyway?"

"My cousin?"

"Your cousin. Come now. How can your cousin be the father of your child when he was in Jamaica? Really, my dear, you must base your stories on more reality than that. It would strain anyone's imagination." In order to mask the hurt that ripped through him, he was striking back in any way he could without thought of what he was doing to her.

Georgiana winced. Then she stood up as tall as she could, looking straight into his eyes. "I borrowed his name, nothing else," she said proudly. "What else was I to do when I found myself with child with your babe?"

Charles stepped back, shocked. "Is that your story now? It is no better than your first one. How dare you suggest that this is my child."

"Have you forgotten that night at the inn? Count the months, Mr. Harcourt." Georgiana threw her head back proudly. "I knew I was wrong to give in to you, to agree to marry you. But I could not help myself. I had been in love with you for years," she said. She held his eyes, refusing to drop her own. "And did I throw myself at you when you reappeared in my life? No! You did the pursuing. I tried to suggest that we postpone this marriage.

You rushed us into it. Think about that!" She whirled
and left the room, slamming the door behind her.

Although he did not change expressions, what she was
saying left Charles shaken. "You should have told me
the truth," he shouted after her. Calling for a fresh horse
and his hat and greatcoat, Charles told the footman, "Tell
my wife if she asks that I will be staying at my estate."
He went out into the cold air, closing the door with a re-
sounding bang. Georgiana's words echoed after him:
Count the months, Charles.

# 14

WHILE her household buzzed with gossip, Georgiana lay in her room weeping. Charles had reacted just as she had known he would. She should have told him. But then he would not have married her; she was sure of that. Look at what had happened today. She thought of the vows they had taken such a short time before and wondered what he planned to do. Could he gain an annulment, she wondered, the tears streaming down her face and sobs racking her body. Could she and her baby be left all alone?

As he galloped down the road to his estate, Charles was filled with anger. How dare she accuse him of being the father of her child. However, beneath his furious thoughts rolled a constant refrain that was echoed in the hoofbeats of his horse: Count the months. In spite of himself, he found himself doing just that. The answer shook him. He spurred his horse forward as though he could outrun his forebodings.

His mother had just sat down to a lonely dinner when he walked in, his face bleak. Holding back her questions, she watched as the servants quickly laid a place for him. When they were alone once more, her son asked, "Are you not interested in what I found out?"

"If I need to know, you will tell me," she assured him. In the time since he had left her, she had done some thinking, thinking she wished she had done earlier. Although she knew that she had no choice but to tell him about the notice that had appeared, now she had to stay out of the quarrel. "Remember. Georgiana is your wife.

What is between the two of you does not have to be shared with anyone else. I would have hated it if your father had told anyone else about our quarrels."

"How do you know we have quarreled?" her son asked belligerently.

"My dear, your face told me. I have not seen such black looks since we sent you off to school." The footmen reentered the room. "Now eat your dinner. Good food never hurt anyone." Keeping the conversation well away from his marriage and the newspaper article, Mrs. Harcourt watched her son push his food around his plate, eating only a little.

"Will you join me for tea?" she asked finally when she realized that he would eat nothing else. He glanced longingly toward the bottles of port that lined the serving table; then he sighed and nodded.

As soon as the tea tray arrived and the door had closed firmly behind the servants, she poured two cups and held out one to him. He took it and put it on the table beside his chair. He leaned forward and put his face in his hands. She longed to take him in her arms but knew that would not be the right thing to do. "What am I to do, Mama?" he asked.

"About what?" she asked, knowing the answer but wanting him to verbalize it.

"About Georgiana. About our marriage. I have made such a mull of this."

"Nonsense. Do not be so hard on yourself. You did not get into this situation alone. Take some time to think about it. You do not have to make any decisions immediately," she said. Although she wanted to rant and rave about the horrible woman who had put him through such misery, she kept silent. If he decided to stay with Georgiana, she would have to welcome her no matter how much she resented her.

"She lied to me, Mama. She admitted it," he said in a voice that broke.

"She did?"

He stood up, his eyes bleak. Walking heavily as

though he were an old man, he crossed the room. "I will see you in the morning, Mama." He did not notice the tears that glistened in her eyes.

In spite of the fact that he was exhausted both mentally and physically, Charles did not sleep well that night. His bed, the bed in which he had slept comfortably for weeks, seemed too big. He dropped off to sleep only to wake up reaching for someone who was not there. Finally he rolled over on his back, staring at the bed hangings above him. Could Georgiana be right? For the second time since she had flung the words at him, he counted the months. His mouth tightened. Even if it were true, he told himself, she should not have lied.

And what else was she to do, his better self asked. He had gone blithely on his way, never wondering if the night had had any repercussions. What must she have felt like when she realized what had happened? He thought of her elderly aunt and knew that Georgiana would not have shared her trouble with that lady. Who had she turned to when she discovered she was pregnant with his child? His child? The question kept him awake for a long time. He heard the clock strike three before he drifted off to sleep.

Georgiana's night was also restless. She could not get comfortable. Finally, she rose, put on a dressing gown, and wrapped her warmest cloak around her to protect her from the cold. Then she picked up a candle and slipped into the nursery. Opening the chest, she took out the tiny garments that rested there, inspecting each one, and refolding it before she put it back in place. As she did, she wondered if her child would ever know its father. She blinked back the tears that brimmed in her eyes, not wanting to stain the garments she held.

All this pain for a moment of madness. Was it worth it? She smiled as she thought of that night. Even if she had never met Charles again, she had something to remember, to hold on to in the darkness. If he never forgave her, she would still have that. She stroked the lace on the top of the small dress she held. "But I want more," she whispered, "much more."

When the maid came to build up her fire early in the morning and found her gone, she hurried to the kitchen with her news. "Search the house," Mrs. Smythe demanded when she was told. "She does not need to be wandering around at this time." The servants scurried to do her bidding. "That husband of hers must be a brute to leave her alone like this," she later confided to the cook. That woman merely nodded her agreement, her mind already planning a light breakfast that might tempt her mistress. When Georgiana had refused to eat the evening before, the cook had not been pleased.

As one, Georgiana's servants blamed Charles Harcourt for their mistress's despair. Had he been there he would have suffered from their disapproval: cold water to wash with, food that was undercooked or burned, fires that smoked or went out. Digby, forgotten when Charles left the house so hurriedly the day before, held his tongue, although he privately wondered what the lady had done.

When they found Georgiana in the nursery, she lay dozing on the narrow bed that had been installed for the nurse. Awakened by the noise of someone opening the door, she sat up and looked around herself in amazement, wondering how she had gotten there. Then she remembered. Her face crumpled with unhappiness. Almost as though she had no will of her own, she allowed them to take her back to her own room and put her to bed. She lay there looking at the hangings that had been installed only a few months ago. Too full of despair to cry, she simply stared into nothingness.

Her behavior frightened her maid. As soon as she knew that Mrs. Thomas was awake, Daisy hurried to her room. Surprised and alarmed by the news, the older lady hurried into her clothes. "Send for the doctor," she told the maid. Then she walked down the corridor to Georgiana's rooms. Slipping quietly inside, she walked toward the bed. The utter stillness of the younger lady made her wish the doctor were already there.

"Mrs. Harcourt, Georgiana," she said. She saw her employer's eyes blink, but Georgiana did not look at her. "Cook has prepared a lovely breakfast. Shall I have something sent up?" Georgiana merely shook her head. "Surely you would like a cup of tea or chocolate," she suggested brightly. Again Georgiana shook her head. No matter what Mrs. Thomas tried she could not get any other response from her employer.

When the door flew open and the doctor came in, she breathed a sigh of relief. "How long has she been having contractions?" he asked, putting his bag on the table.

His wife-to-be drew him to one side. "That is not why we called you," she said in a voice that was only slightly more than a whisper, too low for Georgiana to hear.

"What is wrong?" he asked, looking at the still figure on the bed.

"I do not know what happened. Mr. Harcourt left for a time yesterday. When he returned, I think they quarreled. And he left again. He told the footman he was going to stay at his estate," Mrs. Thomas said. "She refused supper and has eaten nothing this morning. A maid found her in the nursery and called me. She refuses to say anything."

"Hmmm. Is this their first quarrel?" he asked. She nodded. He walked up to the bed to inspect his patient. The lack of color in Georgiana's skin alarmed him. He picked up her wrist and checked her heartbeat. For all the notice that Georgiana gave him, he could have been invisible. He put his hand on her abdomen, felt the baby kicking, and gave a sigh of relief. He checked Georgiana's ankles and legs for swelling. When he had finished, he asked, "Have you had any pains yet?" She ignored him as though he were not there. "Mrs. Harcourt, you must answer me." He reached down and gave Georgiana a shake. She blinked her eyes and then seemed to come out of her trance.

"I will be fine, Doctor. You worry about preparing for

your wedding," she said weakly. Her voice sounded as though it came from far away. The effort of speaking seemed to exhaust her. She closed her eyes.

"Mrs. Harcourt, I want you to rest a while and then get up," he said sternly. "And for the sake of the child, you must eat to keep your strength up." She opened her eyes once more. "Did you hear what I said?" the doctor asked sternly.

"I must eat," Georgiana repeated.

"Good. I will have someone bring a tray to you immediately. Sleep if you can until it comes." Catching his betrothed by the arm, he led her into the sitting room and closed the door. "How long has she been like this?"

"I do not know. Yesterday she shut herself into her room and would not allow anyone but her maid in. Is there something wrong?" Mrs. Thomas asked, reaching up to smooth a wrinkle from the doctor's lapel.

"I am not certain. She acts as though she has had a great shock. Do you know what she and her husband quarreled about?" She shook her head. "Call her maid. I need to talk to her." But when Daisy appeared, she could tell them nothing more than they already knew. Her mistress had changed into a nightgown and then had gone to bed. Daisy thought she had been crying.

As she walked the doctor to the door, Mrs. Thomas asked, "What should I do?"

"Keep an eye on her. If she continues acting strangely, send for me. If I am called away, I will send word where to find me."

"You think something is wrong, don't you?"

"I do not know," he told her. "I simply do not know." He kissed her cheek and took his hat and cloak from the footman. "Remember to send for me if anything changes." Mrs. Thomas nodded. As soon as he had left, she walked back up the stairs, arriving at Georgiana's room just as the breakfast tray was delivered.

"Come and see what Cook has sent up," she called to her mistress. "I think she has included all of your favorites."

Remembering her promise to the doctor, Georgiana slipped from the bed and allowed her maid to help her into her dressing gown. She glanced at the tray and picked up a muffin. Mrs. Thomas poured her a cup of tea and took one for herself. Georgiana took a bite or two and then put the muffin down.

"You must eat more than that," her companion protested. "Cook's feelings will be hurt." Georgiana walked back over toward the bed. The tumbled covers made her think of the nights she had spent there with Charles, and she backed away.

"Find me something to wear, something comfortable," she told Daisy. "One of my gray dresses will do." Daisy and Mrs. Thomas exchanged worried glances.

"What about something brighter. The dressmaker finished the dark green kerseymere you ordered. It arrived yesterday," Daisy suggested.

"The gray," Georgiana said. Quietly, she stood while Daisy tied the tapes and adjusted the dress about her. When the maid had finished, Georgiana stood there for a moment. Then as though the dress has been shield against the world, she turned to face her companion. "Shall we inspect the china, Mrs. Thomas. I think the housekeeper mentioned that we were short of certain dishes."

The rest of the day the two of them counted cups and saucers and matched soup bowls to platters. When she was busy, only Georgiana's quietness gave a sign that she was not happy. When she was still, her body seemed to shout her grief. Her steps were heavier than they had been, and she moved about slowly and carefully as though she ached.

Charles's day began no better than his wife's. After too few hours of sleep, he awoke and had to remind himself where he was. Then the memory of the previous day came washing over him. His lips tightened. He forced himself out of bed by reminding himself that he could not hide from his problems no matter how bad they seemed. The light of day had not softened the problem any. Georgiana had lied to him and to the world. And she was his wife. His wife. Had he not been so hasty, so determined that she would not escape him once more, he could have avoided this issue. He rang for his valet, forgetting that he had left him behind the day before. When a footman appeared, he looked up in surprise. Then he glanced around the room once more. His clothes lay where he had thrown them the night before. "I need hot water and someone to shave me," he told the man who waited. "I wonder if I have anything to wear?" he muttered to himself, opening cabinets and looking in the wardrobe. Fortunately, he found a pair of smallclothes and a shirt that must have been in the laundry when Digby left. And folded away in the bottom drawer were the clothes he had been wearing to hunt in. They would have to do until he could send a message into town.

That thought made him stop. What was he going to do? Was the child really his, or was she lying again? Once more he tried to remember the exact details of that evening at the inn. She had seemed unskilled; he remembered that and the warm, enveloping way she had welcomed his advances. His body began to react in spite of himself. Cursing, he forced himself to remember the afternoon before. She had been so white, so innocent-seeming. Yet she had lied about being married, about the child.

When he entered the breakfast room sometime later, he had achieved some of the calm Georgiana had displayed. His mother was there before him, her eyes revealing her own sleepless night. He kissed her cheek and then took his seat. She searched his face but was disappointed by the lack of emotion there. Knowing that he, like his father before him, did not like to talk before he had finished breakfast, she applied herself to her own meal.

"What would you like to do today, Mother?" he asked as though she were a guest and he responsible for entertaining her.

"I thought I might read or catch up on my correspondence," she said, her head tilted to one side as if to inspect him more closely. "Do not worry about me. What do you plan to do?" she asked, hoping he would act sensibly.

"I have sent for my estate manager. Even though I have checked the books for this property, I have not learned enough about my tenants," he said, remembering how much he had missed at home. Because he only visited Yorkshire to hunt or fish, he was certain he had much to learn about these people. They would fill in the time.

"Are you going to, to . . . Harrogate today?" his mother finally asked. The longer it was before he faced the problem squarely, the harder it could be.

"No." His answer was so uncompromising that she did not try to ask him any further questions. Before long, each left the room to go about his or her own pursuits.

When Digby arrived at the estate in response to his master's message, Charles was in his library. His valet inspected him while he waited for his master to issue his orders. "How is she, Digby?" Charles asked, feeling like a fool.

"Who, sir?"

"My wife." His master glared at him. Digby shifted uncomfortably.

"The staff, I believe, is quite worried about her. The doctor has been there twice already today."

"To see Mrs. Thomas?" Charles asked, knowing that the servants already knew about that match.

"To see Mrs. Harcourt."

"Is it time for the baby?" Charles asked, his face anxious. He stood up and walked to the fireplace where the bellpull was, ready to give orders to prepare a horse so that he could ride back to town.

"I do not believe so. Apparently Mrs. Harcourt was not acting her usual self, and Mrs. Thomas was worried."

"Is my wife all right now?" Charles demanded. His face was as white as his shirt.

"As far as I know," his valet assured him. He inspected his master carefully once more. "Shall I have a bath run for you, sir?"

Charles nodded. When he was alone once more, the memory of what he had lost haunted him. How could she have done it? Why had she not told him the truth?

During dinner that evening and the next few days, Charles could not forget Georgiana. The longer he was away from her, the more he thought about her. Words that he had said earlier came back to haunt him: If the child were only mine. But was it? The question was one he could not answer.

After several days of watching her son struggle with the problem and waiting for Charles to turn to her for help, Mrs. Harcourt decided to return home. "Why leave now, Mama, before anything is settled?" her son asked.

"But I think it has been."

"What do you mean?" her son asked. "I have not made up my mind." He stretched his arm along the mantel and picked up the Meissen figurine that stood there. The girl had russet curls like Georgiana's.

"I think you have," his mother assured him. "Why are you still here?"

"Because you are here."

"No. Do not put that burden on me, my dear. You are still here simply because you cannot bear to go any further away from your wife," his mother said quietly. "But you cannot go on as you have been doing. You need to talk to her." She stood up and walked over to him. "When you have worked everything out, bring her to me." In the days that had followed her revelation, she had regretted bringing the matter to his attention. She hoped Georgiana never learned who had tried to wreck her life.

"She lied to me, Mama," he said in an anguished voice.

"Have you asked her why?"

"I know. She was afraid to tell me the child was mine."

"Yours?" The answer was not what she expected. "Are you sure?"

"That is what she said," he explained, rubbing his forehead with his hand. "I do not know whether to believe her this time."

"Is it possible? You assured me that the child was not yours." Her head was spinning with questions, but she tried to sound as calm as she usually did.

"That was when I thought she was married."

"Charles, I do not understand everything that is between you and Georgiana. You obviously know more than you are willing to tell me. What you must decide is whether you think she is telling the truth."

"If I knew that, would I still be here with you?" he asked angrily. "I have asked myself that question over and over again. But we were together last spring." He saw her begin to mark off the months on her fingers. "Yes, Mother, I have done my arithmetic. It is possible. But can I live with the uncertainty? What if she is lying again?"

"If you think she is, you have some decisions to make. Are you planning an annulment?" his mother asked, her face shadowed with despair.

"An annulment? On what grounds? She would only have to appear in court for the case to be laughed out."

"She lied to you. There is a lie on the license."

"If lying were a crime, most husbands and wives would be separated," he said bitterly.

"As I said before, I think you have already decided. I am leaving for London in the morning. I would be happy with your escort at least until Harrogate. No. No. Do not try to persuade me to stay. I have caused quite enough disruption in your life already. If you wish to bring her to me later, I will welcome her as your bride." She smiled ruefully. "But do not wait too long. Accept her as your wife or set her free. Neither of you need to live in a prison of your own making. You can find the way." Her words echoed throughout the room even after she had left.

The next morning Charles was dressed and waiting for her when she got ready to leave. "Are you sure you will not stay longer?" he asked, drawing her hand through his arm.

"For what?"

"To meet your new daughter-in-law," he said with a smile. During the last evening the question had truly clarified for Charles. As far as he was concerned, the main problem was whether or not he believed he was the father of Georgiana's child. Her other lie had been used to keep the first secret. When he acknowledged that the child was his, the lie had seemed much less important. What he did resent was her lack of trust in him. But even that could be explained. How could she trust a man who went around making love to other men's wives. What she must have thought of him. Of course, if she ever looked at another man or dared tell him another lie, that would be another story.

His mother simply looked him in the face and then smiled, pleased with what she could see. "I will meet her when you bring her to London," she said quietly. "And let me know about my grandchild." He helped her into her traveling coach and then climbed onto his own horse.

They had traveled only a short while when they met a rider spurring his horse onward. When the man caught sight of Charles, he pulled his horse to a stop. "Mrs. Thomas said to tell you that you must come, sir," the groom said to his master. "It's the child."

Despite Georgiana's specific instructions to the contrary, Mrs. Thomas had sent for Charles as soon as the doctor had arrived. "Mr. Harcourt did not change my orders when he left," she explained to the housekeeper when the woman questioned her. "He told me to send for him."

"I hope you have not raised the mistress's hopes for nothing," Mrs. Smythe had said, glaring at Mrs. Thomas.

"He will come. And I have not told Mrs. Harcourt I have sent for him," she said, raising her chin. But when she was alone once more she wondered if she had made the right choice.

If she could have seen Charles's reaction when he heard the news, Mrs. Thomas would have been pleased. He leaned forward and grabbed the other man's bridle. "Is she all right? Is anything wrong?" he asked frantically. But the groom could tell him nothing.

"Let the man go, Charles," his mother called. "You ride on ahead. I will follow." Nodding, he bent low over his horse's neck and urged it forward.

As he pounded along the road, Charles thought about the child, about Georgiana, about himself. He had wanted to resolve all of their problems before the child was born. Would he be too late? Then a horrible thought struck him. What if something happened to Georgiana? Women did die in childbirth. Every year someone was in mourning for just such a reason. Would it happen to his wife? The thought made him shiver. Using his spurs, he forced his horse to go faster.

When he arrived at Georgiana's house, he was off his horse and up the stairs almost before the servants knew he was there. "How is she?" he asked as he walked into the sitting room where the doctor and Mrs. Thomas were talking quietly.

They saw him, and both of their faces seemed to brighten. "Just the man I want to see," Dr. Mackensie said, patting him on the shoulder.

"How is she?" Charles asked again, his face serious.

The doctor and Mrs. Thomas exchanged worried glances. Charles looked from one to the other; a feeling of cold that had nothing to do with the weather crept up his spine. "We may be worried over nothing," the doctor began.

"Worried? What is wrong?" Charles asked, his worst fears becoming reality. He started to go into the bed-room, but the doctor held him back.

"It is almost as though she has given up," the doctor

said. "She lies there in a world of her own, and nothing we do or say can reach her. She worries me."

"She has eaten almost nothing for the last few days," Mrs. Thomas added. "A few bites here and there when I reminded her that she and the baby need nourishment. She must be starving."

"Go in to her, man. Talk to her. See if you can get her to respond," the doctor told him, pushing him to the door. Although he usually refused to allow the husband into the room with the wife, in this case someone had to reach Georgiana before she slipped so far away they could not reach her.

Charles opened the door and entered the room. The curtains had been thrown open, but the weak sunlight did not give him much light to see by. He walked up to the bed, the bed he and Georgiana had shared for such a brief time. His first sight of his wife sent shivers through him. She was so pale. Lying there with her eyes closed, she seemed more a corpse than a living woman.

For longer than she had been willing to admit, Georgiana had known that the baby was coming. Early in the dark hours around midnight, the pains had begun. She had not called anyone until her water broke and she needed to change into something fresh. At first the pain had seemed like it was happening to someone else. Now, however, she could not block them out. All she could do was endure. Another pain gripped her. She clenched her fingers around the sheet and bit her lip until it began to bleed. When it was over, she lay there panting, too tired to open her eyes. Her maid wiped the sweat from her forehead.

Charles had been about to speak when the pains began. He stood there, his hands clenched, watching her suffer. When the pain subsided and her maid had finished, he took Georgiana's hand. She recognized his touch and stiffened. Then she opened her eyes slowly, afraid of what she would see, what she would hear.

"Charles?" He reached up to smooth away the damp

curls that clustered around her face, noting the way the pain had plunged lines into her usually smooth skin.

"I am here, Georgiana. I am here." He smiled down at his wife. "I thought I told you to send for me when this began," he said lightly.

"I thought you never wanted to see me again," she said weakly. Then another pain attacked her. Charles reached out and took her hand. Her fingers gripped his so tightly that both of their hands began to turn white around the knuckles.

"Do you want me to get the doctor?" he asked.

"No. Do not leave me," she begged, holding on to him tightly.

"I promise I will stay," he said soothingly. "I will stay," he repeated when he discovered those words brought a smile to her face even in the midst of her pain. Georgiana did not hear his words, only the sound of his voice. But she hung on to the sound, using it as a focus against the pain.

In the interlude between pains, she looked up at him. "Are you still angry at me?" she asked.

"Yes." The animation in her face disappeared. He hurried on. "You should have trusted me," he explained. "I suppose I am angry because you did not. Georgiana, you can tell me anything." She looked at him in disbelief.

"But you were not there to tell," she reminded him, her voice rising in the stillness.

"I know. You must have felt so alone, so lost. I wish I had been there," he admitted. "I am sorry you had to go through this on your own."

"If there had been any chance of seeing you again, do you think I would have done what I did?" she asked, taking a deep breath. "I was so frightened when I saw you again. Why do you think I fainted?"

"I thought fainting was normal for a lady in your condition," he said quietly. He could see her fighting against the pain. "Hold on to me. Do not bite your lips like that."

"I do not want to cry out."

"Why not? I would be if I were suffering as you are."

She laughed weakly. "Men are such terrible patients. I remember when my father was recovering from falling off a horse; he complained constantly."

"And probably got well faster. What you have to do is follow his example." Charles smoothed her hair back from her face once more, wishing that he could do more than just stand there and talk to her. But his being there seemed to help; even he could do that. Georgiana had more energy than before. "Have you thought about names for the child?" he asked, searching for some way to get her mind from the pain.

"Not recently. I wanted you to help me, but, but . . ."

"But I was acting like a bear with a sore paw. I am sorry, my dear." He bent and kissed her gently. Her cracked lips clung to his as though afraid that if she let them go she would never feel them again.

"Not your fault," she said through clenched teeth as another pain hit her.

"I do not know how you can say that. If I had been more of a gentleman, this would never have happened. You should have slapped my face that night in the inn." In the midst of her suffering, what he had done seemed very wrong. "Should I get the doctor?" he asked, realizing that this pain had gone on longer than the others.

"Do not leave me," she cried, grabbing his hand.

"I promise. I will stay." He nodded to the maid and at the door. She hurried out. In the few moments they were alone, he bent down close to her and whispered for her ears only, "You are mine. This child is mine. I will never leave you again. I love you, Georgiana." Even in the midst of the worst pain she had suffered, he could see how she relaxed and tried to smile.

Then the doctor walked up to the bed, noting the improvement in his patient immediately. He smiled at Charles. "If your husband will leave us alone, we have a baby to bring in this world."

"No!" Charles said, glaring at the doctor.

"Do not leave me!" Georgiana tightened her grasp on Charles's hand.

Dr. Mackensie looked from one to the other, his face impassive. He nodded and turned back to his work.

# 15

WHILE all the members of the household tried to go about their usual tasks, every time the door to Georgiana's chambers opened or closed, they stopped. When no news was forthcoming, they would go back to work. Even the footman at the front door was not as alert as usual. He did not even hear the coach that pulled up to the door and jumped when the knocker sounded.

When Mrs. Harcourt swept into the hallway, he did not know what to do with her. "Show me someplace to wait, and send me the housekeeper," she said firmly. "I plan to wait until the child is born."

Showing her to the drawing room, the footman then hurried to find the housekeeper. "She came in like this were her house," he explained. "I did not know what to do."

"Did you send for Mrs. Thomas? Perhaps she knows who this lady is. She is a lady?" The footman nodded vigorously. "I will order a tea tray and take it in when Mrs. Thomas arrives."

Charles's mother looked around the drawing room, noting the tastefully chosen furniture. She stood before the mirror in the room and pulled her pins from her hat. She was about to ring for a servant to take it away when the door opened.

"I am Mrs. Thomas, Mrs. Harcourt's companion. I am sorry I was not here to greet you, but the household is in turmoil today," the lady said, wondering how she could get rid of an unknown visitor.

"As well it should be with the mistress in childbed."

Mrs. Thomas stepped back, surprised. "I am Mrs. Harcourt, Charles's mother," she explained. "I know I am imposing, but I simply could not leave without knowing something about the child. Is Georgiana all right? My son was so worried."

Her companion had to bite back the angry retort that sprang to her lips. She nodded. When the door opened and the housekeeper, followed by a footman and a tea tray, entered, she sighed with relief. "This is Mr. Harcourt's mother," she explained, "come to wish the child well." The housekeeper inspected the intruder carefully and said nothing. She watched while the footman placed the tray on the table in front of the settee and then glanced at Mrs. Thomas. With a slight shake of the head, Georgiana's companion signaled her to leave.

"I do not think she approves of me," Mrs. Harcourt said as she took her seat in front of the tray as though she were the lady of the house. "One lump or two?" As they waited for news of the birth, the two ladies made polite conversation, each wishing the other gone.

Upstairs the time was measured as pain or between pains, the intervals between growing shorter and shorter. Hours after Charles arrived, the child was born. Although Georgiana had gained strength by holding his hand, Charles was feeling weak. He held on to Georgiana's hand as though it were a lifeline to reality, letting go only to take the small, wiggling bundle that was his daughter. "She's so, so tiny," he whispered, rubbing his hand over her small fingers. She opened them and closed them over his.

"Give her to me, sir," Daisy said. "I will clean her up. Then you can show her to her mother."

Charles bent over his wife, who once again was as pale as the pillow she was lying on. "Are you sorry she is not a boy, Charles?" Georgiana asked, her voice a whisper.

"Of course not. She is as perfect as her mother."

Georgiana laughed weakly. "Now I know I am dreaming." The baby began to cry as Daisy washed her. "What is wrong?" Georgiana tried to get up, but the doctor pushed her flat again.

"Nothing. The lady is just trying out her lungs. It appears she does not like her bath. She will be ready to be presented to you soon," he promised. He inspected the pallor of her cheeks, not liking what he saw. "As soon as you can,.I would suggest you have something to eat. You need to build your strength back up." He stretched and then smiled as Daisy brought the baby back, tightly wrapped up. "I will leave you to get acquainted."

Georgiana reached out for the small bundle while Charles hovered over her. Lifting the blanket, she inspected the small face, running her hand over the dark eyebrows and thick crop of golden brown hair. Then she finished unwrapping her, checking her fingers and toes. The baby, released from the tight wrappings, waved her hands happily. "Oh, Charles, she is perfect," Georgiana said, looking up at him with a smile that reminded him of those the Italian masters had painted on their Madonnas. Then she yawned wearily.

"Let me take her for a while. You eat something and go to sleep," he said. "We will take care of everything. Let Daisy take care of you." He bent over and kissed her. Then he picked up the baby. "We are going to have to think of a name for you, sweetness," he told her as he wrapped her up carefully.

"You will not go away, will you?" Georgiana asked, her eyes shadowed with remembered pain.

"Only as far as downstairs. There is someone anxious to meet you, sweet," he whispered. "Say good-bye to your mama." He held her where Georgiana could kiss her cheek. "We will be right back."

The hall outside Georgiana's rooms seemed crowded with people. Charles held his daughter up proudly, letting the servants gathered there take a good look. Then he hurried down the stairs. "Mama?" he called.

"In here," she answered. "Is that she? Let me see her," Mrs. Harcourt hurried to his side. The doctor had already given them the news. Mrs. Thomas was not slow to follow. "Ah, she is precious."

The doctor, who had been drinking a cup of tea when Charles arrived, stood up. "She should be upstairs in her nursery. It will not be long before she will need her mother or her wet nurse." The ladies laughed and nodded, cooing at her once more.

Before he left, Charles quietly asked his mother, "Are you staying?"

"Not here. But I will return to the hunting box. When Georgiana is ready for some company, send for me. Shall I send Digby to you?" she asked.

"Yes," he said quietly. His daughter whimpered. He smiled down at her. Then he smiled at his mother. "Thank you," he said quietly.

"For what?"

"For being here. For coming when I needed you." He looked down at the baby in his arms. "I hope I will always be there when she needs me," he whispered. His mother looked at him fondly and smiled. She patted his cheek and then called for her hat, cloak, and carriage.

When the door had closed behind them, Mrs. Thomas collapsed on the doctor's chest. "What is wrong?" he asked, putting his arms around her.

"Nothing really. I was just so uncomfortable. She kept calling the baby her grandchild. Yet she had to know how recent the wedding was," she explained.

"Maybe it was merely her way of accepting the situation, of acknowledging the child's position," he suggested. He bent and whispered in her ear. She blushed and shook her head. "Why not?" he asked.

"Mrs. Harcourt might need me."

"She has her husband," he reminded her. "Surely, she can spare you for a single evening."

"A fine help he has been over the last few days. What if he decided to leave again?"

"Georgiana should sleep most of today and tonight. And after seeing that man with her this afternoon, I do not believe he is going anywhere she does not go. Most men would have collapsed this afternoon. He was as strong as the best foundation. I was proud of him."

"That is another thing. Why did you let him stay? It was not right," his fiancée said angrily. "I had promised to be with her."

"You could not reach her; he did," he reminded her. "As soon as he arrived, she began to improve. I will tell you, my dear, that I had begun to despair."

"What?"

"That gentleman probably saved her life." He sat down and pulled her onto his lap. "Now how long are you going to make me wait?" he asked as he kissed her neck.

The next several days were restful ones for Georgiana and Charles. They spent hours in the nursery to the consternation of the nurse they had hired. "It is not natural," she told Daisy one afternoon. "Why did they hire me if they will not let me do my job. You should see them. Unwrapping the child, playing with her fingers and toes. She will catch her death of cold."

In spite of the nurse's complaints, the baby showed no ill effects because of her parents' attention. In fact, everyone who saw her commented on how healthy and happy she was. Georgiana, too, looked better than she had in months. Her color was good, and she had regained some of her strength.

That strength was her salvation the afternoon that Charles's mother came to call. Georgiana had known she was staying at the hunting box. Everyone from the housekeeper to Mrs. Thomas had been at great pains to make sure she knew. She had hoped, however, to have Charles's support when his mother arrived to see her. But as fortune would have it, he had gone out just before Daisy came in with the word of her arrival. "Shall I tell her you are sleeping?" Mrs. Thomas offered. She had been sitting with Georgiana more to keep her company than for any other reason.

Georgiana longed to accept her help but knew she must not. "Please show her in, Mrs. Thomas. And ask

Cook for a tea tray. You will have to serve," she said, wishing that the doctor had allowed her to get up so that she could greet her mother-in-law properly. "Do I look all right?" she asked her maid.

Assured that she did she lay back on her pillows, watching the door apprehensively. She wondered just how much her husband had told his mother. When the lady entered, Georgiana's eyes opened wide. The lady was almost as tall as she was and looked so much like Charles that Georgiana would have known her anywhere. "Oh, I hope my daughter looks like you," she said impulsively. Then she blushed.

"Our brown eyes and brown hair do tend to breed true," Mrs. Harcourt said with a smile. Mrs. Thomas, who had entered the room in time to hear the last remark, looked from one to the other puzzled. Noting the surprised look on the other lady's face, Mrs. Harcourt quickly changed the subject. "Did my son tell you I was here the day the baby was born? Are we still calling her the baby? Or have you decided on a name?"

Georgiana sighed. "I wanted to call her Charlotte, but Charles would not agree," she explained.

"My son shows better taste than I thought. You can do better than name her for the Queen."

"Not for her. I wanted to name her in honor of Charles, but he objected," Georgiana explained. She leaned back on her pillows, feeling much more at ease. Her mother-in-law was nothing like she had expected.

"I suppose you could call her Caroline, but with the Princess of Wales acting as she is, I would not recommend it." Mrs. Harcourt took off her hat and laid it to one side. She, too, was pleasantly surprised at the sight of her daughter-in-law. She had been prepared to be cordial but had not expected to like the lady.

The next few minutes passed easily as they discussed the merits of various names while they drank the tea that Mrs. Thomas poured. Then Mrs. Harcourt brought up the real reason for her visit. "As soon as you are able to travel, I want you to join me for the Season. I will put your name down to be presented as soon as I reach London."

"Presented? I did that ten or more years ago," Georgiana said nervously. She shook her head when Mrs. Thomas asked if she needed more tea.

"As a married lady. You will want to take your rightful place in society." Charles's mother put her cup down and frowned at her daughter-in-law.

"I want nothing to do with society," Georgiana quickly corrected her. The thought of having to face his friends, to entertain them in her home perhaps, made her want to run and hide. How would she explain what she had done? They would condemn her without listening.

"You intend to allow Charles to participate in the Season without you?" her mother-in-law asked, her eyebrows going up.

"What do you mean?"

"Surely you and Charles have discussed . . ."

"Discussed what, Mother?" he asked as he walked up to his wife and kissed her. Only then did he give his mother her customary kiss on the cheek. Using his entrance as her excuse to escape, Mrs. Thomas hurried from the room, her forehead creased. They should be allowing Georgiana to rest instead of upsetting her.

"The Season. I was telling Georgiana I would sign her up to be presented as soon as I reach town."

"Only if she wants to, Mother." He glanced at his wife, noting the white line around her mouth. "She did not enjoy her last experience."

"There was nothing to enjoy," Georgiana said bitterly.

"My dear, things will be different. You are different," her mother-in-law said forcefully. "I can see where the insipid fashions of the very young would not become you. But you will pay for dressing. I have just the mantua maker in mind."

"Mother, before you get the bit between your teeth, perhaps you should ask Georgiana," he said firmly. Then he changed the subject. "Have you seen the baby today?"

"That is another thing. You cannot call that sweet child simply the baby. She needs a name. Her own name," his mother said firmly.

"I agree," Georgiana echoed. "Something that fits her."

"I wonder if there is a name that means cranky when hungry?" Charles asked, grinning. His mother and his wife glared at him. "Shall I rescue our lady from her nursery?" he asked. They nodded.

When he returned, they inspected the baby closely. "She already looks like you, Charles," his mother said, reaching down to touch her granddaughter's dimpled cheek. "Her eyes will definitely be brown. Yours were like that when you were born." She smiled as the child grabbed her finger and held on tight. Her words sent chills up Georgiana's spine. She leaned back against the pillows, white and pale with fear. Charles glanced at her, opened his mouth to ask her what was wrong, and then decided to wait. He pulled his daughter loose from her grandmother and laid her in her mother's arms.

"Have you ever seen two such lovely ladies, Mother?" he asked proudly.

"Never." Mrs. Harcourt smiled indulgently. "But what are we to call her?"

"Charles calls her sweetness," Georgiana said as she smiled up at her husband.

"Can you imagine what it would be like when she was announced at a ball?" her grandmother asked. She assumed the tones of a majordomo. "Mr. and Mrs. Charles Harcourt and Miss Sweetness Harcourt." The three of them dissolved into laughter.

When they were serious once more, Georgiana said, "I do like the way it sounds with her last name."

"I will not permit it," Charles said firmly. "She would be the laughing stock of the ton."

"As if I would. I merely meant I like the combination of sounds. What are some names that start with s?"

"Sylvia," Mrs. Harcourt suggested.

"I knew a girl named Sylvia once; she was a gossip," Georgiana explained as she shook her head.

"Susanna, Susan, Samantha," Mrs. Harcourt continued. At the last name Charles and Georgiana looked at each other. Then the baby chose that moment to coo. Looking up from the list she was making, Mrs. Harcourt smiled at the sight they made, their heads together over the baby.

"Wonderful, Mama," Charles said. "You have done it."

"Done what?" she asked confused. She looked from one to the other.

"Found a name for Samantha," Georgiana said with a smile. "Tell your grandmama thank you, Samantha." She held the baby out to the older lady, who took her immediately.

"Samantha," Mrs. Harcourt said, rolling the name across her tongue. "Introducing Mr. and Mrs. Charles Harcourt and Miss Samantha Harcourt," she said grandly. "Yes, that will do nicely." They all laughed. Before long, the visit Georgiana had been dreading was over. And to her relief, they did not discuss her return to the ton any further.

When Samantha was once more in the care of her nurse and he had walked his mother to her coach, Charles walked back into Georgiana's bedroom, a bedroom he was no longer sharing because of Dr. Mackensie's orders. Pulling off his boots, he climbed up on the bed beside his wife. He put his arm around and pulled her close. She put her head on his shoulder, listening to the steady beat of his heart. He stroked her hair.

"She is nice," Georgiana finally said. "I thought she would hate me."

"Only if you made me unhappy."

"Does she know?" Georgiana's voice was soft. As calm as she tried to make it, he could hear a quiver in it.

"Yes." His arms tightened around her. She hid her face against his neck. He could feel the tears that ran down her face. "What's wrong?"

"I am so ashamed," she whispered. "What must she think of me?"

"Of you? Remember, my dear one, you were not alone. I think most of the blame was mine. I pursued you."

"But I should have said no."

"Well, I am glad you did not. I would not be here with you then," he reminded her. He kissed the top of her head and waited for her response.

"Oh, Charles, I could not bear it if I lost you," she said, raising her head and throwing her arms around his neck.

"What brought this on?" he asked, tilting her chin so that he could look her in the eyes.

"I do not ever want to return to the ton," she said emphatically. "Never."

"What about when Samantha needs to be presented? My mother may not be alive to do it."

"Oh." She ducked her head again, taking refuge in his shoulder.

"Georgiana, this is not like you. You are the bravest lady I know."

"Me?" She looked up and smiled.

"Yes, you." He kissed her gently. "It took courage to come to Yorkshire by yourself."

"It was not my idea," she told him. "My sister thought of it."

"Your sister. How many others knew of your situation?"

"Only my brother-in-law."

"Will he tell anyone?"

"No, but he will probably cut me."

"I doubt that. Not since you are married to me," Charles explained. "Have you written to your sister since we married?"

"The day after. But there has been no time for a reply." Georgiana's face went pale as she remembered the last letter her sister had sent her.

"What is wrong?" Are you ill?"

"Nothing."

"Do not try to fob me off. Tell me why you look as you do?" he demanded, giving her a little shake. "You promised no more secrets."

"She, she is the one who told me about the notice in the papers," she explained. "Oh, Charles, everyone will be talking about us."

"Everyone? Who is everyone? You said only your sister and brother-in-law knew."

"And your mother and your friends," she reminded him, taking a shaky breath.

"My friends. Are you worried about them? About what they will say?" he asked. Once more he tilted her face so that he could see it clearly. "You honestly are worried about them." She nodded, too choked up to speak.

"Georgiana, most of them will not even remember your name. You were never formally introduced, and when I spoke of you, which I rarely did, I referred to you just as Georgiana. How will they know what happened. Most of them never read the death notices anyway."

"Are you sure?" she asked, hopeful for the first time in several hours.

He bent his head and brushed her lips with his. "Very sure. I would never do anything to cause you the least embarrassment," he promised. He would have to write John Wentworth he admitted to himself, but John would keep their secret.

Georgiana sighed with relief and smiled up at her husband. "Is the Season so important to you?" she asked. He could still hear the uncertainty in her voice.

"I enjoy it," he admitted. "But I will enjoy it more if you are with me. We can dance together."

"As we did ten years ago. You were my hero then," she explained, wrapping her arms around his neck and bringing his head close to hers.

"Only then?"

"And now." She kissed him, and the desire between them built until they were almost engulfed. Trying to gain control, Charles pulled back. He took a deep breath and smiled at her.

"Dr. Mackensie would not approve," he said with a smile.

Knowing he was right, Georgiana simply stroked his cheek, her lips curving in a mysterious smile. He took her in his arms once more and slid behind her so that she rested against him instead of the pillows.

"About returning to London," he said finally. He could feel her stiffen. "Would you have any objection to postponing our return until the Little Season? You will have to wait to be presented," he said quietly. "That will allow you time to recover fully and to help Mrs. Thomas with her own wedding."

"Objection? I would put it off forever if I could," she admitted. "But I suppose for the sake of Samantha I must."

"And our other children," he whispered in her ear.

"Our other children?" She turned so that she could look at him. He smiled at her and lay back against the pillows, pulling her to him, holding her close until she dropped off. Although he knew he should let her go and return to his own room, he shut his own eyes and settled her more comfortably against him. Then he opened them again as if afraid she were merely a dream. "Mine," he whispered. "All mine." He closed his eyes once more and drifted off to sleep.